"GOD, I JUST DON'T KNOW WHAT YOU WANT ME TO DO."

The brook's slow-moving current produced a calming effect on Chance as he skipped tiny pebbles across the water's surface. The tip of the sun peeking over the pine trees was a beautiful sight . . . though it also brought back many memories. He used to come to this secluded spot with his wife, where they would sit and hold each other, watching the sun rise over the horizon . . .

The nagging theme of purpose weighed on his mind heavily . . . So many families and lives changed. So many churches who now prayed for their sick and shut-in members not merely as a formality, but with a fervent faith, that *believed* God could heal them. All because he had stopped by their church and prayed over someone with an impossible-seeming condition. But now, the past few days had produced too much pain.

"I just want to love again," Chance whispered. "I just want to stop running from my past . . . I'm tired of the pain, God. I'm tired . . ."

"This story taps into God's unlimited power and . . . stresses the importance of believing that God, in His sovereignty, can do what is naturally impossible."

—YOLONDA TONETTE SANDERS,
author of *Soul Matters*, on *Brother Word*

"Authentic . . . intriguing . . . four stars!"

—*Romantic Times BOOKclub Magazine*
on *A Man Inspired*

Also by Derek Jackson

A MAN INSPIRED

DESTINY'S CRY

BROTHER WORD

Derek Jackson

West Bloomfield, Michigan

WARNER BOOKS

NEW YORK BOSTON

Published by Warner Books with Walk Worthy Press™

Warner Books
Hachette Book Group USA
1271 Avenue of the Americas, New York, NY 10020

Walk Worthy Press
33290 West Fourteen Mile Road, #482, West Bloomfield, MI 48322

Visit our Web sites at www.HachetteBookGroupUSA.com
and www.walkworthypress.net.

Printed in the United States of America

First Edition: April 2006
10 9 8 7 6 5 4 3 2

Library of Congress Cataloging-in-Publication Data

Jackson, Derek.
Brother word / Derek Jackson.
p. cm.
Summary: "A mysterious stranger, gifted with the power of healing, appears at a small South Carolina church service"—Provided by the publisher.
ISBN-13: 978-0-446-69349-3
ISBN-10: 0-446-69349-9
1. Healers—Fiction. 2. Church membership—Fiction. 3. South Carolina—Fiction. I. Title.
PS3610.A348B76 2006
813' .6—dc22

2005023745

Book design and text composition by L&G McRee
Cover illustration by Carlos Aponte

To the city of Sumter, S.C., the site of
my childhood wonder years . . .

acknowledgments

To my Lord and Savior, Jesus Christ—thank you for another opportunity to shine for You.

To my parents, Doris and Nokomis Jackson Jr.—your support and encouragement have been amazing. My writing is a testament to how you raised me.

To Denise Stinson—thank you for always keeping me on my literary and spiritual "toes."

To Marina Woods, as always, this may have never happened without you—I'll never forget that.

To Peggy Hicks and the great team at TriCom Publicity—thank you for your tireless efforts.

To all the wonderful people at Warner Books, and in particular Frances Jalet-Miller and Mari Okuda—thank you for helping me "shine" on all the pages!

Dr. Courtney Walker—a true brother and encourager. Thank you for sharpening me like iron sharpens iron.

Rev. Maceo Smedley—I cherish your friendship. God is doing great things through you.

Bishop T. D. Jakes—your ministry has tremendously impacted my life.

Bishop Shelton Bady and Sis. Kim Bady—thank you for speaking words of life to me.

To W. G. Daniels and the Pilgrim Valley family—I'm grateful for the foundation you gave me.

To my big sis, Stacy Pryor—thank you for the encouragement and for keeping me sane!

To Salem Baptist Church of Chicago—"the greatest church in the world!" Thank you for the support and incredible ministry experience.

Ivy McGregor and YVI Enterprises—your encouragement has been such a blessing.

To Debra Aboagye and CorZone Marketing Solutions—thank you for marketing me across the World Wide Web.

To Alicia Johnson, for opening so many doors for me!

To Sharen Watson, Linda Kozar, and the Words for the Journey group—thank you for continually reminding me what this journey is all about.

To Frank Peretti and Ted Dekker—just because.

To the May and Jackson families, for your support and prayers.

And last, but in my heart you all are first, to the readers and everyone who has supported me from day one—thank you!

BROTHER WORD

prologue

"IT'S CRAZY WE SHOULD BE so in love with each other." Nina snuggled even closer to her husband in the bed. "We're so different, you know?"

"Why is that crazy? Opposites attract, right? Our differences are what make us right for each other." He took her hand in his, gently caressing the wedding ring he'd placed on her finger just twenty-four hours earlier. "Did you know I had my eye on you ever since the eighth grade?"

Nina laughed. "How could I not—I could practically *feel* those eyes staring at me, since you always sat behind me."

"Your last name was Harris. Mine was Howard. The teachers always sat everyone in alphabetical order for homeroom—I thanked God every single day for that blessing."

"I bet. Still, we never really talked until Spring Break of our senior year. If you were interested in me all that time, why didn't you ever tell me?"

He shrugged as he now rubbed the wedding ring on his own finger. "Because I'm not like you, remember? I wasn't able to speak my mind as freely as you did . . .

as freely as you *still* do. Getting rejected by you would have been too hard for me to deal with."

"But that's just it—I wouldn't have rejected you. In fact . . . I was *waiting* for you."

"God, it feels so good to hear you say that. And now that you have me, was it worth the wait?"

Nina smiled and traced her finger down his chest. "Lord knows it was."

Chapter One

Four years later

HE SAT IN THE FOURTH ROW, in the seat nearest the aisle. With a faint sigh, he propped his right arm on the edge of the pew, resting his head on his thumb and forefinger. Slowly, almost lazily, he moved his long finger lying just under the bridge of his nose up and down, stroking the three-day-old stubble covering the jut of his chin. Though he was only in his late twenties, his skin was already creased with the wrinkles of a man approaching middle age. His eyelids opened and closed wearily, like someone battling the first stages of sleep, but true sleep—the deep, restful sleep that complements a satisfied, peaceful life—had eluded him over the last few years. Such rest had become foreign to him; indeed, it was a luxury he had forgotten he'd ever enjoyed. At any rate, he was not the least bit tired at the moment. How could he be? His present surroundings could only be described as . . . *electric.* On this morning, as was the case every Sunday morning, the devoted, Spirit-filled congregants of Hope Springs Church were actively participating in their pastor's call-and-response sermon.

"God is getting His house in order, church!" Pastor Smallwood chortled, gripping his handheld microphone with both hands and seemingly holding on for dear life. "This ain't the time for playing games! We gonna have to be ready to board that train for glo-ory! All aboard now, come on!"

"We're ready, Pastor!" a member in the front row exclaimed. "We're right behind ya!"

The man in the fourth row watched the exchange with a slightly bemused look on his face. This particular member had been shouting just as loud, if not louder even, than Pastor Smallwood all morning.

Pastor T. R. Smallwood was now in the last stages of his forty-minute, hair-raising, suit-sweating, glory-packed sermon. Every Sunday, it was exactly forty minutes, the ending always punctuated by either taking Jesus from the cross to resurrection or by cajoling his members to board the train bound for glory.

"This train's leaving the station!" he now whooped, bending his arm and pulling it down like a real train conductor. "Get ready, now! Make sure you got your ticket! Make sure you got your bags packed! Because there ain't no looking back now! Next stop . . . glory!"

Brother Sanderson, the minister of music, leaned forward on his seat at the Hammond B-3 organ and played a B-flat chord. The well-timed musical assistance added fuel to Smallwood's fire and the revved-up preacher retrieved a handkerchief from inside his suit pocket and mopped the sweat running down his face.

"Oh, I see those precious pearly gates now!" he crooned, his voice perfectly in tune with the octave of the organ's previous note. "We're about to enter the glory!"

At sixty-one years of age, the seasoned country pastor still thought himself in decent shape, and as the music intensified in volume he began energetically swaying back and forth. Then, with a reverential glance outward at his small but devoted congregation, he immediately drew strength from the signs of how the church's faith was growing.

In the front row, Brother Jefferson Embry stood with his hands lifted above his head and tears coursing down his face, a complete transformation from the foulmouthed, drunken wreck of a man who'd first stumbled through Hope Springs's doors three years earlier. Smallwood had personally nurtured Embry's growth as a new believer, teaching, exhorting, and praying with him until the man received his complete deliverance. And the fruit of that labor was evident to all—nobody in the church now worshipped with more passion and abandonment than Jefferson Embry.

He who has been forgiven much, loves much, Smallwood thought, smiling at Brother Embry.

Two rows behind Brother Embry, and filling the entire length of the pew, sat the eight members of the McCullum family. T. R. Smallwood had baptized all eight of them, a family that now spanned three generations with the recent birth of Diedra McCullum's baby girl. By Smallwood's count, the McCullums had not missed a Sunday service in the past twenty years.

I'm blessed to have such faithful members . . .

"Church, are you ready to enter the glory?" Smallwood asked once more, relying on one of his greatest vocal assets as a preacher—repetition. His other asset was knowing how to expertly tune his voice that he might capitalize on the ultimate destination of all his sermons—boarding that precious train to glory.

"Yeeessss!" he exclaimed. "I see those angels awaiting, and the glo-oory is filling the whole room! Those trumpets are sounding, so we must bow before the King of—"

Suddenly, Pastor Smallwood bent over in mid-sway, with both hands still clutching the microphone. Trembling ever so slowly, like a wobbling infant on unsteady legs, he sank first to his knees, and then until he lay in a prostrate position. Brother Sanderson continued to play an angelic-sounding melody as the fifty-member congregation followed their pastor's lead, apparently in worship.

But T. R. Smallwood was *not* presently worshipping. His dramatic shift in posture was the result of a sudden, stabbing pain to his chest. Silently and urgently under his breath, he began praying.

"By the stripes of Jesus, I am healed . . . by the stripes of Jesus I am healed . . ."

The entire congregation, however, seemed oblivious to Smallwood's situation. They had all knelt down as well, their faces touching the wooden floor of the sanctuary. Even Brother Sanderson had closed his eyes at his perch on the organ, though his fingers and feet were still producing the angelic-sounding melody.

Heart disease ran rampant in Smallwood's family line; his grandfather had succumbed to a heart attack at age sixty-three, and his own father at age sixty. Two uncles had been robbed of life in their late fifties. Smallwood had been having chest pains on and off for the past month, but he had refused to concentrate on them. Not only had he preached divine healing through the blood of Jesus, but he also had confessed several healing scriptures over his life every day.

But strong faith in the area of healing or not, his present chest pains were real. *Painfully* real. Unfortunately, the entire congregation was oblivious to his agony, because they were too far gone in worship as they boarded the glory train.

"Lord, help me," Smallwood whispered with great difficulty, his chest heaving. "Your Word says I can be healed . . . help me, Lord."

After what seemed like an eternity had passed, he dropped the microphone to the floor and resolutely closed his eyes. If this was his time to meet his Maker, then so be it. It was no small consolation that at least he was *ready* to meet the Lord.

• • •

THE MAN NOW STOOD from his fourth-row seat. He touched the ring on his finger, tugged briefly on the lapels of his checkered suit jacket, and then began making his way toward the front of the church. His unhurried gait was as relaxed as the expression adorning his face. When he was twenty feet from the prostrate preacher, he bowed his head and clasped his hands behind his back, still walking slowly.

Soon, he was close enough to touch the preacher,

and he knelt down, his face inches away from the praying man.

"Sir, do you believe you are healed through the blood and by the name of Jesus Christ?" he asked. The confident delivery of his words belied his casual demeanor.

Smallwood stopped praying, opened his eyes, and weakly looked up, his wizened face contorted in pain.

Maybe . . . maybe it's not my time . . . he thought, with a bittersweet pang. To be absent from the body and present with the Lord had long been one of his desires. He just hadn't wanted a heart attack, of all things, to be the means of making that desire a reality.

With much effort, he nodded his head. "Yes, I do." He paused to take a few short, ragged breaths. "I believe I am healed in the name . . . of . . . Jesus."

"Then according to your faith, receive your healing in the name of Jesus," the man responded, gently reaching out and placing his palm on Smallwood's heart.

Instantly, the pain . . . *ceased.*

The throbbing ache in the center of Smallwood's chest quickly became a distant memory, almost like it had never happened at all.

Praise God! Smallwood thought to himself. He felt like rejoicing out loud, but the suddenness of it all had rendered him momentarily speechless. *Praise His holy name!*

And just as slowly and casually as he had come, the man turned around and walked back down the aisle, pausing only to pick up an old black leather Bible resting on the fourth-row seat. Continuing on, he walked out the front doors of the church and into the brilliant afternoon sunshine.

Chapter Two

LYNN HARPER HAD EVERY REASON to be in a bad mood. The repairs to her car were going to take two days longer than expected, the air conditioner in her town house was on the blink again, she was having a bad hair day, and if that weren't enough, there was a noticeable, full-length run along the back of her nylons. She noticed this small tragedy with a sigh as she happened to look down, running her comb through her unmanageable hair once more.

Lord, I'm needing serious help today . . .

Determined not to get too frustrated with both her hair and her hose, she peeled off the sheer nylons, figuring she would have to make do by putting Vaseline on her legs today, like she did when she was a little girl. And that might even be better, seeing as how she didn't have anywhere real important to go today. And who was watching, anyway?

Despite her misfortunes, she wouldn't allow herself to think negatively. Not today. Today, thank God, signaled the start of her summer vacation—one week of absolute freedom from her seemingly never-ending responsibilities as outreach director for Faith Community

Church. Her vacation was sorely needed, because she knew from personal experience that ministry and emotional burnout mixed together like oil and water. And getting burned out was not an option for her. Even as a child, she'd known her life would be lived to help others, if for no other reason than the abundant joy and fulfillment she felt meeting the needs of others. And as the years had passed and she'd grown into a young woman, God had furthermore blessed that youthful desire by giving her life a clear sense of purpose and direction.

Presently, however, her guiding light of direction was doing nothing for her unruly hair. After wasting another few frustrating minutes, Lynn grudgingly began to face the sobering reality of a bad hair day. At least her hair had grown long enough now for her to tie it into a short ponytail, which actually didn't look all that bad, once she really thought about it.

Again: who's watching, anyway?

She playfully stuck out her tongue and made a few funny faces at herself in her bathroom mirror as her youthful face stared back at her, a face that belied her thirty years of age. Even without any foundation or makeup, her healthy, almond–chocolate brown skin positively glowed, for which Lynn was thankful. She considered herself blessed to have such good skin tone, primarily because she had neither the time nor the patience to spend hours in front of the mirror fixing herself up.

But what was she fretting about her hair for, anyway? Without question, her eyes were the best things she had going for her. Unquestionably passed down from her mother, her riveting, beautiful brown-and-hazel eyes were positively Natalie Cole–like. Much to her irritation and annoyance at times, she was forever telling people that no, she didn't wear contacts and that yes, she knew she was the spitting image of Nat King Cole's daughter.

After a few more minutes, Lynn came out of the bathroom, grabbed her purse and keys off her sofa table, and headed out the front door. In her mind she hurriedly ran through her much-too-long list of things to do today, one day before she would blissfully take off to Myrtle Beach, where she then would do absolutely *nothing* for seven days.

Take overdue library books back, place newspaper subscriptions on hold, pick up clothes from cleaners, check on Mom and Dad . . .

She allowed herself a small smile as she opened the door of the rental Dodge Neon. It was a small wonder anything got done in her normal workweek.

Columbia, South Carolina, was a delightful place to live, in her opinion. She'd been born and raised in Sumter, located forty minutes east of the capital, and she'd long held that the city's hustle and bustle were just right for her. With a population of just a little more than one hundred thousand, Columbia retained that southern small-town feel that had attracted Lynn here in the first place. Though she'd been proud to have received an acceptance letter to prestigious Emory University in Atlanta, she'd opted to save money and stick closer to home. The decision to attend the University of South Carolina had paid off handsomely—after majoring in religious studies, she had found a position in outreach at nearby Faith Community Church. And after three years in that position, she'd been promoted to director.

"You're our right-hand person in outreach," Alonzo Gentry, the senior pastor, had told her on the same day he announced her promotion. "And I know everyone always says anyone can be replaced, but I honestly don't know what this church would do without you."

Now, running through the preset radio buttons, she longed once more for her beloved Camry with her much-used CD player. A great thrill and added joy of driving for her was the opportunity to worship while she drove by listening to her old-school and new-school favorites. If she had known this rental didn't have a CD player, well, she certainly *would not* have agreed to drive it, no matter if it *was* free of charge with her own car still being worked on. She had a big *hunch* why it had been free, too!

How in the world does one drive without music?

After a few minutes of frustrating radio surfing and wondering aloud more than a few times why Columbia did not have a good gospel station, she reluctantly settled for an old Aretha Franklin classic.

The temperature was forecasted to reach the mid-eighties on this clear Saturday and there was not a cloud in the June sky as she approached the downtown theater district.

Perfect weather for lazy days on the beach, she happily thought to herself. She could endure waiting for the repairs to her car, temporarily forget about her air-conditioning problems, and even deal with the kinks in her hair because of that one blissful, luxurious thought.

Hitting the high notes perfectly, she sang "R-E-S-P-E-C-T" aloud with Aretha as she navigated into a parallel parking space. Oh yes, her rest and relaxation would get some much-needed respect soon. Myrtle Beach was waiting.

• • •

THE TAN-COLORED PICKUP truck steadily made its way beyond the outskirts of Sumter, heading west toward Columbia. Traveling in the right-hand lane, at first glance there was nothing unusual about its progress. Upon closer inspection, though, the late-model truck was slightly weaving and bobbing in and out of the slow lane. This was not a major concern, though, since there were not many cars on Highway 76 today.

Inside the cab the old driver vigorously rubbed his bloodshot eyes, forcing them to remain open. He wasn't having much success, however, and every five miles or so he was reduced to jerking the steering wheel hard to the left or right, pitifully attempting to stay in the center of the lane.

He drained the last of the beer down his throat and tossed the empty can out his window. On the radio an old country-and-western tune was blaring, some melodramatic jingle about a jilted ex-lover from Nashville, but that was not helping him stay alert. Opening his eyes and having to jerk the wheel again after weaving to the left, he narrowly missed sideswiping a sedan that was passing him. The driver of that car shouted a few choice words and gestured rudely.

The old man cursed back, sleepily and drunkenly

slurring his words. He knew he shouldn't be driving in his present condition, but he was only ten or so miles out of Columbia; there wasn't much farther to go. And besides, how else was he supposed to get home? Walk?

"I don't know why my da-ahling left me . . ." the Nashville crooner droned on the radio as the pickup truck wobbled and weaved along the highway. Normally an avid country-and-western music fan, the driver was so conked out, he didn't even hear the song. That he was even navigating the pickup as ably as he was constituted a small miracle.

• • •

FORTUNATELY, LYNN SPOTTED HER a good thirty seconds before she would be approaching her rental car. The dreaded meter lady.

Thank goodness I didn't stop to chat with Marianne, Lynn thought as she increased the speed of her walking gait. Marianne was Lynn's favorite librarian, but the elderly, good-natured busybody always had endless stories to tell. Usually Lynn had the patience and time to humor her, but since she'd been facing a thousand items on her to-do list today, she had consciously avoided Marianne while returning her four overdue books. And also, apparently, avoided this parking ticket. She breathed a sigh of relief.

"I'm leaving, I'm leaving," she cheerfully called out as she visibly and loudly jingled her keys, much to the meter lady's displeasure.

The old woman glanced up, a disappointed smirk

plastered on her face. "You're lucky I'm in a good mood today, missy. You're over your time limit."

I'm not lucky; I'm blessed . . . "Sorry!" Lynn replied, flashing her best smile. "I was really trying to make it."

The meter lady grunted under her breath and moved on to the Mercedes-Benz parked behind Lynn's, which was also over the limit. The driver of this sleek luxury car would not be as fortunate.

As she made a right and merged into light traffic on Hampton Street, Lynn's cell phone rang. A sideways glance at the caller ID showed that it was Arlene, so Lynn quickly put the call through.

"Hey, sis, I've got a thousand things to do today. What's going on?"

Arlene's bubbly laughter filled her ear. "Easy, Lynn. Just because you're taking a whole week off doesn't mean you can just blow your best friend off."

"I wouldn't think of doing such a thing. But . . . uh, make it quick, now."

"Don't make me put you on my prayer list!" Arlene responded, still laughing. After a moment, she added, "I'm just calling to see if you're coming back to the office before you take off to Myrtle Beach."

"Now why would I do that? I love y'all, but do I need to remind you that I'm going on *vacation*?"

"You'd do it because Sister Margie made some banana pudding and brought it to the kitchen this morning," Arlene answered. As the minister of music at Faith Community Church, Arlene had an office just down the hall from Lynn's. "And I know you would kill me if—"

"You got that right!" Lynn exclaimed, slapping her

hand atop the Neon's dashboard and licking her lips for added emphasis. "That woman of God's banana pudding is so good, it ought to be a sin to eat it!"

Arlene laughed again, a sound that blended harmoniously with her natural voice. Perhaps that was why Lynn liked her so much—Arlene literally knew how to count everything as joy. "I take that to mean you're coming by the office, then?"

Lynn looked at her watch. As it was, she was already running a tight schedule, but how could she pass up a chance to score a helping of her favorite dessert, made by one of the best cooks this side of the Mississippi?

"I'll swing by in about an hour, Arlene. Don't you let them eat it all up, you hear?"

"You got it, girl!"

Ten minutes later, now traveling east on Highway 76, Lynn calculated in her mind that if she really focused she just might get everything done today, *including* getting that dish of banana pudding. And she certainly didn't mind pushing herself to be productive, because in a few days the only meaningful tasks she would be engaging in would be clicking a remote control and dialing out for room service.

Breakfast in bed . . . my own personal masseuse . . . sunsets to simply die for . . .

Those tempting thoughts instantly made her giddy with anxiousness. She sighed and stretched her neck, daydreaming ahead to future massages and tantalizing hours spent in the Jacuzzi . . . so she really wasn't concentrating on driving . . .

As a result, she only casually noticed the tan-colored pickup truck to her left as she approached the three-way intersection, at which she had the right-of-way. She thought nothing of it. Because after all, she *did* have the right-of-way. But had she been more focused on driving, and driving defensively for that matter, she probably would have observed that this truck was not going to heed the stop sign.

Her mind still captivated by spas and her awaiting Jacuzzi, too late she saw that the truck was not stopping. The acute shock of the impending driver's-side collision was too much for her senses to handle and she screamed.

Then her entire world faded to black.

A split second later, she felt nothing when the truck plowed into her compact car. Didn't even feel a thing.

Chapter Three

FIVE MINUTES SHY OF TWO O'CLOCK found the sun finally forcing its way past the thick, cotton-like clouds that had enveloped the sky all morning. The air was not yet humid, though, a small relief to the man sitting along the banks of the Congaree River. This stretch of the river and its surrounding land, located twenty miles southeast of Columbia, had recently been designated a national park, in part because the swampland preserved the largest intact tract of old-growth floodplain forest in North America.

The man was interested in neither the park's serenity nor its beauty, however, as he leaned against a bald cypress tree towering one hundred feet into the sky. He longed for the rest that still eluded him.

God, this place is beautiful . . .

Though he'd stumbled onto this park almost by accident, he couldn't imagine being anyplace else. After conducting a little research at the public library a few days earlier, he'd found that no other place in the eastern United States held a larger contiguous area of tall trees. And since tall trees equaled privacy and seclusion, this park had quickly become his outdoor sanctuary.

His old black leather Bible lay open in his lap, the pages turned to a highlighted passage of scripture he'd spent years poring over—Isaiah 53. He knew the passage so well he could have recited it just as easily backwards as forwards.

"Surely He has borne our griefs and carried our sorrows; yet we esteemed Him stricken, smitten by God, and afflicted. But He was wounded for our transgressions, He was bruised for our iniquities; the chastisement for our peace was upon Him, and by His stripes we are healed."

"The suffering servant, Jesus Christ," the man muttered through clenched teeth. "On the cross, You bore my sins and iniquities . . . my infirmities so I wouldn't have to. Then tell me this, God. Why . . . why do I still have all this pain? If You bore all my pain, then why am I still *suffering*? I shouldn't have to feel all this pain."

A few minutes passed by, and when there was no answer, the man cried out in anguish.

"*Why!* Why, God? Why did my love have to be taken away? What did I do to deserve this? Are You hearin' me?"

Again, no answer. Not that he was expecting one. He had a thought to shake his fist toward the heavens, but resisted; he knew the fine line between anger and stupidity in questioning the Almighty. Though he might never understand why God had allowed Nina to be taken away, God was still . . . *God*. And who was he to challenge that sovereignty?

"Why'd you even give me this?" he asked quietly, looking down at his hands. He turned them around and over with the fascination of a newborn baby, looking at these ten-fingered appendages as if for the very first time. They looked normal enough—five fingers to either hand with two joints on each finger. The underside and palms were slightly callused from years of outdoor manual labor.

"Why'd you even give me this gift, if it's not for the people who mean the most to me?"

Tilting his head back against the tree, he closed his eyes, inviting sleep to mercifully take him away from his reality. But sleep would not come. Gnats whined and buzzed around his head incessantly, and he spent several minutes swatting at them to no avail. Frustrated and tired, he slid down the base of the tree. His mind traveled back in time to the happiest day of his life. His wedding day.

Oh, God . . .

Most people considered weddings to be the happiest day of a *bride's* life, but the same was true for the groom, at least when such a man was deeply in love.

And he had been—as he'd watched Nina gracefully sashay down the aisle, the white veil covering the loveliest face he'd ever laid eyes on, he was unaware that he'd been temporarily holding his breath.

Due to circumstances beyond their control, their wedding had only been a small affair. But it didn't matter who had been invited to witness their celebration of love—this was his and Nina's special day.

"Do you take Nina Reneé Harris to be your lawfully wedded wife?" the minister had asked, looking earnestly into his eyes. "To love and to cherish, to have and hold from this day forth, in good times and bad, in sickness and health, till death do you part?"

"I do," he had answered, speaking two of the most

important words he'd ever been honored to say.

"I. Do."

• • •

"THE REHEARSAL SOUNDED GREAT from where I'm sitting, Sister Arlene," Pastor Gentry remarked, looking up from his daily devotional. "But I'm not sure I recognized the voice on the solo. Who was singing?"

Arlene walked farther into the office, gently placed a manila folder on the desk, and took a seat opposite her pastor. "That was Sister Dana—doesn't she have the most amazing voice? I've been trying to get her to lead out for months now, and since we're rehearsing some Milton Brunson classics for the concert series, there was no way I was letting her wiggle out of leading. I'm telling you, Dana sounds just as good as Kim McFarland, if not even a little better."

Pastor Gentry smiled at his choir director before leaning back in his chair. "That's a bold statement. I won't mention to Kim that you said such a thing next time I see her—Kim and I go back a few years, you know. Anyway, 'I Tried Him and I Know Him' is one of my all-time favorite songs. And it's going to sound even better once we get our state-of-the-art audio equipment installed in the main sanctuary in three weeks."

Leaning forward again, he opened the manila folder and scanned the pages inside. After a minute or so had passed, he nodded his head. "Everything looks to be in order for the fall choral concert."

"Thank you, sir. We're getting more churches from

the surrounding counties involved this year—it's going to be a tremendous event."

"I have no doubt of that. I take it the public relations committee is ready with their advertising?"

"Absolutely."

Gentry smiled and closed the folder. "It's enough to give God praise for having you over the choir. It's such a blessing to never have to worry about a thing concerning the music ministry—you run a tight ship."

Arlene respectfully lowered her head and was about to respond when the red light on Pastor Gentry's phone began blinking.

"Excuse me," he said, before picking up the receiver and swiveling around in his executive chair.

With Faith Community's current status as the fastest-growing church in the Carolinas, all of its members had grown used to the pressing demands on Pastor Gentry's time. It had nearly gotten to the point where one was deemed fortunate just to have an uninterrupted meeting with the man. Arlene understood this as well as anybody, busying herself with picking imaginary lint from the fabric of her pantsuit while her pastor spoke softly into the receiver from a few feet away. She assumed it was merely another routine business call, but when he quickly swiveled back around and almost dropped the phone back into its cradle, she immediately sensed something was wrong.

"Lord Jesus, have mercy," Pastor Gentry breathed, closing his eyes as he pinched the bridge of his nose.

"Pastor? Is . . . is something wrong?"

Ten seconds passed before he opened his eyes. "Sister Arlene, please gather the intercessory team together—we need to pray as a church family. That was Brother and Sister Harper, on their way to the hospital."

"The Harpers? The *hospital*? Wha-what happened?"

"It's Sister Lynn," he said slowly. His voice was now notably strained. "There's no easy way to say this," he began, measuring his words. He knew how close the relationship was between Arlene and Lynn. For that matter, he regarded Lynn Harper as his own daughter. "She's been in an accident."

All the color drained from Arlene's face. "Oh, God . . ."

Chapter Four

THE DOUBLE DOORS OF Palmetto Memorial Hospital electronically burst open, clearing the way for the lead paramedic to rush through, communicating on a walkie-talkie. In seconds, two nurses appeared from around the corner, ready to assist the first responders.

"Woman, five-nine . . . early thirties," the paramedic announced in rat-tat-tat staccato. "Auto collision, driver's side. Trauma to head, concussion, possible internal bleeding. Broken left leg . . ." Seconds later, a gurney rolled through, carrying the body of an immobilized woman. An oxygen mask covered the woman's face and her neck was secured in traction. The entire left side of her body seemed to be covered in blood.

"Get her to trauma room 2," boomed the voice of one of the nurses.

Not far behind the stretcher, Leonard and Jeannette Harper stumbled through the double doors. Leonard half held, half supported his wife as they moved as quickly as they could, the end result looking like a pairing in an awkward three-legged race. Jeannette's eyes were wide and darting around inside their sockets, and she was incoherently mumbling to herself.

"Excuse me, Mr. and Mrs. Harper?" The lady at the front desk called out, standing and raising her hand in a futile attempt to gain their attention. But the Harpers weren't about to be slowed down by some woman behind a desk. Not when their only daughter was clinging to life mere feet away from them.

"Mr. and Mrs. Harper!" the receptionist called out again, more loudly this time. At the sound of her voice, one of the nurses turned around to see the couple attempting to gain entry into the trauma room.

"I'm sorry, but you two *cannot* come past these doors," the nurse sternly cautioned, holding out his hand to block their path before they reached the doors leading to the operating room.

"My daughter!" Jeannette screamed. "Get out of my way! My daughter is back there!"

"I understand, ma'am," the nurse replied gently, holding his ground. His facial expression radiated the perfect blend of sympathy and sorrow. "But I can't let you past these doors. The doctors are doing everything they can for her right now."

Jeannette sagged against the nurse's arms, her screams now turned into a mournful wailing. "You've got to let me . . . my daughter . . . Lynn . . ."

Leonard placed his hands on his wife's shoulders, gently leading her away from the doors. "It's in the Lord's hands now," he whispered.

"My baby . . . Lynn . . . oh, sweet Jesus . . ." Jeannette continued mumbling.

"I know . . . I know," Leonard repeated, encouraging himself as much as his wife. "But we're going to make it through this."

They slowly made their way back to the desk, where the receptionist offered them a sympathetic smile. “If you’ll just fill out these insurance forms . . .”

• • •

THIRTY-FIVE MINUTES LATER Pastor Gentry, Arlene, and four ministers from the intercessory prayer team arrived to find Leonard and Jeannette sitting in the waiting area, holding each other.

The pastor walked over to them, briefly placing his hand atop Leonard’s shoulder. He’d known Leonard for thirty years, dating back to when they were both students at Morris College. Alonzo had been the chaplain for the Baptist Student Union, and Leonard had been the first man he’d led to the saving knowledge of Jesus Christ. The two had remained close friends ever since, and Leonard had been one of the charter members when Alonzo had founded Faith Community Church. Alonzo had also introduced Leonard to his future wife, Jeannette, at a church barbecue, he had been in the hospital for the birth of their daughter, Lynn, and he was known to stop by a few times a year for Jeannette’s delicious German chocolate cake. Jeannette had long since returned the favor by introducing Alonzo to her longtime friend Shanice; the two had been married now ten years.

“Leonard, this is . . . this is a shock to us all,” Alonzo began, sitting down in the chair next to Leonard. He allowed a few seconds to pass in contemplative silence. “But I want you to know that we are all here for you. Have the doctors said anything further about Lynn’s condition?”

Leonard shook his head. "We don't know anything yet. The . . . the impact on her left side . . ." He shook his head as his voice trailed off. He had seen Lynn lying on that stretcher—a sight no parent should *ever* have to see.

Pastor Gentry closed his eyes and squeezed Leonard's hand. "Father, we know that You are Jehovah-Rapha, the Lord that healeth us. We pray that You would now touch the hands of the doctors who are in the operating room as we speak. We know that nothing is too hard for You, and we release our faith for a complete healing for Lynn Harper. We ask that You would strengthen our hearts in the midst of this crisis. Above all, though, we pray Your will be done. In Jesus's name, amen."

Chapter **Five**

DURING HIS PAST FOUR YEARS as a staff writer for the *State*, the bulk of Travis Everett's articles had gone largely ignored by readers. It was not that he was a bad writer; indeed, his colleagues regarded his literary acumen as above average. Instead, his lackluster reporting skills meant that he was assigned the garden-variety stories that languished in obscurity on the fourth page of the Metro section. In the editor's all-important opinion (since story placement was ruled on with an iron fist), Travis simply was not a good enough reporter to handle the kind of hard-hitting political and community-interest stories commanding priority in Metro.

Outwardly, Travis acted as if this stepchild-like treatment didn't affect him. He claimed to be perfectly satisfied collecting a paycheck for pounding out two eight-hundred-word features a week, no matter where his stories were placed. In truth, though, he longed for the recognition that came from penning an important and interesting story that would dominate not only the front page of Metro, but also the front page of the entire newspaper.

But where would he find such a story? By his own admission, he was a lazy reporter. He often researched data on the Internet instead of cold-calling sources and physically traveling to various parts of the state to collect eyewitness accounts. His boss, Ryman Wells, had noticed his tendency to cut corners almost immediately, handing Travis the thankless job of covering the likes of community bake-offs and town hall meetings.

Glancing at his watch, Travis now saw he had three more hours until the deadline for submitting his next piece, a yawner of a story about the proliferation of summertime gnats. The article's subject—gnats—aroused as much interest as tickets to watch a family of turtles sprint around the Darlington Raceway, but Travis could care less. For all intents and purposes, the article was already written; it just needed a little polishing.

Nobody's gonna read it, anyway . . . why even bother?

He popped another salty pretzel into his mouth and washed it down with a swig of diet Pepsi from the can always perched next to his keyboard. He didn't even know why he was addicted to this particular soda, since it didn't taste better than the diet brands of the other soft drinks. Maybe it was the baby blue and red colors. It certainly had nothing to do with dieting—Travis's five-foot-eight-inch body perpetually fluctuated between 250 and 280 pounds, depending on how many trips he made to Damon's Clubhouse in a given week.

Speaking of Damon's . . .

The pretzels weren't doing anything to appease his growing hunger. He glanced at his watch again and greedily calculated that he had time for one of Damon's tasty barbecue sandwiches. And maybe a slice of cheery cheesecake to satisfy his sweet tooth. And, of course, another diet Pepsi to wash it all down.

As he stood and retrieved his Clemson Tigers baseball cap, his arm accidentally knocked the framed picture of his nephew Eddie onto the desk, causing the glass frame to shatter. He automatically cursed, but was nevertheless relieved to see that his half-full diet Pepsi can hadn't tilted over and spilled onto his keyboard. That had happened once before, earning him two weeks of Ryman Wells's unrelenting wrath. Hadn't the old buzzard ever heard of the word "accident" before?

He reached over to pick up his wastebasket, then placed the metal receptacle at the edge of his desk. Carefully he swept the tiny shards of glass into the trash, idly wondering how much damage a piece of glass could inflict upon a keyboard's internal wiring.

"Hey, Trav, everything alright?"

The question came from Benny Dodson, a fellow staff writer whose cubicle was adjacent to Travis's. If Travis's stigma was being Ryman Wells's whipping boy, then Benny Dodson was the polar opposite. Benny kissed up to Ryman any chance he got, a tactic that the veteran editor loved. Partly due to such brownnosing (and to the fact that he was probably a better journalist than the other staff writers), Benny regularly saw his articles grace the Metro's front page.

"Yeah, Benny," Travis responded, contemplating scattering a few shards of glass all over Benny's chair. Now wouldn't the chaos from *that* make for an interesting, exciting article? "Everything's alright—go back to thinking of new ways to suck up to the boss."

Benny sighed loudly and Travis could visualize him rolling his eyes. "Give up, Travis. Will ya?"

Travis started to respond with a nasty remark, but at that moment his eyes fell on the picture of his nephew Eddie, grinning in that "what, me worry?" way, a facial expression that was all the more remarkable considering Eddie's medical condition. Eddie had been born with ectrodactylism, a rare birth defect that caused the tibia and fibula in both of his legs to be fused at the ankle, rendering him unable to walk. Eddie's pediatrician had mentioned that only one out of every ninety thousand children in the United States was born with such a defect, causing Travis to sometimes wonder why fate had dealt Eddie such a cruel hand. And if that wasn't misfortune enough, Eddie had also been born deaf. Both afflictions compounded Travis's awkwardness around the kid, especially since Eddie was always reaching out with his arms, looking for hugs from his "Uncle Trav," or pleading for someone to throw the Nerf baseball around with.

The growling of his stomach interrupted Travis's thoughts then, pleasantly reminding him that barbecue and cheesecake were awaiting the attention of his palate.

Chapter Six

HOPE SPRINGS CHURCH had been built at the turn of the twentieth century, during a time when houses of worship were constructed with one basic theme in mind—*Repent, for the Kingdom of heaven is at hand.*

The church was a simple, wooden, one-story shotgun frame touched up with white paint about every ten years. T. R. Smallwood vividly remembered the first time he had walked through Hope Springs's doors, and it was this memory that now caused a smile to spread across his weathered face.

He had been eleven years old at the time, and his father had just relocated the Smallwood family to Sumter for a "missionary" assignment. All of the family moves—eight of them by the time TR reached high school—were *missionary* moves, as TR recalled. To his young eyes, his father had been a preacher without a pulpit, a wandering evangelist with four hungry mouths at home to feed.

"We're doing the Lord's work," his father would always answer to TR's questions of why he couldn't get a real job. "And the Lord will provide for our family."

Sure enough, God *had* always provided for the Smallwoods, a continuing act of providence that played a big role in TR's heeding the same call as both his father and grandfather into full-time ministry.

But on that day fifty years ago, TR had walked into a Wednesday night prayer service at Hope Springs and had been astounded at how the people were behaving. Women young and old were spinning around like colorful human tops, their hands lifted to the heavens and their long, billowy dresses fanning out all around them. The men were shouting and dancing, lifting their Bibles and waving them around like swords. And the pastor at the pulpit, a fiery young man known to all as Preacher Ray, was exhorting the congregation to do the same thing TR now employed as the trademark of his sermons.

"Every man, woman, boy, and girl," Preacher Ray had been exclaiming in his unforgettable raspy tenor voice, "if you're a child of God, then let's board that train to glory!"

"Ah, that glory train," TR now repeated, reminiscing as he stood on the front steps of Hope Springs Church. He looked upward, marveling at the countless number of stars dotting the summer South Carolina sky.

"Lord, You have been so good to me," he began, not caring about the tears coursing down his face. "You've blessed me with a wonderful, loving wife, with a church family that hears Your voice and follows me as I follow You, and most of all, You've blessed me with . . ." His voice began breaking. "You've . . . blessed me with a healthy heart. Lord, I've always believed in divine healing. And now, more than ever,

I'm committed to preaching that message from now until the day You return to this earth. You are the Healer." He lifted his hands and closed his eyes, letting the presence of God wash over him.

"You . . . are the Healer," he repeated.

• • •

AN INTENSE THROBBING in the center of her forehead jarred Lynn awake more convincingly than any alarm clock ever could. Her first reaction was to cry out, but for some horrifying reason she . . . couldn't.

Why can't I open my mouth?

In addition to the headache, it felt as if a thousand cotton balls were glued to her tongue. She tried to open her eyes and found she couldn't do that either. She sensed some sort of bandage covering them.

Oh God, am I blind, too? Relax, Lynn. Just relax . . . try to remember what happened . . .

Surely there was a reasonable explanation for everything. But why on earth couldn't she . . . Then at last, she was able to remember. In an instant, like she was pressing rewind on a monitor and seeing a colorful blur of images flashing before her, the all-too-vivid remembrance of the accident came roaring back to her mind. The sight of that tan pickup truck seconds before it hit her . . . a gut-wrenching shriek . . . and then nothing. Everything after that went blank in her mind. Amazingly, she remembered no pain, no blood, nothing like the gory images of wrecks she always saw in the movies and on television. It was as if God spared her from all of that.

But what about the other driver?

There were so many questions in her mind at the present moment. Obviously, she must be in a hospital of some sort. But how long had she been here? And had someone called her parents? How badly was she injured? What . . . oh, Lord . . . what did she *look* like now?

As she lay there unable to move, see, or speak, though, slowly the profound gravity of her present situation sank in a little more clearly. At once, she was upset with herself for even thinking about something as trivial as her looks. She could have very well . . . she could have very well . . . *died.*

Do you realize how close to death you were?

As it was now, she couldn't even open her eyes and mouth. Or move her legs, she realized with a mounting sense of dread. And those two impairments were beginning to ring slight chords of fear within her heart. What if she could never walk again? Or see again? Or talk again?

Lynn, don't you even think that . . . Finally, after much effort, she found that she could manage to move her arms a little bit.

Oh, thank God for that . . .

A faint whirring noise could be heard to her right. Slowly crossing her left arm over her chest and then inching her hand and fingers along the edge of the hospital bed, she discovered, as she had presumed, that an intravenous fluid line ran from the machine into her right arm. Because her eyes and mouth were not any help at the moment, she had to rely more heavily on her other senses to get a feel of the room. The door was not far away; if she strained, she could just hear footsteps and other noises every other minute or so. The sounds were muffled, though, so the door more than likely was not fully open.

Aside from the electrical whirring of the various machines on both sides of the bed, there were no other sounds. She was alone, utterly alone in the room and unable to open her eyes or mouth. That sobering reality would have given her a valid reason to be afraid, if not for the fact that surely a nurse was regularly checking on her.

At least I'm alive, she thought, before a wave of dizziness overtook her and she lapsed back into unconsciousness.

• • •

"LYNN?" THE VOICE SOUNDED GARBLED and far away, like the person was speaking underwater via sonar. "Lynn, honey, can you hear me?"

Lynn tried opening her eyes but they were still bandaged. Her tongue didn't feel like cotton balls, peanut butter, and Superglue anymore, however, so she attempted to speak.

"Daddy?" she weakly croaked, her voice sounding like a frog. "Is that you?"

"Yes, honey, it's me. Your mother and I are both here. Oh, Lynn, it's so good to hear your voice."

But I sound like a frog . . .

Leonard Harper didn't seem to mind one bit what his only daughter's voice sounded like. "We came just as soon as we could, honey. It's so good to . . . so good to . . ." His voice cracked. "You're . . . you're gonna be okay, baby. Don't you worry about a thing."

"Lynn? Lynn, oh God, we're so glad to hear you," came her mother's voice. From the sound of it, Lynn could tell her mother had been crying.

"Mom, how . . . how long have I been in here?"

"Two weeks, baby."

Two weeks!

"You were in a coma for six days, and for a while it was touch and go. The doctors didn't know if you were gonna make it. But everyone was praying, Lynn. We knew God was going to get you through this somehow."

Oh my God . . .

"Lynn, I'm Dr. Sherman Winthrop," she heard another voice say. "I'm very glad to see you awake and talking, although I'm afraid we are going to have to limit that."

"My eyes," Lynn broke in. "Why . . . why are my eyes bandaged?"

"Some glass splinters from the driver's-side window pierced your eyelid and the surrounding uveal tissue. We're waiting for the tests to come back on a diagnostic procedure we performed, and until then the bandages are a protective measure."

"What about . . . what about my other injuries?"

"Lynn, it's best that you get your rest right now," Leonard interjected. "You'll be fine and out of here in no time at all."

"I feel so sore, Daddy . . . and what about the other driver . . . and—"

"Lynn, shh . . ." Leonard soothingly interrupted

her. He glanced quickly at Jeannette, who shook her head. Neither wanted to tell their daughter just yet that the other driver, whose blood alcohol level had been two times the state's legal limit, had not survived the accident. "The most important thing is that you're alright," Leonard said instead. "Everything is going to be alright."

Daddy's always right, Lynn thought to herself, taking a deep breath. *He's always . . . right . . .*

Chapter Seven

LYNN'S NEXT FEW DAYS passed by in a medicated haze. It seemed to her that doctors and nurses were stopping by her room nearly every hour, monitoring the equipment around her bed, pricking her with needles, or taking her temperature. The bulk of her injuries stemmed from her rental car not being equipped with side-impact air bags, leaving her with a concussion, two broken ribs, and minor damage to her tibia and lower left leg. Although those were severe injuries, they were not life-threatening. She was expected to make a full recovery in a matter of months.

The injury that concerned the doctors and her family the most, however, was the trauma inflicted on her eyes. Both her left and right corneas had suffered extensive abrasions and vitreous hemorrhaging from the shattering of the driver's-side window at eye level, delicate wounds for which surgery would not guarantee a restoration of sight.

"Y-you mean . . . you mean I'm going to go blind?" Lynn now whispered, her voice faltering as she contemplated what it would be like living in permanent darkness the rest of her life. She thought about her

Natalie Cole–like eyes, her best facial feature, and how they might now appear lifeless and cloudy gray. She thought about being unable to read (her favorite pastime), or never again enjoying the brilliance of sunsets, sunrises, and rainbows. She thought about never again gazing through the stained-glass windows of Faith Community Church while in the throes of intimate worship.

"Yes, there is a chance you could completely lose your sight," Dr. Winthrop responded.

Lynn couldn't help but wonder if all of this was merely a test of her faith. Perhaps it was a boomerang effect from all the times she'd taught about faith during Christian education classes, encouraging believers to only believe the report of the Lord when facing trials such as a terminal illness, a job termination, or parenting a prodigal child.

But *blindness*? How on earth could she live and function in a complete state of darkness?

"It is also possible that you may lose only a percentage of sight, or perhaps your peripheral vision. At this point, we just don't know how your eyes will respond to the treatments."

Lynn tried once more to visualize Dr. Winthrop's face, just as she'd been doing with everyone she hadn't already known who visited her room. The doctor's voice had always been calm and soothing, almost grandfatherly. She sensed he was in his fifties, and had heard nurses talking about his "big tufts of white hair," so she fancied him as the old colonel who'd founded the KFC restaurants.

Come on, Lynn . . . get a hold of yourself . . .

Is this what her life was to become? Imagining what strangers looked like? Straining for the scent of someone's perfume or cologne?

Oh God, I just can't do this . . .

". . . going to do everything we possibly can to get you well," Dr. Winthrop was saying as Lynn snapped out of her despairing trance.

"I know, Doctor. Thank you."

"Your parents, Arlene, and a few members from your church are waiting in the lobby, as always. Do you feel up to a visit?"

Lynn nodded. Visits from her family and friends were the highlights of her day, since there was no need for visualizing what *they* looked like.

• • •

"TRAVIS! TRAVIS, GET IN MY OFFICE NOW."

The gruff, steely voice barking on the other end of the phone line couldn't have sounded much angrier, Travis thought, as he replaced the receiver on its base. He'd e-mailed his second weekly story to Ryman Wells twenty minutes earlier, and apparently the old guy hadn't liked it.

What else is new?

Travis guzzled the last of his diet Pepsi and tossed it in the wastebasket along with the two earlier cans he'd already polished off. Slowly, he got out of his chair, exited his cubicle, and plodded down the carpeted hallway leading to the editor's corner office. Ryman was waiting for him, glaring at him from underneath brooding eyebrows. An ex-marine who'd returned to the newsroom after the first Gulf War, Ryman Wells was about as approachable as a pit bulldog. And about as friendly, too. Accordingly, he ran the Metro section as though he were dictator and it was his own personal kingdom.

"Travis, what the devil is this?" he barked, holding up what looked like a copy of Travis's latest submission.

"Looks like my story," Travis replied, his face blank.

"What it *is*," Ryman corrected, "is a piece of trash. Our readers do *not* care about the reproductive nature of *gnats*!"

"It's a follow-up, sir, on last week's story about the proliferation of gnats in greater Richland County. In the summer, they're—"

"Your writing on that was trash, too! Last week's story was only printed because we didn't have enough community announcements to fill up the fourth page."

Travis didn't even blink at Ryman's tirade. He wasn't hearing anything new from the grumpy old editor; Ryman *always* hated how Travis's stories were written.

"I've never given you an ultimatum," Ryman continued, "but I'm past fed up with this. I've had it with your juvenile efforts at quality journalism. If your next story is not *significantly* better in both style and content, you'll be given your marching orders."

"My marching orders . . . sir?"

"Let me spell it out for you, Everett. I will fire you quicker than an AWOL soldier finds himself in trouble with Uncle Sam. I will *not* have juvenile stories cluttering up my Metro section. Do I make myself clear?"

Travis resisted the urge to salute the ex-marine. He

could never remember if it was supposed to be done with the left or right hand.

• • •

"THIS IS AMAZING, TR. I've never seen anything like it in my life."

T. R. Smallwood grinned broadly and lifted his gaze to the ceiling as his personal physician for the past twenty years, Hank Mitchell, studied his most recent heart scan.

"God is good, ain't He, Hank?"

Hank coughed and pushed his reading glasses farther up on his nose. "Y-yes, God is good, but your arteries have had significant blockage for years. You've been doing a decent job with your diet and exercise, but this radical reversal on your heart is . . . is simply *unprecedented.*" He held out the readout from the heart scan. "I'm looking at the heart of a thirty-year-old here."

"Well, glory to God!" Smallwood shouted. "All praise to God for His miracle-working power!"

Hank was a Christian and generally believed in the power of God to do the miraculous, but for Smallwood's heart to change (and rejuvenate, even) virtually overnight defied all medical and scientific logic.

"TR, now let me get this from you one more time," Hank began, lightly scratching the back of his head. "You're saying a man walked up to you, in the middle of your heart attack, touched his hand to your heart . . . and . . . and that was it? The pain, the shortness of breath—it all stopped?"

Smallwood nodded. "But the man of God first asked me if I believed I was healed through the blood and by the name of Jesus. And Lord knows I do! I've been preaching that at Hope Springs for years! In the gospel of Mark 16:18, Jesus says that we will lay hands on the sick, and they shall recover!"

"Yes, that's true," Hank replied, still scratching the back of his head. "But except for the miracles in the book of Acts, I've never seen this sort of thing."

"Oh, come now," Smallwood said, still grinning. "Instances of divine healing have happened before—maybe I should refresh your memory a bit. Surely you've read about the Azusa Street revival in Los Angeles? William Seymour led that great move of God back in 1906, which drew people all over the world to an old renovated livestock stable on Azusa Street. Folks were healed of all manner of sicknesses and were filled with the Holy Spirit by the thousands. Glory to God! And you've heard of Kathryn Kuhlman, right?"

Hank took off his reading glasses. "Name sounds familiar."

"It should. She was a mighty healing evangelist who packed auditoriums and arenas all over America in the forties and fifties. People from all over the world testified of being healed through her services. And right around that same time, God raised up Oral Roberts, whom I know you've heard of because your daughter-in-law Gracie graduated from Oral Roberts U. His tent healing services in the fifties and sixties impacted who knows how many lives. I know one thing—it impacted mine. I attended one of 'em in 1954, and it changed my life forever." Smallwood sighed contentedly and slapped his knee. "So many others—Smith Wigglesworth, John G. Lake, Charles and Frances Hunter. I tell you, Hank—the gift of healing is alive and well in the body of Christ!"

"Well yes, that seems to be true . . ."

"Ah, Hank, I still sense some doubt in you. But you've got the proof there in your hand! A personal encounter with the miracle-working healing power of God! Glory to His name! I'm beginning another series at our church on divine healing starting this Sunday. You should stop by. They don't preach that at your church, do they?"

Hank shook his head. "Well, n-not exactly."

Smallwood stood and placed a hand on Hank's shoulder. "The Bible defines faith as the substance of things hoped for and the evidence of things not seen. But you've *seen* those images of my heart. And you've been my physician for the last twenty years. I'd reckon that's more than enough evidence, wouldn't you say?"

"I-I really don't know what to say, TR."

"Have faith, Hank. Have faith in God."

• • •

LATER THAT EVENING, TR stared at his reflection in his bathroom mirror, vacillating between longing and wonder at the aging process. His hair had once been full and jet-black, but it was now gray and thinning. It was amazing how the years had flown by. The bald spot at the crown of his head was seemingly growing larger with each passing month, but TR refused to get hair implants, or hair injections, or whatever those late-night infomercials kept advertising. He was content to grow old gracefully, now that he felt a greater assurance that he was *going* to grow old.

Still looking at the mirror, he touched a finger to the spot on his bare chest. It was the same spot where that mysterious man had placed his hand and spoken the healing words of Jesus over his heart. Slowly, almost reverently, TR began circling that spot with the tip of his index finger, silently mouthing praise to the Lord. He'd long wrestled with the fear of succumbing to the heart disease that ran in his family line, mainly because his father and grandfather had both preached divine healing, just as he now did. And what did it say about a preacher who preached great faith in the pulpit, only to lie awake at night wrestling with the spirit of fear?

Says you're human, jus' like everybody else . . .

Yet God had heard him, and answered his prayer!

"I don't know who that man was that walked into Hope Springs, Lord, but I'm so glad he was listenin' to Your precious Spirit and was obedient to come forward when he did," TR said, the same prayer of thanksgiving he'd been saying every day since the healing.

"TR, what are you doing standing there looking at yourself in the mirror?"

TR jumped slightly, initially thinking the voice of God was responding to him. But unless God was now speaking in a gravelly "Weezy" Jefferson vocal inflection, then it was not the Almighty. Rather, it was his beloved wife of thirty-three years, Estella.

"I'm marvelin' at what a fine specimen of manhood the Lord wrought when He made ol' TR," he answered, chuckling.

Estella appeared in the bathroom doorway and laughed along with him. He turned around to face her, and it was only then that he noticed Estella was wearing his favorite nighttime outfit, a silky black gown that accentuated the graceful curves of her body. Even at fifty-two years old, Estella Smallwood sported a figure that put an hourglass to shame. For a second, TR forgot all about what a fine specimen of manhood the Lord had wrought. The woman standing in front of him conjured up more pleasant, and urgent, thoughts.

"Well now, that outfit's been known to keep me young," he remarked, walking over and taking her into his arms.

"Amen to that," Estella purred.

Chapter Eight

DR. SHERMAN WINTHROP studied the eye examination data that had been returned to him after he'd sent copies to a respected ophthalmologist at the University of Alabama–Birmingham. The diagnosis from that doctor was the same as his.

Lynn Harper . . . would never see again.

The surgery team at Palmetto Memorial had been successful in removing the glass debris from both of Lynn's eyes, but the damage to her corneas had been too great. Her left eye certainly had no chance of restoration, and her right eye was not much better.

The red light on his desk phone began blinking, a sign that he was being paged.

"Winthrop here."

"Dr. Winthrop, Lynn Harper's mother and father are here."

Nodding, Sherman set the papers down. His face took on a grim expression as he stood. "Tell them I'll be right there."

• • •

LYNN HEARD THE FOOTSTEPS approaching her door fifteen seconds before anyone entered her room. Her hearing had been sharpened tremendously, as had her senses of touch, smell, and taste. She'd known, in an academic sense, that a human being's other four senses were heightened during a prolonged state of blindness, but to experience the phenomenon over the past few weeks was almost too much for her to bear. She wanted—*needed*—her sight back.

"Lynn, how are you feeling this morning?" she heard Dr. Winthrop ask.

"A little better," she replied, smelling first her mother's perfume, then her father's aftershave as they came in the room as well. "I can lift my left arm higher now," she added, demonstrating with a thumbs-up gesture.

"That's terrific! You'll be whipping it around like it was brand-new once you're assigned to physical therapy."

"Baby, we've all been praying for you at church," Jeannette spoke up, grasping her daughter's hand. "Pastor Gentry called all of us to pray and fast for your healing and recovery."

Several church elders had visited her as well, following the scripture in James 5:14, where the elders of the church were called for, to pray over and anoint those who were sick in the name of the Lord. Lynn's own faith had strengthened as a result, prompting her to lay her right hand over her eyes in the middle of the night, confessing healing scriptures from the Word of God.

"Lynn, I'm afraid I have some bad news," Dr. Winthrop continued. "Additional tests showed that the corneal damage to your left eye was so severe that there is no chance of sight restoration to that eye. Your right eye fared a little better. The optical nerve was not severely damaged; in a surgical procedure called temporary keratoprosthesis vitrectomy, we remove the injured cornea and place a clear, artificial cornea over your right eye. Retinal surgeons will then transplant a donor cornea."

"Wait a minute," Lynn interrupted, unsure of what she'd just heard. "Are you saying there's a chance . . . I could remain blind? *Permanently*?"

In the brief silence that ensued, Lynn heard Dr. Winthrop rustling some papers and quiet sniffling from her mother. It was the respectful silence normally reserved for funeral parlors.

"Yes, Lynn, there is a chance of permanent blindness," the doctor finally answered. "However, the technology for treating ocular trauma has grown in leaps and bounds over the years. The finest eye trauma surgeons in the country are in Birmingham, Alabama, at UAB's ophthalmology department. I have a colleague there who has successfully performed this procedure hundreds of times. Making arrangements is no problem at all. The Callahan Eye Foundation Hospital in Birmingham is just a five-hour drive away."

Though Dr. Winthrop's words were reassuring, Lynn was still unable to move past the unthinkable. She . . . could . . . go *blind* for the rest of her life?

No! God, this can't be happening!

"Lynn, honey, maybe we should think about this procedure," she heard her father say.

". . . and you know God is still able," her mother added.

"I'll leave you to discuss the options," Dr. Winthrop said. "I've given your parents a packet with all the information."

A packet that I can't read, Lynn thought despairingly. *A packet that I might never be able to read . . .*

"Oh, Lynn, we're going to get through this," her father said, moving over to the bed and taking her hand in his. "We're just going to have to trust in the Lord. He's never let us down."

Lynn agreed with her father one hundred percent—after all, she'd always been the rock of faith in the Harper family. She'd always known she was *called* to the gospel ministry, even when it was unpopular for women to make such announcements in certain denominations. She'd led in campus ministry at the university, leading many students to Christ, and had fit in easily with the ministry team at Faith Community Church. If anyone knew that God would not disappoint, it was she.

But I can't see, God . . . I can't see!

It was one thing to believe for someone else's healing, she knew. But she was now discovering the unique dilemma of believing in the miraculous when it was *she* standing in the need of prayer.

While her mother cried quietly and her father read over the information the doctor had given them, Lynn began meditating on the Word of God.

"I sought the Lord, and He heard me and delivered me from all my fears . . ."

Chapter Nine

NEWS OF THE SEVERITY of Lynn's condition soon reached Pastor Gentry's attention, causing him to shake his head and gaze up at the small gold cross hanging on his office wall as if to ask, *why*?

Pastoring Faith Community Church had taught him one consistent theme throughout the fifteen years he'd been there—it was inevitable that God's trials befell every one of His children. No distinction was made for those with titles in front of their names, no matter how gifted or anointed they were. In fact, the more anointed a person, the greater the trials. But while Gentry understood the general principle behind trials, he was nevertheless baffled at the current predicament of the church's director of outreach.

"God, I know You have a plan for our lives," he began praying. "And I know Your Word in Jeremiah 29:11 tells us the thoughts You think toward us are designed to give us a future, a hope, and an expected end. Lynn Harper is one of Your precious daughters, and I know Your expected end for her is to bless, favor, and give her the desires of her heart. I do not understand how her being blind fits into Your plan for her life, but Your ways are higher than mine. Your thoughts are higher than mine.

"I pray for her faith, God, that it would remain strong. I pray for her parents, Brother Leonard and Sister Jeannette, that You would encourage their hearts and cause them not to despair. First Peter 2:24 declares that Jesus bore our sins in His body on the tree, so that we might die to sins and live for righteousness, and that by Jesus's wounds we have been healed. I believe in the power of Your name to heal. And I confess that Lynn Harper be completely healed in the name of Jesus Christ."

• • •

THIRTY MINUTES LATER, after Gentry had finished praying for the members of the church, for his wife, Shanice, and finally for himself, he stood and walked over to the refrigerator he kept stowed away in the corner. Retrieving a water bottle from inside, he stretched and glanced at his watch. He was scheduled for a meeting with the altar workers in twenty minutes, then a meeting with his elders before going home for a meeting with Shanice.

That's my most important meeting of all, he thought, smiling.

The phone rang as he was taking a few sips of the water, and he moved closer to his desk to glance at the caller ID. His smile became even broader when he saw the name displayed.

"TR, is that really you?" he asked, settling back down into his chair. "It's been too long since we last got together."

"That's not my fault, Alonzo," T. R. Smallwood replied with a chuckle. "I hear the reports of what's going on over at your church. I'm surprised you even have time to breathe."

Alonzo laughed. Their relationship had begun long before Alonzo had founded Faith Community Church. Smallwood had asked him to preach the summer revival at Hope Springs Church, back when Alonzo was just starting out into full-time ministry. The older pastor had been the first one to publicly recognize his call, for which Alonzo would always be grateful.

"God is good, TR, I can testify to that. How've you been?"

"The best I've ever been, Alonzo!" Smallwood recounted the events of the strange man sitting in his church service, and how God had used him to heal his heart. He ended by saying he was preaching a series of healing sermons, beginning next Sunday.

When TR finished talking, Alonzo felt goose bumps along his skin. Was he hearing this right?

"TR, I've just finished praying for the healing of our church's outreach director. You remember the Harpers, right? Their daughter was in a car accident and lost the sight in her eyes. Everyone at our church is believing for the miraculous, and hearing your testimony has just charged my faith."

"Praise God!"

"You have *no* idea who that man was?"

"Nope. Not a clue. I've been looking for him ever since, though. God's given the gift of healing to all believers, but some operate in a greater level of faith. I remember attending an Oral Roberts tent meeting back in 1954, where I saw legs growing out, the lame getting out of wheelchairs and walking, and tumors disappearing right in front of my eyes! But when this man laid hands on me . . . my God! It was the touch of glory itself!

"And, I'm telling you, Alonzo—this man . . . he has it. He has the gift."

• • •

"THIS MAN" SAT A MERE FIVE MILES away from Faith Community Church, eating dinner at Five Points Diner, unaware that he was the current subject of conversation between two preachers.

"Would you like a refill on that iced tea?" the waitress asked, stopping next to his table.

He shook his head.

"Not real thirsty, huh? That's a shame. We serve great tea. You from out of town?" She seemingly had not caught the subtle hints that he wished to be left alone. After introducing herself with a boisterous, "Howdy, I'm Florence," she had taken a lengthy pause by his table each time she walked by.

"Yes."

Florence grinned. "I can spot 'em a mile off! Where ya from?"

"Here and there. No place in particular." He smiled, then cut another piece of waffle, dipped it in syrup, and placed it in his mouth. Florence seemed to get the hint this time and moved on to the customer two booths back.

The man finished his meal, left a decent tip for Florence, and strolled out the door. He headed for the bus stop, which would take him back to his encampment along the Congaree River. He had money for a rental car, but he preferred riding the bus. It catered to his need for privacy—no paper trail that way.

He took a seat at the very rear of the bus, and was instantly reminded of the time he and Nina had taken a bus to go sightseeing in Washington, D.C. They were there on a high school field trip, but had both decided to take an unofficial detour from the recommended itinerary and spend time together. Though they had money for a taxi, Nina had thought it would be more fun to ride the bus.

"Let's just ride and see where it takes us," she'd said, her big brown eyes lighting up at the prospect of the adventure.

He had agreed (though at that point he would've agreed if Nina had asked him to accompany her to Mars), and for the first fifteen minutes they'd been treated to excellent visuals of the White House, the Lincoln and Jefferson memorials, and the Capitol. But in ignorance they had neglected to get off the bus, and were thus taken to the seedier streets of the nation's capital—areas not represented in all the glossy tourist brochures. Upon seeing their predicament, the bus driver had just smiled and advised them to stay on the bus until he reached the station and could transfer them to a connecting route back to the Mall.

"You're not scared, are you?" Nina had asked, her brown eyes still sparkling, when he'd suggested they both move to the seat directly behind the bus driver.

He'd affected a macho shrug. "'Course not."

"Good. Then let's sit in the back instead."

Before he could protest, she had scrambled all the way to the rear of the bus, never once glancing back to see if he was following her. In retrospect, he realized it was at that point that he'd begun falling in love with Nina. He'd never known her to be this incredibly spontaneous, so vigorous and full of excitement. She was a live wire to his more reserved personality, and the more time he spent with her, the more he knew this was the woman he wanted to spend the rest of his life with.

"Hey, buddy," a rough voice said, breaking up the man's nostalgic trip down memory lane. "Somebody sittin' here?"

He shook his head and moved closer to the window, allowing the passenger to take the aisle seat. The man hadn't realized how crowded the bus was becoming as it traveled its circuitous route through the streets of downtown Columbia. Closing his eyes once more, he sought relief in the sweet sanctuary of memories.

Chapter Ten

LYNN'S RELEASE FROM THE HOSPITAL, nearly one month after her debilitating accident, should have been cause for celebration, if not for one major unresolved issue. Though she was thankful for the great care she had received from Dr. Winthrop and others at Palmetto Memorial, the likelihood of permanent blindness was a bitter pill she still could not swallow.

Gingerly and hesitantly, she now walked out the front doors with the support of a cane and the aid of her mother's arm.

"Your father has the car ready, just a few more feet," Jeannette whispered, leading her step by step.

The dark sunglasses Lynn wore hid the cloudy, almost lifeless irises of her eyes, but they could not stop the tears that began rolling down her cheeks.

"Lynn?" Jeannette noticed the tears, and quickly took a handkerchief, still damp from her own tears, from her purse to wipe her daughter's face.

"Mom . . . why?" Lynn's grip hardened on her mother's arm. "Why did this happen to *me*?"

"I don't know, baby. Sometimes, God . . ." Jeannette paused to look away. If Lynn had been able to see, she would've seen the utter heartbreak on the face of a parent unable to comfort a hurting child.

"Lynn, I don't know why this happened," Jeannette finally managed. "I know the Bible says God won't put more on us than we can bear, but this . . . this is right to the limit. This is right to the breaking point. But somehow, we'll get through this. Somehow."

Lynn was already preparing herself for the words of sympathy and faith she was sure to receive; well-intended expressions from others to try and comfort her and reassure her that everything would be alright.

But how can everything be alright? I . . . cannot . . . see!

The simple act of walking twenty feet from the hospital's front door to the circular driveway turned into, literally, an act of blind faith.

How am I going to live? How am I going to take care of myself?

The rational part of her brain told her that millions of people all over the world functioned without eyesight, so it *could* be done. The faith in her told her that with God, all things were possible, and to never stop believing for her healing. But at the moment, optimism and faith were no match for *reality*. The reality was that her life had been forever changed by the act of a drunken driver.

"Lynn, I'm right here," she heard her father say now as he helped her into the backseat.

"Thanks, Daddy," she replied, the tears still rolling down her cheeks.

God, I know You can do all things . . . but I need a miracle . . .

• • •

KNOWING THAT STAYING in her town house was no longer a viable option, Lynn remained quiet as her father turned east on Highway 76.

Sumter was an idyllic town of around twenty thousand residents, a rural community where people flew kites on breezy Saturday afternoons in their front yards, where neighborhood barbecues were frequent occurrences, and where the pace of life remained unhurried and laid-back. Lynn had countless memories of her parents' old, two-story home on Millwood Avenue, including the time she'd almost burned down the kitchen while frying a skillet of catfish, and the time she'd climbed the large pine tree in the backyard as a child, only to get her left leg wedged between two tree limbs. She'd remained stuck in that tree for almost two hours before her mother had come home from work. Twenty-five years she'd lived here, and she knew every twist, turn, crook, and crevice in this house, both downstairs and upstairs.

But her first blind steps inside the front foyer were the teetering, unsteady movements of a toddler learning to walk. She hadn't truly known how important sight was to balance and equilibrium; Dr. Winthrop had assured her that it might take a while to master the transition, but somehow he hadn't mentioned how frustrating it would be, running into walls and bumping her knees on table ends.

"We've got your room ready," her mother said, gently leading her by the elbow. "It's just as it was before, except the large dresser is all the way against the wall now."

Lynn knew this relocation of the dresser was so she wouldn't stub her toe against its claw-footed legs while stumbling about in the darkness. Her parents had probably rearranged most of the furniture downstairs to accommodate her, for which she was both thankful and a little ashamed. She didn't want to become a burden on the two people she loved most.

"Pastor Gentry and a few members from the church are going to be by in the morning," her mother continued to say as Lynn sat down on the bed. "We're all still believing that God will turn this all around."

Lynn sighed and flopped back onto the pillow. The pillowcases smelled laundry-fresh, like they'd just been taken out of the dryer. "Mom, this is all so . . . hard. I know I'm supposed to have faith, and I do, but . . . but every day when I wake up, it's still the same. Why is this happening to me? What did I do wrong?"

"Oh, baby, you didn't do anything wrong. None of us can ever know why some things happen. But we just have to trust that God has a reason for it all. This isn't the first time something like this has happened to you, remember?"

"I recall only what you told me. I was too young, remember?"

The winter before Lynn's second birthday, she had contracted pneumonia. After a week of intensive care at the hospital, the doctors were giving up hope for any chance of recovery. Her immune system was not strong enough to fight the disease, they said. During this same time, there had been a request from one of the nurses, who'd been a devout Christian, to ask the prominent healing evangelist Floyd Waters to stop by the hospital.

Waters had been conducting a healing crusade in nearby Greenville, and was known to oblige such requests. He had arrived late in the evening on that seventh night of Lynn's stay and had gone alone inside Lynn's room to pray for her.

"I'll never forget him walking out of your room," Jeannette now recalled. "That man of God's face was glowing as he declared your body to be healed by the power of Jesus's name. He said you would grow up to be a mighty champion for souls, and that the devil was trying to thwart the plan of God for your life. The next morning, the doctors informed us your temperature was going down and your vitals were returning to normal. Glory to God!"

"I've always accepted God's call over my life, Mom. What better way to walk in that call than as outreach director for Faith Community Church? But . . . if I'm . . . blind . . ."

"We're *never* going to stop believing for your healing, baby. This is simply another test—the Bible tells us that many are the afflictions of the righteous, but the Lord delivers us from them all."

Chapter **Eleven**

THE LIGHT RAIN rhythmically splashing against the bedroom window stirred Lynn from her light slumber. Her eyelids fluttered open, and she blinked for several seconds before it horribly dawned on her that she still was unable to see. She'd imagined this whole tragic affair to be a nightmare—that truck plowing into her car, the subsequent weeks in the hospital, the doctor's diagnosis that she would never see again. A terrifying nightmare, to be sure, but one that she would eventually awaken from.

But as she lay in bed, listening to the rain, an enormous weight of despair slowly settled over her, threatening to crush all remaining hope from her spirit.

Why me, God? Why . . . me?

What on earth had she done to deserve such an unthinkable fate? Hadn't she been taught all her life that if she lived right, if she loved and served God, and if she treated others as she would have them treat her, then God would certainly bless her? Had all those feel-good Sunday school lessons been nothing more than lies?

C'mon, Lynn . . . you know better than to think like that . . .

Sighing, she rolled to her right side, carefully letting her legs first dangle, then drop to the floor. She took a few tentative steps in the direction of the door, thinking of how difficult it would now be to perform the simplest tasks she'd always found pleasure in—taking a bath, washing her face, brushing her teeth, combing her hair. The degree of difficulty for those tasks had now been ratcheted up several frustrating notches.

Oh, God . . . I could look like a total mess and if nobody says anything, I wouldn't even know it . . .

Around nine o'clock, Lynn heard several church members come to her parents' door while she sat outside on the backyard patio. Growing up, she had always read her devotional Bible outside on the patio with a cup of coffee, enjoying the sun as it rose in the sky. There was something glorious, almost majestic, about communing with the Lord while surrounded by nature. Out of habit, she had come outside on the patio today for her devotional, but it hadn't felt the same since she could neither read her Bible nor behold the morning sun.

"Good morning, Lynn," she heard her pastor say behind her. She turned around in her seat to his voice.

"I'm here with Sister Arlene, Sister Margie, and Brother Charles," he began. "We wanted you to know how much we care about you, and that we're believing God is with you."

Lynn heard the intercessory team leaders begin praying in the Spirit as Pastor Gentry laid his right hand on her shoulder.

"Lord Jesus, we boldly come before the throne of grace to ask for help in this time of need," he began.

As he prayed the Word of God over her, with the chorus of intercessors praying behind him, Lynn's faith became strengthened as she focused her heart on an awesome God—a God who had created all things with the power of His Word and for whom nothing was impossible. She recalled every prophetic word that had been spoken over her, every time she'd asked God for a miracle on behalf of someone else and He'd provided, and every revelation she'd gleaned from countless hours studying the Word. Every time, God had proven Himself to be true in her life, and He had always been in her corner. Who was she to doubt Him now?

". . . and we thank You for hearing and answering our prayers. In Jesus's name, amen."

A full minute passed before anyone spoke, such was the heaviness of the Spirit all around them.

"I . . . I needed that," Lynn finally acknowledged, wiping her tears away with a handkerchief. "I . . . I didn't realize how *much* I needed that."

"Prayer is the lifeline to God, Lynn," Pastor Gentry began. "And in a time like this you need the saints collectively interceding on your behalf."

"Amen," Arlene concurred. "Lynn, you know how much we care about you and are praying for you."

"In addition to prayer," Pastor Gentry continued, "I'd like for you to come with us to Hope Springs Church. A pastor I've known for years, T. R. Smallwood, has a marvelous testimony of divine healing, and he's conducting special healing services beginning this Sunday night."

Lynn looked up at her pastor, unable to see his face

but clearly sensing the conviction in his words. He was not only her pastor but also a spiritual father whose faith in Christ had always been a shining example for her to follow. If he believed that attending this healing service would help her, then there was only one correct response to his request.

"I'll be there."

• • •

"CAN I GET YOU SOME MORE iced tea?" Florence asked the man, who had stopped by the diner for the second time that week.

He hesitated slightly before handing her his glass.

"It's good, isn't it?"

He agreed that it was.

"Made it myself. The secret is to keep a pitcher out in the sun— Wait a minute, I'm not supposed to tell you that!" She started laughing.

The man smiled. "Don't worry about it. I won't tell a soul."

"I can believe that—you don't strike me as much of a talker. You like the pancakes?"

He nodded. "You make them, too?"

"No, I just stick to the tea. It's what I do best." She put a hand on her hip and leaned against the table. "You know, I couldn't help but remember that big ol' tip you left for me last time. Things like that'll brighten my day like gettin' roses on Valentine's Day. You, uh . . . you going to be around town for a while? I wouldn't mind showing you around."

"Thanks, but I'm just passing through."

Before walking away, Florence scribbled her phone number on his copy of the bill, just in case, and flashed him a big grin.

The man took another bite of the buttermilk pancakes and wiped his mouth with the corner of his napkin. He leaned his head slightly to the right, listening to the conversation at the adjacent table. The whole time he'd been at the diner, he'd been overhearing the family of three discussing the health of their seven-year-old son, Eddie.

Eddie was seated at the table in a wheelchair. His legs were deformed below the knee, unnaturally twisting inward so that his ankles almost laid flat on the wheelchair footrests. As far as the man could perceive without frequently turning around, Eddie was also deaf in addition to his physical handicap. He gleaned this from the conversation between his parents, Andrea and James.

"I don't know what more we can do," the husband said to his wife. "We've gone to every specialist and doctor in the region. We've been praying every night. I just want our son to have a normal childhood."

"I know, James. But we have to keep believing . . . we have to keep trusting in God's will for Eddie's life."

"I want him to walk, Andrea. I want him . . . to know what it is to catch a baseball with his father. I . . . want him to be able to hear me say . . . I love him."

"He knows you love him, James . . ."

The man took another bite of his pancake, chewing slowly. More than most people, he empathized with Eddie's parents. For he, too, had been put in a position where a loved one's physical ailments were beyond a doctor's care. He knew what it felt like to see a loved one's life slip away and be powerless to do anything about it.

However, he'd also been given a gift of healing that he could not deny little Eddie or his parents, if they had the faith and if it was the will of the Lord.

Lord, is it Your will? he asked silently. *Here? In this restaurant?*

The man turned around as Eddie pounded his fork and spoon against his plate, looking at his parents with the lovable smile only a seven-year-old can make.

The man stood up from his seat, left another nice tip for Florence, and approached the table where James, Andrea, and Eddie sat.

"Excuse me," he gently interrupted. "I couldn't help but overhear your conversation about your son. I understand that you're praying for him."

James looked at the man somewhat warily before nodding. "Yes. We pray every day for God to heal Eddie. Are you a doctor?"

The man shook his head. "No, I'm not a doctor. I'm a believer in Jesus, like yourself. I believe God not only can heal your son's legs, but also He can open Eddie's ears."

"Well, we know God can certainly do that," Andrea commented, eyeing the stranger with a mixture of interest and a little concern. "God can do all things."

"Yes, He can," the man replied. "Do you mind if I pray for Eddie?"

Andrea leaned over and whispered in James's ear.

"We believe in prayer," James said. "We pray for him every day, but—"

"I understand your concern," the man cut in, "since I'm a total stranger to you, and you don't know what I might speak over your son. Here's what I believe, though, and what I will speak over your son. I believe in the healing power of Jesus. I believe that His act of love on the cross not only atoned for our sins, but also took away the curse of infirmity and disease. I believe in the laying on of hands, as Jesus commanded His disciples, that the sick might be healed."

"Well, we certainly believe all of that," James said, looking a little more relieved. "Uh, no . . . no, I don't think we mind if you were to pray for Eddie. Eddie?" James leaned over and, using sign language, communicated with his son. Eddie looked up at the stranger, smiled, and nodded his head.

The man walked over to the little boy and knelt down. Florence, leaning against the bar counter, observed the scene with great interest.

"Hello, Eddie," he signed, the extent of his knowledge of the language for the hearing impaired. Reaching over, he placed his hands over the boy's ankles.

"Lord, be glorified today. I come to You in the name of Jesus. Your Word declares that these signs shall follow those who believe: they will lay hands on the sick and the sick shall recover. I stand in agreement with James and Andrea, who have been praying for the health of their son. Lord, You said the effectual fervent prayer of the righteous avails much. As I lay hands on Eddie, I speak life and health to these ankle bones. I command his ears to be opened in the name of Jesus. I speak health over his body, and command his entire physical body to line up with the Word of God that says we are healed by the wounds of Jesus."

After saying these words, the man stood up straight, looked briefly at James and Andrea, and then calmly walked out the diner's front door and into the afternoon sunshine.

Chapter Twelve

TAP, T-TAP, T-TAP, TAP . . .

Travis's fingers furiously danced over his computer keys, moving to a mindless rhythm all their own as he hurried to beat the deadline for his next story submission. Despite his chubby frame, he'd always been an excellent typist, thanks largely to his long fingers. They were the fingers of a pianist, his mother had once told him when she'd tried to convince him to take piano lessons many years earlier. That forgettable fiasco had lasted all of one and a half lessons, as Travis possessed neither the patience nor the desire to master anything remotely as complicated as a piano.

And not that he was really *mastering* journalism, for that matter, but at least it constituted a job. A job that held enough respectability to keep him from being the butt of all the jokes at the family reunions. His two older, ultra-overachieving siblings, Maynard and Andrea, had both been valedictorians of their respective high school classes, and both had the complementary charisma and good looks to have everyone oohing and aahing over them like they were heirs to royalty.

Travis, naturally, provided dead-on meaning to the notion of a family's black sheep. His last name might have been Everett, but that was where the comparison to Maynard and Andrea ended. He'd barely made it out of college, but he hadn't really cared. He would have been more than content to find a minimum-wage job somewhere, peddling for enough pennies to indulge his gluttonous habits. But his father would have none of that embarrassment and had pulled some strings to get Travis this job at the *State* six years earlier.

With a sigh of relief (and five minutes to spare), Travis typed his final period and pressed the key command to save his article. Seconds later, Benny Dodson popped his head over the top of his cubicle. Benny, no doubt, had been listening for the cessation of Travis's typing.

"Just finished, huh?" Benny asked smugly. In all likelihood, Benny had finished his article much quicker and would probably enjoy another front-page byline.

Travis looked up nonchalantly, as if Benny's insults had no effect on him. "Just finished what? Oh, you mean my article?" He waved his hand dismissively. "Nah—I finished that two days ago. I've been working on something else all morning. Something *big*."

Benny laughed, exposing two rows of perfect white teeth. Could *anything* about Benny Dodson not be perfect?

"Yeah right, Travis," he replied, still laughing. "Perhaps this time Ryman will put it on the third page, instead of the last page."

Travis gritted his teeth, using every bit of his willpower not to reach up and strangle perfect Benny's little neck. And maybe knock out a few of those perfect teeth while he was at it.

"You keep laughing," he muttered instead, in a tone of voice Benny couldn't hear. "One day you're gonna be reading my byline on the front page of not just Metro, but the whole newspaper."

• • •

"LORD, TAKE ME ON THAT TRAIN to glory . . . I got my boarding pass . . . I'm ready to go this evening . . ."

T. R. Smallwood's prayers centered on one theme as he walked the inside perimeter of Hope Springs Church—*glory*. Anyone who might've walked in on him, unfamiliar with what was going on, would've thought Smallwood crazy at the very least, delusional at the very most. But T. R. Smallwood was oblivious to anything outside the scope of his eyesight, currently fixated on his open Bible as he walked the sanctuary's floors. The Bible had been opened to his favorite passage of scripture, 2 Chronicles 7.

"When Solomon had finished praying, fire came down from heaven and consumed the burnt offerings and the sacrifices; and the glory of the Lord filled the temple. And the priests could not enter the house of the Lord, because the glory of the Lord had filled the Lord's house."

"Ahh . . . yes! That's what I'm praying for," TR exclaimed, rejuvenated as he reread the passage aloud.

"Lord, let Your glory be so thick in this place that miracles will spring forth like the dawning of a thousand sunrises! Let cancerous tumors dry up the second they come inside this place! Let broken bones and broken hearts be healed inside these holy walls! Let blinded eyes be opened and deaf ears be unstopped! Lord, I know that You are the Most High God and that nothing is too hard for You. I believe that there is an anointing in this church to heal the sick and afflicted, and I thank You in advance for a great outpouring of Your power and glory at the healing crusade."

This was the secret, Smallwood knew. It all revolved around this—*prayer*. Every aspect of his ministry, in all the years he'd been in full-time ministry, had been bathed in prayer. His late father had taught him that in both word and deed.

"Doing ministry work without prayer is like driving an automobile without gas," he was known to say. "You can be lookin' fine on the outside with that car all washed and waxed, but if you're running low on gas, pretty soon that car's gonna be sputtering, and then it's gonna stop altogether. Prayer is the gasoline that fuels a ministry's engine. So when you want to go far in God, fuel up with some high-octane prayer!"

TR's prayers were not only high-octane now, they were also further supercharged with *personal experience*. God had answered his prayer for a personal healing in dramatic fashion—healed right during the middle of a heart attack! There was a huge difference between praying something you *believed* and praying something you *knew*. T. R. Smallwood had moved past the realm of belief and into the realm of knowing.

"I know You as Jehovah-Rapha, the Lord that healeth me," he now prayed, placing his Bible on the steps of the altar and raising his hands. "I pray this community, and then this whole state, and then this country and world may come to know You as their Healer as well."

TR felt the power and presence of the Lord even more strongly then, and he fell, trembling, to his knees. The glory train had pulled into the station, and TR didn't need to be told twice to get on board.

Chapter Thirteen

THE FOLLOWING EVENING, the arriving crowd at Hope Springs Church was large enough to create a mini traffic jam for travelers in their cars heading south on Highway 15. The buzz around town had been further fueled by Pastor T. R. Smallwood's weeklong proclamation that the evening's healing crusade would be "an opportunity for God's glory to shine like never before in Sumter County!" After preaching his usual "glory train" sermon in the morning, he'd handed out packets of healing scriptures, encouraging the membership to commit the passages to memory and begin speaking them aloud everywhere they went—the grocery store, the gas station, in their homes, and on their jobs.

"God responds to His Word," he reminded the congregation. "When you speak that precious Word and come into agreement with what He's already said about healing, you create an atmosphere for miracles to happen."

Now Brother Sanderson began playing a warm-up melody on the organ while the ushers scrambled to seat what would surely be the largest crowd they'd ever seen. The small sanctuary of Hope Springs comfortably sat 150, but about twice that many people were expected to attend.

Lynn had arrived early enough with her parents, Pastor Gentry, and the intercessory team leaders to secure seats four rows from the front. After praying over her again, Pastor Gentry had gone to meet with T. R. Smallwood, leaving Lynn with a growing sense of anticipation as she heard the crowd gathering all around her.

Was this to be her night of healing?

Lord, I believe that You are a healer . . . I believe my sight can be restored in Jesus's name . . .

She heard someone on the organ softly playing "What a Friend We Have in Jesus," prompting her to quietly sing along. She heard people steadily coming into the sanctuary, but the noise level remained respectful, almost hushed. It was the anticipation, she thought. Among the whisperings, she heard some people praying in tongues while others spoke healing scriptures aloud.

T. R. Smallwood's testimony that he not only had been supernaturally healed during a heart attack but now also had been given the heart of someone half his age had swept through the town of Sumter like fire blazing through a stack of dry kindling. It was common knowledge that heart disease had run through the Smallwood family line, and though TR had been preaching divine healing for years, few people, even Christians, actually thought the old preacher would be living, breathing *proof* of such healing. In a town where the average age was in the forties and the elderly outnumbered the young almost two to one, healing and health were important topics of discussion.

"Saints, are we ready to board that train for glory?" T. R. Smallwood's voice now thundered from the pulpit.

The congregation stood and began shouting and clapping in response to the pastor's trademark call to worship.

"My Bible tells me that in the glory there is no sickness! In the glory there is no disease! In the glory there are no crutches! And the glory shall fall in this house . . . *tonight*!"

The shouts from the congregants lasted for several minutes, spurred on by Brother Sanderson's well-timed organ chords.

"Many of you have heard my testimony of how God healed my heart," Smallwood continued. "He used an anointed man to lay hands on me and curse that spirit of infirmity, that spirit of sickness, and drive it right back to the depths of hell!"

More shouts from the congregants.

"Though I have not seen that man since, God has clearly chosen this time as a season of healing for all who will receive it in the name of Jesus Christ. Tonight, those who are sick, those who are lame, those who are blind—we will lay hands on you and declare you healed in the name of—"

"Oh my Lord!" A woman's voice suddenly pierced the air. "Oh my Lord!"

Lynn turned her head at the sound; it seemed as if the woman was sitting behind her a few rows back.

"My son can hear!" The woman screamed. "And his ankles! His ankles have been straightened out! Lord Jesus, it's a miracle!"

Pandemonium broke out all over the sanctuary. As Brother Sanderson began playing chords on the organ, Lynn heard the beating of tambourines, shouts, and handclaps around her. It was as if a spiritual dam had been broken, and a river of praise had been set free for everyone to swim in.

"Praise God!" someone yelled.

"What a mighty God we serve!" another exclaimed.

The spontaneous praise lasted for a few minutes, until Smallwood asked everyone to settle down and directed the woman to testify to what the Lord had done.

"My name is Andrea Everett," the woman began, "and this here is my son, Eddie. He was born deaf and with ectrodactylism, a birth defect that fused the bones in his legs together, making him unable to walk. The doctors gave my husband, James, and me all the results from hundreds of medical studies, saying how impossible it was for Eddie to ever walk or hear, but we never stopped believing that God could turn it around for us. We knew that nothing was too hard for the God we serve."

"Praise God, sister!" Smallwood exclaimed. "That's exactly right! And he was healed just now?"

"Y-yes, well . . . I just happened to look down and notice that Eddie was rotating his ankles around, something he'd never been able to do before. I was about to ask him in sign language how he was able to do that, but . . . but then his eyes just lit up and he said that he could hear! He said that he could . . . hear . . . everything around him, and that he had started to get strength in his ankle bones two days ago."

"Two days ago?"

"Let me explain. Two days ago we were eating out at a diner in Columbia, and this man came up to us and asked if he could pray over Eddie. I was kind of hesitant at first, but he prayed everything you've just been talking about—that Eddie was healed by the stripes of Jesus and that his physical body must line up with what the Word of God says."

"Glory to God! Saints, are you hearing this? The Bible tells us in Mark 16 that we shall lay hands on the sick, and they shall recover!" Smallwood turned his attention to the young child.

"Eddie, can you hear me?"

"Yes, sir," the boy answered.

"Glory to God! Eddie, would you like to run down the center aisle, touch the door, and come back?"

"Yes, sir!"

"Have you ever run before?"

"N-no, sir."

"Well, Jesus has healed you, so you can now run for His glory!"

The bedlam of praise erupted throughout the sanctuary once more as the center aisle was cleared for Eddie. Lynn clapped her hands along with everyone else and wished she could see the jubilant expression that must've been all over the little boy's face.

"Saints, the Healer is here," Smallwood declared, amidst the joyous shouts of the congregation. "Come forward now to receive what God's Word says is yours!"

Lynn got to her feet. Using a cane that she tapped out in front of her, she carefully made her way to the front, where she heard a concert of voices praying all around her.

The altar workers must have already been lined up, she thought.

"Sister, I'll pray for you," Lynn heard a woman's voice say. Walking in the direction of the voice, Lynn reached out her hand. A soft hand enclosed hers.

"My name is Sister James. I'm here to pray for your healing."

The woman's soft, grandmotherly voice sounded faint and quivering, and for a second Lynn felt a pang of disappointment. The sharp contrast in demeanor from the fiery T. R. Smallwood to the soft-spoken, gentle Sister James didn't mean this lady possessed less faith, but Lynn nevertheless had wanted someone a little more radical to pray over her.

"What are you standing in need of, sister?"

Lynn swallowed. Wasn't it obvious what she was standing in need of? "I'm . . . I'm blind. My prayer is that the Lord would restore my sight."

Sister James clucked her teeth together. "Oh dear," Lynn heard the old woman whisper.

Oh God, Lynn thought, sensing a spirit of doubt in the old woman. It was a spirit she knew all too well. *Help her unbelief* . . .

• • •

TEN MINUTES LATER, Lynn returned to her seat, still unable to see. Sister James had prayed over her (and

Lynn had been praying, too), but her sight had not been restored. All around her, she heard random shouts of people testifying of their healing.

Then why not me, Lord? Why . . . not . . . me?

Did she have a lack of faith? Was there unconfessed sin in her life? Had she done something to *warrant* being in that accident and losing her sight? Maybe God's mercy had already been shown on her behalf by allowing her to live while that other driver had died.

These thoughts bombarded Lynn's brain like a barrage of cannon fire, and for the first time since the doctor had said she might remain permanently blind, her faith began to waver.

"Lord, please help me," she whispered. "I know that You can heal me. You opened that little boy's ears and healed his legs. You healed Pastor Smallwood's heart. I know You are not a respecter of persons; if You did it for them, You can do it for me . . ."

Thirty minutes later, Lynn got to her feet again.

"Are you going to the front for more prayer?" her mother asked.

"No. I'm . . . I'm just going to the restroom."

"I'll go with you."

Lynn was in no position to refuse her mother's help, especially since she had no idea where the bathroom *was.* It turned out the church's lone restroom was at the rear of the building, and at the moment it was fortunately empty.

"I'll be right outside," Jeannette said.

"You don't have to wait, Mom. I'm getting better at moving around." Lynn didn't voice what she wanted to—her mounting frustration at both losing her independence and the fact that she might never see again. Turning on first the cold and then the hot water from the sink, she splashed her face with the water, letting the warmth mix with the tears that had begun running down her cheeks.

"Lord, I know You can restore my sight. I . . . I just want to see again."

As she turned around, she stumbled and started to fall. At the last second, her hand reached out and grabbed what felt like the door handle. She took a few seconds to calm herself before opening the door.

Immediately, she sensed something was wrong. Instead of the hallway she'd just come from, she sensed the cool evening air on her skin and heard the chirping of crickets around her.

I'm outside, she thought. *How in the world did I get outside?*

Her sense of direction must have gotten turned around when she had stumbled, and she had grabbed the wrong door handle. Not being able to see, and never having been to Hope Springs Church before, she hadn't known the church's small restroom had been built like most country churches built in the early 1900s. There was a door leading in from the outside as well as inside. Lynn turned around and retraced her steps back to the door, but when she grabbed the doorknob, she discovered that it would not turn.

Suppressing the urge to cry for help, she took a few awkward steps to her left, keeping her palm against the outer wall of the church. She took comfort in knowing that if she kept one hand on the wall at all times, it would be impossible to get lost.

• • •

THE MAN HAD BEEN WATCHING her careful trek around the church, and at first it had been like seeing a ghost from his past. He realized that she was blind, but her physical stature, her skin tone, the way she wore her hair pulled back from her face—it all reminded him of someone who'd been taken from his life years earlier.

He would have remained content to watch her and nothing more, had it not been for the garden rake lying haphazardly on the ground a few feet in front of where the woman was headed. Someone had carelessly neglected to set the rake upright, or perhaps it had fallen over—who knew? What the man *did* know was that in a few more seconds, the woman was about to have an unfortunate accident.

Quietly and quickly, he moved to where the rake was and picked it up.

"Who's there?" she called out, just as he was retreating.

Apparently, he hadn't been as quiet as he'd wanted. He'd underestimated this woman's heightened sense of hearing.

"There was a rake lying on the ground," he replied. "I didn't want you to step on it."

"Oh . . . oh, thank you. That was very nice of you." She waited a moment before adding, "Listen, can you help me back inside the church as well? I somehow got locked out of the restroom, and . . . well you can probably see my predicament."

The man cleared his throat. "Of course."

Taking her free hand in his, he began leading her around the church.

"I take it you're here for the healing crusade," the woman said. "What are you doing outside?"

"I guess I just like the outdoors," the man replied.

They had come around to the front of the church when the woman stopped. "Can I ask you something? Do you believe in healing? I mean, everything that Pastor Smallwood is saying—that believers in Christ can lay hands on the sick and they shall recover?"

The man cleared his throat again. "Yes, I believe that we can lay hands on the sick and they can be healed." He hesitated for just a second. "I've seen it happen."

"You *have*? Then would you mind praying for me? I had come here for prayer, but I don't think the sweet old lady who prayed for me truly believed God could restore my sight. You, on the other hand, sound so . . . so different. For some reason, I don't know, I . . . just believe you have faith that God can do it."

"God can do all things," the man responded. "Including allowing you to see again."

"Amen! Then would you . . . would you pray for me?" she asked again.

The man nodded. "What is your name?"

"Lynette Harper. Everybody calls me Lynn, though."

The man nodded again. "Lord Jesus, I come to You on behalf of my sister Lynn. There is nothing too hard for You, and it is with that confidence that I stand in agreement with her faith that You would restore her sight. Your Word declares in Matthew 18:19 that if two believers agree on anything we ask for, it will be done for us by our Father in heaven. Now I confidently stand upon Your Word and ask that You would restore her sight."

He placed his hands over Lynn's eyes. "As I lay hands on my sister's eyes, I speak the healing power of Jesus Christ to manifest with her eyes being—"

Suddenly, the man felt Lynn inhale sharply and begin to fall backward. He had seen this happen before—the Spirit of the Lord had this effect on many people. Looping his arm quickly behind her, he broke her fall as she descended gently on the grass. Lynn was wearing a dress with a hemline that stopped just above her knees, so to respect her modesty he took off his checkered suit coat and draped it across her legs.

Then, with one parting glance at a face that conjured up a host of memories he'd tried for years to forget, he calmly strode off into the evening twilight.

Chapter Fourteen

HE CAUGHT A RIDE BACK into town after flagging down the driver of a passing truck—the locals were extremely hospitable, he was fast discovering. Still, he remained shaken over how much that young blind woman had reminded him of Nina. The physical resemblance had been startling—it was almost as if Nina had a secret twin sister living in South Carolina, though he knew that could not be true. Nina had been an only child.

He looked down at his hands, surprised to see them shaking ever so slightly. There was a loud ringing in his ears as well, and he felt it becoming difficult to breathe.

Stop it . . . get a hold of yourself . . .

The question would not stop ringing throughout his mind—why had he come back to Hope Springs Church? It was the first time he'd ever revisited a church where he'd healed someone previously; ordinarily, he made it a rule never to do that. But he'd felt the leading of the Holy Spirit to come back.

He was reminded of the words of John the Apostle, writing in his gospel that Jesus *must need* pass through Samaria to minister to the woman at the well. It was a similar, strong compulsion that he had felt—was Lynn to be his own "woman at the well" experience?

"Hey, the buck stops here," the truck driver said, stirring the man from his thoughts. "I gotta head on towards Florence, which is goin' east. You going to Columbia, and that's the other way."

The man nodded, unbuckling his seat belt and reaching for the door's handle. "Thank you for taking me this far. I appreciate that."

"No problem. Happy trails, partner." *Partner* came out of the man's mouth sounding like *pahd-nuh.* With a hearty wave, the truck driver pulled away from the road's shoulder.

The man stuck his still shaking hands in his pockets and set off in the direction of the bus station. He needed to get to Columbia, and back to Congaree National Park. Above all, he needed to get back to his personal, private sanctuary.

• • •

"LYNN!"

"My God! Lynn, are you alright?"

The voices, faint at first, then growing louder, reached her consciousness and caused her dream to dissipate. In the dream, she had been sitting on a bench in the Swan Lake Iris Gardens, feeding the graceful swans that swam to the water's edge from her personal bag of bread crumbs. Sumter's Swan Lake, the only public park in the States to feature all eight species of swans, was the place where Lynn had spent many lazy childhood Saturday afternoons, reading, praying, and passing time. Yet the past few minutes hadn't seemed like a dream—it had seemed so *real.* And the most glorious part of it all was that she had been able to see!

But it was just a dream . . .

"Lynn, are you alright?" Her mother asked again, lifting Lynn slowly from the ground. From the intermingling smells of perfumes and colognes and the whispers, Lynn sensed a crowd forming around her.

"I waited for you to come out of the restroom, but when you didn't—"

"I'm alright, Mom," Lynn interrupted. "I just went out the wrong door." She was about to say something else when her eyes fluttered open, as they had done so often during the last six weeks with nothing but blackness greeting them.

This time, however, a burst of color flashed through her mind like a kaleidoscope. Lynn blinked once, twice.

I can see!

She saw the red dress her mother was wearing and the gold pendant swinging from her neck. Looking up, she looked straight into her mother's eyes. Though her mother had the same Natalie Cole–like eyes as she, they had never looked as beautiful as they did at this moment.

Jeannette saw her daughter's eyes, too, and saw that there was no longer a cloudy haze over them.

"Lynn!" she shrieked. "My God, your eyes!"

My eyes! "I can see, Mom! I can see!"

At once, the crowd began shouting and clapping around her—Lynn saw Arlene, Sister Linda, Sister Margie, Brother Charles, Pastor Gentry, and her father giving praise to God—and to *see* them after six weeks of utter darkness was just . . . amazing!

Soon, T. R. Smallwood joined the small gathering outdoors and began to give God praise for another miraculous healing. So far, there had been *fifteen* testimonies of healings that had taken place, and with every one Smallwood had rejoiced louder.

But his expression changed from one of jubilance into one of near shock as he noticed the checkered gray-and-black suit coat Lynn held in her hands.

"Sister, can I ask where you got that coat?"

Lynn looked down at the coat in her hands. "I . . . I don't know where— Oh, it must have come from the man who prayed over me." She looked up, remembering. "A man laid hands over my eyes while I was out here and prayed that my sight be restored."

"Glory to God," Smallwood whispered, practically in reverence. "That's the same coat the man who laid hands on my heart was wearing."

"And the same coat the man who prayed over my Eddie was wearing," a woman spoke up. By her voice, Lynn recognized her as Andrea Everett.

"Glory to God," Smallwood whispered again.

"But why does this man . . . *vanish* after these healings?" Jeannette wondered aloud. "It's as if he wants no recognition at all."

"He wants the recognition to go to God," someone mused.

"Maybe he's an angel," someone else spoke up.

"What's *most* important," Smallwood cut back in, "is that the glory of God is falling around here like never before! It's just like the pool at Bethesda, with the waters stirred up and the healing of the Lord available for all who believe and receive!"

Lynn began rejoicing along with everyone else, her eyes taking in the hues and colors of everyone and everything she could. Still, though, in her mind she couldn't help but wonder—who *was* the man God had used to restore her sight?

Chapter Fifteen

AFTER PASTORING a Spirit-filled church for fifteen years, Alonzo Gentry was hardly a stranger to witnessing modern-day miracles. One miracle he always reflected on had occurred when one of his most faithful members, Brother Michael Williston, had traveled to Atlanta on a business trip. Not sure of where he was going, Brother Michael had had the misfortune of making a wrong turn off I-75, and had soon found himself driving inside the gates of the McDaniel Glenn housing projects. The Glenn was not a place for outsiders; in fact, it was not a place most Atlanta residents dared even venture into without a police escort. Survival in the Glenn was predicated on knowing the law of the streets, a law Brother Michael knew nothing about. Easily identified as a newcomer (and one with perceived wealth, based on the luxury sedan he was driving), Brother Michael had been robbed at gunpoint after he'd compounded his navigation error by making another mistake: he'd stopped to ask for directions.

"He pointed the gun to my chest and demanded money," Brother Michael had recounted. "But I didn't have any cash on me, only credit cards. And this kid—he couldn't have been older than fourteen—starts screaming and cursing at me, waving that gun back and forth to try and scare me. But I wasn't scared. I kept praying in the Spirit the whole time, loud enough for him to hear what I was doing."

Alonzo had been impressed by Brother Michael's boldness, and he personally wondered if he would have possessed that same spirit of boldness. He preached it behind the pulpit, but to pray in the Spirit with an actual gun to your face?

"This kid started screaming louder at me once he saw he wasn't scaring me," Brother Michael had continued. "But that wasn't too smart, because a surefire way to draw attention to yourself while waving a gun is to start yelling. And then the kid puts the gun to my head . . . and . . . and he pulled the trigger."

"Oh my Lord," Alonzo had whispered.

"But the gun *jammed*, Pastor," Brother Michael had said, with tears now rolling down his face. It had taken him almost a minute to regain his composure.

"It wouldn't fire. And not five seconds later, a police car rolled around the corner. It turned out that someone had heard the kid yelling, saw what was going down, and called the police. But God saved me that night—I know that just as sure as I know my name."

"Praise God," was all Alonzo could whisper.

And then there was the miracle involving Sister Margie, one of the key members of his current intercessory team. Sister Margie's daughter Latriece had gone swimming in Stevens Creek one hot summer afternoon while Sister Margie was at work. Latriece, fourteen years old at the time, had swum in Stevens Creek several times, and was an excellent swimmer. However, on this particular day she had dived into a section of the creek and had not seen a rock jutting up from the bottom. After the dive, as she was straightening out underwater, the right side of her head collided with a sharp plane of the rock. Latriece had instantly been knocked unconscious.

"Pastor Gentry, I just *knew* something was wrong," Sister Margie had later recounted, with tears rolling down her face. "I was sitting at my desk at 3:23, and I felt in my spirit that something had happened to Latriece. I started praying in the Spirit, and then I called my next-door neighbor, Etta, and told her to go in my house and get Latriece. Then the Lord showed me a vision of my baby in Stevens Creek, behind our house, and I told Etta to get my baby from that creek bed."

Etta Rosedale was in her late forties, and had probably never swum a day in her life. But like Sister Margie, she was a praying woman of God and she sensed the urgency of the request. While all this had been going on, Sister Margie had told one of her coworkers to call 911 and get the paramedics to her house.

"All because you sensed this in the Spirit," Alonzo had interrupted, just shaking his head. He would never cease to be amazed at the greatness of the God he served.

"That's right, Pastor."

Etta Rosedale, amazingly, had been able to quickly locate Latriece at the bottom of the creek and pull her to the shore. By then, the paramedics had arrived and were able to administer CPR, reviving Latriece. The local media outlets had wanted to credit either the fast-responding medics, the heroics of Etta Rosedale, or the quick thinking of Sister Margie as being responsible for saving Latriece's life, but Sister Margie was adamant about who received the glory.

"The *Lord Jesus* saved my baby," she had stated unflinchingly to all who would hear.

In addition to these unforgettable miracles, Alonzo had witnessed other miraculous events in his congregation. Various members had had their debt supernaturally canceled; others had been healed of numerous diseases; others had received incredible promotions in their businesses; and still others had seen unsaved loved ones come to know the salvation of Jesus Christ.

But the miracle of witnessing Lynn Harper's blinded eyes being opened had literally taken his breath away. He'd believed that it could happen, sure. And he'd wanted it to happen. But to actually *witness* it? After personally knowing and sympathizing with Lynn's desire to see, and then feeling the frustration of hearing the doctors report that Lynn would never see again?

"God, You are such an awesome God," he breathed, closing his Bible and leaning back in his chair. After the healing crusade, he'd gone back to his office, needing time and space to reflect on what he'd just seen. He felt a little like how Moses must have felt after the parting of the Red Sea, or Daniel the morning after spending the night in the lion's den. Like those biblical giants of the faith, it radically stirred his faith to know he served a God who could do *anything*.

Chapter **Sixteen**

THE MORNING SUNRISE greeted Lynn's eyes, transforming her daily devotional time into one of her most powerful experiences ever. Never again would she take for granted the small blessings in life—having all five of her senses working, being in her right mind, and being able to walk and move around without depending on someone else.

Lord, You are so good . . . thank You for restoring my sight . . .

She had spent all morning devouring the scriptures that spoke of divine healing, eager to understand more of the amazing phenomenon she had experienced. If God's Word empowered Christians to lay hands on the sick and heal them, then why weren't more Christians walking in the fullness of that power? All her life, she had read the awesome miracles chronicled in the Bible and subconsciously assumed they were for the biblical times. Some theologians even went as far as to say the miracles in the book of Acts were necessary in the days of the fledgling church to bring more believers into the fold. But once the church had grown and prospered, they said, such amazing miracles had no longer been necessary.

Yet Lynn read in her Bible that Jesus promised "greater works" from the disciples that were to follow Him. And Lynn could not discard the apparent healing power that mysterious man had walked in—just look at all the incredible testimonies that had resulted from his demonstration of faith, herself included!

God had given her a glimpse of a greater dimension of the power of His resurrection, and no matter how strong her faith had been before, she was compelled to increase it.

She checked her watch and saw she had another two hours before she was scheduled to meet with Pastor Gentry at Faith Community. In light of the healing miracles that were taking place in Sumter and Columbia, her pastor had felt a need to restructure their outreach program. What greater way to reach the lost than as Jesus Himself had declared in the power of the gospel—that signs and wonders would follow those who believed?

Faith was stirring in the souls of Christians who were witness to the acts of God's power, which pointed to only one outcome.

Revival.

• • •

TRAVIS WAS INFORMED of his nephew's healing over the phone that afternoon as he typed another boring article on his computer's keyboard. But a yarn about a man walking around healing people was too incredible for him to believe. He was beginning to think his sister was losing her mind.

"You're tellin' me Eddie can now *hear* and *walk*?" he questioned Andrea, suspiciously, as he guzzled down the last few drops of his diet Pepsi. "All because someone laid his hands on him and chanted some abracadabra magic over him?"

"It's not abracadabra," Andrea retorted. "You've never believed in Christianity, but this is one of the benefits all believers in Jesus have—divine healing."

Travis snorted. "Oh, Andrea, you were always the gullible one. Remember the time you thought your Barbie doll was talking to you? Giving you advice on what clothes to wear?"

"Travis, I was just a kid then. But this thing with Jesus is real. Alright, you don't believe me?"

"No, I—"

"Then listen for yourself."

Seconds later, a little boy's voice spoke into the phone. "Uncle Trav?"

Travis almost dropped his can of diet Pepsi into his lap. He'd heard Eddie's voice many times before, but always with that echo-type lisp accompanying the voice of someone unable to hear any sound. But Eddie's voice was now clear in tone; there was no lisp at all.

"Ed-Eddie? That's you? And you can *hear* me?"

"Sure, Uncle Trav. And get this—I can walk and run, too. I'm real fast!"

Travis was speechless. "Um, can you p-put your mom back on the line, Eddie?"

"Sure, Uncle Trav."

"Do you believe now, Travis?" Andrea asked.

Travis didn't know *what* to believe. "I . . . I don't know. Listen, I'm going to stop by the house later on, okay?" He hung up the phone, visibly shaken. Andrea had said someone was walking around healing people of sicknesses and deformities in the name of God. Like any other reasonable, sane human being, he had dismissed the idea as ludicrous. Such people came on television from time to time, boasting about being able to cure people with a touch of their hands. Travis had never believed them—he figured people like that were con artists looking for gullible folk to finance their religious charades.

But his own *nephew*? A child he had personally seen born deaf and having ankle bones doctors had said would be deformed for as long as he lived? How in the world was he supposed to explain something like that?

Reaching for his trusty Clemson Tigers cap, Travis stood and walked out of his cubicle. If it was a good story Ryman Wells wanted, then Travis might finally be able to make good on that delivery.

• • •

"LOOK AT ME, UNCLE TRAV!" Eddie exclaimed, jumping up and down like he were a pogo stick. "Look at me! Look at my legs! I can walk . . . and run, too!" As if to demonstrate, Eddie took off like a lightning bolt down the hallway, his little legs scampering faster than Travis had ever seen them move.

"Th-that . . . is . . . unbelievable," Travis commented, half turning his head to glance at his sister. Andrea was leaning against the kitchen doorjamb, wiping tears from her eyes with a handkerchief as she watched the miracle of her son running.

"But it *is* believable, Travis. That's why I can't stop crying these tears of joy. James and I have been praying to see this day for almost seven years now. What God has done . . . what God has done . . ." Her words trailed off as she continued shaking her head.

"Hold it, now. Wait just a second, Andrea," Travis began. The stubborn agnostic that he was, he wasn't ready to accept his nephew's healing as an act of God. "What proof do you have that this was the work of your Christian God?"

Andrea's jaw dropped open. "My *Christian* God? Proof? Travis, will you listen to yourself? We were all raised in the same church growing up. But why you didn't accept the Lord as your Savior like Maynard and I did remains a mystery to all of us. What more *proof* do you need? James and I have been praying and fasting for Eddie's physical healing for the last seven years—you've watched how we've prayed. We attended a healing crusade, where everyone there was believing God for the healing of their bodies, and through the power of God, Eddie was miraculously healed. You want proof? The proof is the joy written all over Eddie's face. Go ahead, Travis. Ask your nephew what happened."

Travis looked at Eddie, who had now run back to them and had obviously overheard the last part of the conversation.

"Jesus healed me, Uncle Trav!" Eddie blurted out, not waiting for Travis to ask a question.

Travis offered his nephew a pitying smile, feeling more awkward than ever around the kid. He wanted to tell Eddie all this Jesus-talk was a bunch of nonsense, but he dared not in front of Andrea. It was a shame, though. They were probably teaching Eddie to believe in Santa Claus and the Easter Bunny as well. Sooner or later, though, the kid's imaginary bubble would burst and he would have to face the cold, hard realities of life.

"Did He, now?" Travis said instead. Better to keep this dialogue neutral.

Eddie vigorously nodded, in the rapid-fire way only an energetic seven-year-old boy can move his head. "Yep! Jus' like Mommy and Dad said—Jesus opened my ears and fixed my legs. Isn't that cool?"

Travis shifted his weight back and forth between his feet. It was one thing to have to listen to Andrea and Maynard talk about Jesus. But to hear this kind of talk from his seven-year-old nephew?

I don't have to take this . . . "Listen, sport, Uncle Trav's gotta run, okay? I got some things I need to do."

"Okay!" Eddie turned on his heels and bounded back down the hallway. Travis offered a pitying smile to Andrea as well, as he headed in the opposite direction toward the door.

"Travis, I know you can feel the Lord drawing you," Andrea called out behind him.

Travis didn't break his stride until he reached the front door. "Yeah, well, if He's calling me, He's gonna have to speak a little louder. It's great what happened to Eddie, though."

It's gonna make a great story, too . . .

Chapter Seventeen

THE MAN STARED AT NINA'S photograph, once more overwhelmed by the physical similarities to that blind woman he'd encountered at Hope Springs Church.

Same eyes, same hair, same everything . . .

He'd tried repeatedly to get over Nina's loss and somehow move on with his life, but the tragic irony of the whole situation tormented him daily. If God could use him to heal people now, why hadn't He used him when it mattered *most*?

"What do You want from me?" he suddenly cried out, staring upward at a cloudless sky. The heavens were quiet. In his mind, they were silently mocking him. "This isn't the life I was supposed to have. I lost everything that mattered to me. And for what?"

The tenor of his rising voice began to shake as he wiped a hot tear sliding down his cheek.

"Everything was going great with my life. Everything was going great with my family. What did I do wrong? I loved You! I served You! How could You have allowed this to happen!"

He closed his eyes in a futile effort to stem the onrushing wave of painful memories bombarding his mind. *Anything* was better than having to face the memories of the past.

"Oh God," he whispered, sinking to his knees and falling headfirst into the soft grass. But God didn't seem to be presently helping him. This was his cross to bear. Alone.

In a choice that was not entirely his own, he had been given a gift—healing hands used by God, which had wonderfully restored health to so many. Through his hands, broken bones had been instantly fused back together, cancerous tumors had dried up, blinded eyes had been opened, and deaf ears had been unplugged. But for all the good he had done, he was nevertheless paying an incredible price. It was a contradiction of the worst sort; an oxymoronic, cruel twist of fate that threatened to forever define his existence. Not a day went by that he didn't ask himself if it was worth the loneliness and the life of utter obscurity. The nights upon nights spent reliving nightmares, weeping until there were no more tears left in him to shed.

Lying in the grass now, he remembered how excited and ready he and Nina had been to consummate their vows on their honeymoon night. It had been the first time for both of them, and with each new discovery of sensual ecstasy, their mutual love had soared to new heights.

"I'll never love anyone the way that I love you," he had whispered in her ear afterward, gently cradling her in his arms. The scent of their lovemaking was the aroma of sweet honey and wine.

"And I'll never love anyone the way that I love you,"

she'd whispered back, kissing him softly. "Right now, right here—I'm so happy. You make me . . . so happy."

"I live for nothing else, Nina. I want to know what makes you smile and what turns you on. I want to know what makes everything about you come alive."

She'd smiled at him coyly. "Well, I'm a pretty complex woman. Finding all that out about me might take a while."

"We've got all the time in the world," he'd answered. "We've got . . . forever." He'd pulled her closer to him then, ready to make love again.

How was he to know *forever* would be so fleeting?

He rolled over in the grass now, eventually rising to a sitting position with his back resting against a cypress tree. He turned the old black leather Bible over in his hands, slowly rotating it between his thumbs and forefingers. He never went anywhere without it—despite its old age, the spine remained in relatively good shape, as did the gold-leaf pages. It had been the only item of note passed down from his late mother, Jacqueline, a woman who'd probably read every single page of this book a dozen times.

"I want you to grow up to be a man of the Word," Jacqueline had told him when he was seven years old. She had been softly stroking the top of his head, the way she always did when she wanted him to know how special he was.

"Things in this world are fleeting, baby. I want you to always remember that. The grass withers and the flowers will fade away, but the Word of God will stand forever."

His seven-year-old mind hadn't grasped the depth of this statement. "Whaddya mean, this Word will stand forever?" he'd asked. "It's just a book."

"Oh, it's more than just a book, baby. It's *alive*, living and breathing. It reveals our hearts like a powerful mirror. And it's how God talks to us—through this holy Word. Do you want Him to talk to you?"

He'd nodded his head, his eyes growing wide with thoughts of God actually *talking* to him.

"Well then, He will . . . You just keep your heart ready." She'd turned to a bookmarked place in the Bible. "Jeremiah 29:13 says, '*And you will seek Me and find Me, when you search for Me with all your heart.*' He's up there, baby. God is all around you. And one day, you're going to hear Him whisper such special things to your heart."

He shook his head again and came back to the present. The constant flashbacks to the special moments in his past were driving him crazy. Looking down, he opened the Bible, and the pages automatically fell to the book of Jeremiah. The passage his mother had spoken to him over twenty-five years ago remained highlighted in yellow marker.

"I called to You, God," he began, his voice trembling. "Don't You remember? I called to You and prayed that You would bless my family. I prayed for You to watch over Nina and me, and give us the abundant life Your *Word* promises us in John 10:10. So what happened? I know I have no right to question You, but why did it all go away? If I could just know . . . *why*, then maybe I could move past this. Tell me why, God. Tell me . . . *why*."

But the heavens—and likewise, his spirit—remained quiet. No answers seemed to be forthcoming, and he began to fear that none ever would.

Chapter Eighteen

ANDREA'S GOING TO KILL ME *for this*, Travis thought as his nimble fingers flew over the keyboard, typing the words of the best article he'd ever written.

But so what? This is gonna be a front-page story . . .

During the past two days, he'd convinced himself that he was not exploiting Eddie's miraculous healing in any way; he was merely placing attention on some unexplained medical phenomena occurring in the region. Any self-respecting journalist worth his or her salt would do the same. At least, that was the mantra he'd repeat to himself until the story was completed.

Instead of researching background information online and over the telephone, as he'd done in previous articles, Travis had physically gone to every place where he needed a quote. Eddie's pediatrician at Toumey Hospital in Sumter confirmed the boy's ankles had been completely healed and his hearing restored one hundred percent.

"Never seen anything like it," Dr. Erickson had said, shaking his head. "The bones in Eddie's body were strong and miraculously transformed; almost as if they'd never been fused together. I wouldn't have believed it, but X-rays don't lie. And his once withered leg muscles have gained strength as well." Though Toumey's entire medical staff had been baffled as to what had happened, the proof of healing had been undeniable. To say nothing of the fact that Eddie could now *hear*!

Travis had also learned of the other healing testimonies from the crusade at Hope Springs Church, and like Detective Columbo (his favorite television detective) he'd tracked down four people who'd been healed at that crusade—T. R. Smallwood, Jefferson Embry, Wayne McCullum, and Lynn Harper. After talking with the three men first, he discovered they were all eager to testify about what had happened, maintaining that they had been healed through the power of Jesus Christ.

The concept of unexplained medical phenomena was not unheard of, as Travis had discovered during his research. Two years previously, a respected network TV news program had centered its entire evening news segment around the theme *Prayer and Healing—Does It Work?* After that story aired, several magazines and news journals had conducted surveys in the hope of establishing a pattern between religion and healing. And while the results had not produced definitive conclusions, they nevertheless inferred a positive link between those who prayed and/or attended church and the speed of medical recovery from various illnesses.

But the speed of medical recovery was one thing. Having blinded eyes opening, cancerous tumors vanishing, and deformed ankle bones straightening out was entirely another.

"This is unbelievable," Travis muttered to himself, reading over the latest doctor's confirmation while guzzling down another diet Pepsi. Though it was growing late in the evening, he had one more contact he needed to make before he would call it a night—Lynn Harper. He'd wanted to personally meet with her, but he hadn't been able to find the time during the past two days. And with Ryman Wells's deadline for the story set at noon the following day, his time was running out for using her as another source. Dialing her number (which he'd semi-illegally obtained), he leaned back in his chair and finished off the last of his soda.

• • •

THE PHONE RANG just as Lynn was settling in to watch *Casablanca*. Along with a million other reasons to give God praise for her sight, one was that she could still enjoy curling up underneath her covers with a bowl of popcorn to watch classic movies from yesteryear.

Her first thought was that it might be a telemarketer; she'd neglected to place her home number on that "do not call" list, and lately she'd been getting heavily bombarded by those persistent phone pesterers.

But what if it's Mom or Dad? Or Arlene?

It *could've* been her parents, calling to make sure she was alright. But her mom and dad were good about leaving messages on her machine; she would let it go to voice mail and pick the phone up if it was them. If it was Arlene, well, Lynn would let it go to voice mail.

Arlene normally talked her ear off, and Lynn wasn't in the mood tonight. Tonight was a night for watching Humphrey Bogart and Ingrid Bergman.

I should really get caller ID on my bedroom phone . . .

"Hello—Lynn Harper?" asked an unfamiliar male voice on the answering machine. "My name is Travis Everett from the *State*. I apologize for calling so late but I'm working on a story for Tuesday's paper about the recent medical healings in Sumter. I've obtained some good quotes from Pastor Smallwood from Hope Springs Church as well as Mr. Embry and Mr. McCullum, and I was hoping to ask you a few questions about—"

More out of curiosity than anything else, Lynn reached over and picked up the phone. It wasn't often that a newspaper reporter called her house.

"This is Lynn," she cut in.

"Ms. Harper? Oh, I'm sorry. Did I wake you up?"

"No, I was up," she replied, pressing the pause button on her DVD remote. "How can I help you, Mr. Everett?"

"Well, as I was saying, I'm doing a story about the healings taking place in Sumter, and I understand you . . . ah . . . that you were *blind* but now you can see?"

Lynn couldn't help but smile at the salvation symbolism of the reporter's words. "I was in a car accident almost two months ago," she began, briefly outlining the injuries she'd sustained. She described how the doctors had been unable to help her damaged eyes, save for a relatively new procedure performed at UAB that might have partially restored vision to her right eye. As it had turned out, she'd never had to try that new procedure. At the healing crusade, she recalled how a man laid hands over her eyes, and how her sight had been completely restored not long after.

"My doctor, Sherman Winthrop from Palmetto Memorial, was absolutely floored by the retinal scans of my eyes taken after the healing," she said in conclusion. "He says it's like nothing had happened to them at all."

"That *is* rather amazing," Travis said. "If I didn't already have doctor confirmations on these . . . these *healings*, I don't know if I could believe them myself. And for the record, who are you attributing your healing to?"

"To Jesus Christ," Lynn replied without hesitation. "I give Him all the praise."

"And what of the mysterious man who touched your eyes?"

"Well, I don't know who that man was."

"That's interesting. Both Pastor Smallwood and my sis—ah, I mean, another lady—speak about this mysterious man as being instrumental to their healings. Don't you find it a little odd that nobody knows who he is?"

"I do sometimes wonder who he is, but that's not really important. When he touched my eyes and prayed for me, his words lined up with both the teachings and the example of Jesus on praying for the sick."

"So, you're saying . . . this man said what . . . *Jesus Christ* would have said?"

"Well . . . yes. Yes, you could say that. Jesus instructed his disciples that they would lay hands on the sick and the sick would be healed."

"Right. Uh, listen, I think I got what I needed for my story. I appreciate you taking this call so late in the evening."

"You're welcome, Mr. Everett. It was my pleasure."

Lynn hung up the phone and returned to watching her movie, having no idea how much she'd regret having ever talked to Travis Everett.

Chapter Nineteen

THE HEADLINE DOMINATED the front page of Tuesday's Metro section in big, bold lettering—"Man Calling Himself Jesus Christ Heals Several in Sumter."

As Lynn unfolded the newspaper with her morning cup of coffee, her eyes bulged disbelievingly. Were her newly healed eyes suffering from some sort of optical illusion?

But this was no illusion—the first Travis Everett story to make page one of Metro had landed there because of its controversial subject matter. Apparently, a feature about some man claiming to be Jesus walking around healing people in Sumter, made all the more credible by the corresponding doctors' statements, was too sensational to place anywhere except on the front page.

Still, the worst was yet to come. Lynn's eyes grew wider with shock as she began reading the article. Her name was mentioned three times in direct quotes saying this man had claimed to be Jesus Christ.

"I never *said* the man claimed to be Jesus!" she screeched, slamming her fist down on the table, in the process spilling her coffee. What Travis Everett had done was beyond betrayal—she felt violated, almost unclean, as she held the newspaper in her hands. Travis had written that the aura of mystery surrounding the man strengthened the argument that he might be delusional. Furthermore, the reports of what this man looked like were slightly conflicting (Pastor Smallwood had not gotten a good look at his face; Lynn, being blind, had never seen him), which added to Travis's hypothesis that the man might be disguised. What reasonable man, Travis wrote, would confuse people by not being straightforward about his identity? If he possessed some sort of healing gift, why shroud himself in secrecy?

Lynn's hands were shaking when she finally set down the newspaper. How could this reporter have tarnished something so precious and beautiful by clouding the truth with shameless innuendo? What was happening in Sumter was not some freakish sideshow circus; it was a move of God! It planted the seeds of a great revival!

"God, what have we done? This reporter misquoted all of us and twisted this story around to make us look absolutely foolish."

Instantly, however, the Spirit began speaking to her and a certain scripture came to her mind, 1 Corinthians 1:27.

"But God has chosen the foolish things of the world to put to shame the wise, and God has chosen the weak things of the world to put to shame the things which are mighty . . ."

Falling to her knees, Lynn began praying aloud in the Spirit, finding comfort that the Lord would speak to her at this moment.

• • •

THE LEADERSHIP at Faith Community had been likewise praying throughout the day, and when Lynn arrived at the church for her weekly meeting, she was met with words of encouragement.

Arlene met her in the hallway with a hug. "Listen, you don't let that newspaper article bother you, Lynn. Alright? Look at it this way—an amazing miracle happened to you. The doctors said you would be blind for the rest of your life, but look at God! *Nobody* can take that away from you."

Lynn nodded. "Thanks for always reminding me of that. And you're so right—every day when I wake up and I can see my alarm clock and the sun peeking through my curtains, all I can do is give God a praise!"

Lynn walked farther down the hallway, which led to the administrative wing of the complex. As she passed the sanctuary, she could hear one of the musicians playing "Great Is Thy Faithfulness" on the organ, and she paused to whisper another prayer of thanksgiving. Experiencing total blindness for seven weeks had radically altered her sense of the *proper* time and manner to praise her God. And during that dark time, she had vowed to the Lord that if He restored her sight, she would never cease to praise Him. Some meaningless article in the state's largest newspaper that had distorted her words could do nothing to dampen her spirits.

"Good evening," Pastor Gentry greeted her as she walked into the conference room. Not once, in all her time attending these weekly meetings, had she ever arrived before Pastor Gentry. She knew he prided himself on punctuality, but just *once* she wanted to arrive first.

"Are you holding up well?" he asked.

Lynn nodded, managing a small smile. "After what I've been through the last two months, everything else is small potatoes."

Pastor Gentry matched her smile. "I know what you mean. The trials we face in life make us either better or bitter. Your particular trial has strengthened you in ways you don't even know yet.

"I've talked to several area church leaders today," he continued, "and there is some concern about any . . . well, any *fallout* from this article. Personally, I don't think anything will come of it. As the saying goes, today's news is tomorrow's trash."

"Except this wasn't news," Lynn commented, settling down into a chair. "It was wrong how that reporter twisted our words to make us sound . . . to make us sound . . ."

"Sound like what, Lynn? Crazy?" He smiled again. "Anytime . . . every time a great move of God happens, there is resistance from the enemy. It's spiritual warfare 101. When I first heard of my friend T. R. Smallwood's miraculous healing and then the other healings, I immediately began warfare praying—praying not just for revival but praying against every demonic attack and hindrance."

"This newspaper article is part of a demonic attack?"

"I don't know if it's that, but it is definitely a hindrance. What's most important for us now is not to magnify the problem, but magnify God in the midst of this. Our God is so much greater than anything the devil can do, plus we know that He is sovereign. If He has ordained something to happen, then it *will* happen. You can count on that."

• • •

"TRAVIS, I CANNOT *BELIEVE* you would write something like that!" Andrea practically yelled to her brother over the phone. "And I can't believe the newspaper would print it!"

"What're you talking about?" Travis calmly answered, pausing to sip his diet Pepsi through a straw. He was no longer gulping his precious drink. On the contrary, after writing an article worthy of the front page, he was feeling extremely relaxed.

"I thought the story was pretty good," he continued. "And Ryman did, too—he gave me the front page. The front *page*, Andrea!"

"Travis, you saw with your own eyes the miracle of Eddie's healing—it was the hand of God! Yet you all but discredited it with this story of some delusional mystery man."

"Look, I admit that what happened to Eddie is beyond my understanding, but my reporting was solid on this. The fact is, *nobody* knows who this man is."

"But why did you have to make him out to be crazy? Do you want your own nephew to read about this years from now and wonder if some crazy man had something to do with his miracle?"

I really don't care . . . "Like I said, I don't know what happened to Eddie. Apparently, the doctors don't either. But I was facing a written ultimatum from my editor. He wanted a good story, and he likes articles that spice things up a bit."

"Spice things up a bit? Travis, I've been praying for you the past twelve years that you would come to know the Lord. And even though you haven't yet, I still thought your morals were in the right place. Obviously, I was wrong."

"My *morals*? What's that supposed to mean? Just because I don't accept this neatly packaged notion of God you're always cramming down my throat? I didn't do anything wrong in writing my article, and in the process I probably saved my job. People will draw their own conclusions—they always do, no matter what we write in the papers. But the facts are the facts. There have been some unexplainable medical healings with this mystery man involved in a good number of them. Yet nobody knows who he is."

"But you wrote that this man claimed to be Jesus Christ. That's not true!"

Travis shrugged and sipped some more of his diet Pepsi, refusing to let Andrea dampen his joy. "Depends on who you ask."

Chapter Twenty

AWAKENING WITH A JOLT, the man groggily turned over in the bed. The Motel 6 bed's comforter and sheets were scattered haphazardly on the floor and the pillow behind his head was damp. It was the evidence of yet another restless, fitful night, something that was becoming all too common for him.

The dream remained vividly etched in his mind as he yawned and pulled the pillow over his head. But it was so much more than a dream—it was the vivid recollection of the last time he and Nina had been together. The last time he'd seen her alive.

"Are you doing anything special today?" she had asked, a question she posed to him every day. She had always been interested in his activities.

"I'm going fishing with Pop," he'd answered, just before kissing her on the forehead. Her skin was soft and warm; he'd always loved the flushed way she looked first thing in the morning.

"Your pop will like that. You two don't spend enough time together anymore."

He nodded, but he didn't want to talk about Pop—a man who had far too many issues for him to deal with. But the activity of fishing had always been their great equalizer. It was just two men out on a boat, surrounded by nature's splendor.

"I'd rather spend the day with you," he said. And he certainly *would* have, if he'd only known . . .

"No, you go fishing with Pop. I'll be at the firm most of the day, finishing some last-minute things for the case. The trial starts Monday."

He groaned, pulling her closer to him. "Don't remind me. I know how you get during court cases. Once that trial begins, I'm not going to see you for two months."

She laughed. "That's not true! We may not have as *much* time together, but I'll plan to make the time we do have as meaningful as possible."

"Let's start right now," he'd said, his passions stirring.

"Start what?"

"Making time as meaningful as possible."

• • •

THE RAMIFICATIONS OF the newspaper article didn't impact him until later that morning, after he'd walked into Five Points Diner for breakfast and had taken his usual booth next to the window. The buttermilk pancakes were especially fluffy this morning, and he enjoyed a quiet twenty minutes alone with his thoughts, gazing out the window.

That all changed, however, when Florence burst through the diner's doors, pointed in his direction, and exclaimed, "There he is!"

Startled, he looked up. The ten or so patrons also looked up from their meals, though most of them were regulars and accustomed to hearing Florence's loud voice.

"You're the . . . Ohmigod, you're the man from that article!" Florence hurriedly made her way to his table.

"I'm sorry," he replied, confused. "I'm not sure what you're talking about."

"There was an article in yesterday's paper about a man claiming to be Jesus walking around healing people in Sumter. It mentioned an incident here in Columbia, though. A little deaf boy with deformed ankles who can now walk and hear—it was you! I remember you praying for that boy in here last week."

He coughed nervously and wiped his mouth with a napkin. "Yesterday's paper?"

"Uh-huh. Here, I kept a copy." Florence walked to the bar counter. He was conscious now of several pairs of eyes peering at him from over coffee mug rims.

This isn't good . . .

Florence returned, waving the paper above her head like a bingo game winner's card. "Here it is, right on the Metro section's front page."

He took the newspaper and quickly scanned through the article. Everything he read was precisely the kind of attention he sought to avoid.

"They're talking about you, right?" Florence pressed, reaching out slowly and touching his arm the way a devout Catholic might touch the arm of the pope. "You're really not . . . *Jesus*, are you?"

He jerked his arm away and picked up his glass.

"Uh . . . listen, Florence, can I get a refill of iced tea? It tastes really good this morning."

Florence nodded and walked to the counter.

Still aware of several stares fixed in his direction, he stuck his hand into his pocket, pulled out a twenty-dollar bill, and left it on the table. Then he stood to leave.

"Hey!" spoke up one of the regulars seated two tables over. "Where you going, mister? I wanna hear about how you healed them people."

"Maybe another time," came his hurried reply as he beelined toward the door.

"Hey!"

"Hey, mister!" someone else shouted.

Outside now on Harden Street, he strode quickly north, keeping his head down and staying in the shadows of building overhangs. Anger, like a slow-rolling fog, began creeping into his thoughts.

They wrote an article! They wrote an article about me!

And if writing an article alone wasn't bad enough, that reporter had written a ridiculously false account of what had happened. He had *never* claimed to be Jesus—he had just invoked the Lord's name each time he'd laid hands on someone. To claim to be Jesus Christ was . . . crazy!

He stopped walking and leaned against a bus-stop sign. Looking down at his hands, he felt the palpable urge to spit on them, curse them for having been unable to help the one person who needed the healing most. At any rate, he knew he had to get out of Columbia. Too many people at that diner had gotten a good look at his face, though no one knew his name.

Running away like a fugitive on the lam wasn't a move he wanted to make, but it was the only thing to do. The fewer people who knew who he was, the better.

• • •

TRAVIS RECEIVED A CALL later that morning from Florence, claiming the mysterious man had shown up at the diner.

"Whoa, whoa," Travis replied, nearly choking on his diet Pepsi. He was already on his third can, at a quarter to noon. "You're saying the mystery man—the man I wrote about in my article—stopped by Five Points Diner?"

"That's what I just said, Mr. Everett. You hard of hearin'?"

"Uh . . . no. It's just that—"

"And not only did he come by here," Florence continued, "but several of us got a good look at him!"

In his haste to grab a pen and his reporter's notebook from the corner of his desk, Travis knocked his Clemson Tigers cap and several knickknacks over. The noise caused Benny Dodson to peer over the top of his cubicle suspiciously, but Travis didn't care. Now that he had gotten the front page for the first time in his career at the *State*, perfect little Benny Dodson no longer intimidated him.

"Y'all got a good look at him?" Travis asked, managing to simultaneously glare at Benny. "What'd he look like?"

"Are you going to put my name in the paper, too?"

The not-so-subtle way Florence asked the question

made it clear she wanted to be quoted. Travis suppressed a chuckle—seemed like everybody wanted their fifteen minutes of fame, no matter where or how that fifteen minutes came.

"Sure, Florence. I'll quote you."

"Hot dog! Well now, let me remember. I'd say he was around six foot two, medium build. A black man, but handsome, like he could be a model for one of Belk's department store catalogs."

"What was he wearing?" Travis asked.

"A navy polo shirt and some Levi's."

Travis scribbled furiously on his notepad. "Did you see where he was going when he left?"

"No, not really. Mystery man got outta here pretty quick after I showed him yesterday's newspaper."

Travis nearly choked again. "You w-what?"

"Well, sure! I wanted him to know he was famous round these parts, so I showed him your article."

"And the man read the whole thing?" Travis was starting to get a sickening feeling in the pit of his stomach, a feeling that had nothing to do with the hearty stack of pancakes he'd polished off two hours earlier.

"He sure did. But it was the strangest thing—he acted all spooked afterwards. He got outta here like he was in trouble with the law or something. Left me a twenty-dollar tip, though."

Travis cursed. Florence had just run his front-page story right out of town. "Thanks, Florence," he finally managed through clenched teeth as the gears in his brain began churning. What would Detective Columbo do in a situation like this?

"Did I do something wrong?" Florence asked.

You betcha, babe . . . "No."

"You're still gonna put my name in the paper?"

"Yeah, sure." Travis hung up the phone, a hundred thoughts bombarding his brain. The mystery man was leaving the area—that much he was sure of. But Travis just *had* to get his picture—that would be another front-page story, to be sure! Ryman Wells loved this story and had already indicated that he wanted follow-ups.

The thing with tasting success, Travis was quickly finding out, was that it inevitably created a thirst for more success. Whereas he once was a self-described lazy reporter satisfied with getting paid for below-average work, those days were long gone. After all, his byline had appeared on the front page of Metro! What if he could do even better and land a story on the front page of the *entire* paper?

Talk about your fifteen minutes of fame . . .

"You going somewhere?" Benny asked, his head reappearing over the top of Travis's cubicle.

Travis sneered at him, reveling in the thrill of now being the alpha dog, and Benny just another nameless member of the pack. "Sure am," he replied. "I'm going to snare another front-page story."

Chapter Twenty-one

TRAVIS IMMEDIATELY SET OUT for Five Points Diner, the goal firmly entrenched in his mind like a vision of one of Damon's mouthwatering barbecue sandwiches.

I've gotta get a picture of this mystery man . . .

His initial plan was to canvass the area around the diner, hoping for clues as to where this man might have gone. Somebody on the street had to have seen him; surely he hadn't vanished into thin air like a ghost.

Parking his car one block from the diner, Travis got out and started walking. It was nearing two in the afternoon, and the sun was now high and hot overhead. Sweat soon began trickling down his face and back, but he continued on, undeterred. His determination for getting the scoop on this story derived from a variety of places. Forever the black sheep of the family who'd never tasted the successes of Maynard and Andrea, well, now he would show them. And while he was at it, he would show Benny Dodson, Ryman Wells, and everybody else who had ever told him he would never amount to anything.

Directly across from the diner was a gas station with

a convenience store, and Travis stopped in for a couple of cold diet Pepsis. Determined or not, his body just wasn't used to being out of air-conditioning for too long. To say nothing of *walking* . . .

He paid for the sodas (one for his pocket and one for his immediate pleasure) and stepped back outside. He'd no sooner twisted off the top of the bottle when he happened to look up and notice the security cameras positioned atop the filling station. One of the cameras pointed north, in the direction of the front door of Five Points Diner.

Detective Columbo, eat your heart out . . .

Travis turned on his heel and walked back inside the store. The young man working the cash register looked up at him.

"Hot out there, huh?" the clerk said. "You want another Pepsi?"

Travis shook his head. "Look, this is gonna sound strange, but those security cameras on top of the building—how many hours back do the tapes cover?"

The young man shrugged. "I think Mr. Bettis told me the film loops over every twenty-four hours, or something like that."

"Mr. Bettis . . . that's the owner?"

The young man nodded.

"Is he here?"

The young man started shaking his head, then stopped and gave Travis a suspicious look. "Hey, mister—what's with all the questions?"

Travis held up his hands. "I know, I know. This must all sound pretty strange to you . . . uh, what was your name again?"

"Sammy," the clerk replied, still giving Travis a suspicious look.

"Sammy, my name is Travis Everett." He pointed to the stack of newspapers arranged by the cash register. "Do you read the *State*?"

"Just the headlines sometimes, when business gets real slow."

Bingo . . . "Did you happen to read the top headline in Tuesday's Metro section? About the man claiming to be Jesus going around healing people?"

Sammy's expression perked up. "Yeah, I read that. Pretty crazy stuff."

"Yeah, well I wrote that article, Sammy."

"Yeah?" The suspicious look gave way to one of curiosity.

"Uh-huh," Travis said, reaching into his pocket, pulling out his wallet, and flashing his press credentials. "Listen, that man was in Five Points Diner earlier today, and I've got a strong hunch that camera taped him coming out. A picture like that would be pretty valuable, if you . . . ah . . . if you get my drift."

"Oh, I get your drift, but Mr. Bettis don't like for me to mess with those tapes."

"Is Mr. Bettis here?" he asked for the second time.

"Naw. He's off today."

Travis moved in closer to the counter. "Then it's just between you and me, alright?"

Sammy started biting on his lower lip, his curious look now giving way to nervousness. "What's in it for me?"

Travis reached for his wallet again, knowing Detective Columbo would never stoop to do something like this. But so what? The mystery man was on that videotape—Travis could feel it in his bones.

• • •

TWENTY MINUTES LATER, his wallet one hundred dollars lighter, Travis was seated inside the store's small security room, looking at the images on one of the TV screens. After rewinding the tape from camera #3 to the beginning, he'd spent the last ten minutes watching the images in fast-forward mode. He watched as people entered and exited the diner, moving like little ants; he was searching for someone matching Florence's description of a black man in a navy polo shirt and Levi's jeans.

"C'mon, c'mon," he muttered, his nerves tingling and standing on end. He couldn't remember when he'd felt more excited in his whole life. It was the thrill of the hunt, he reasoned—after writing an article that everyone in the area was *still* talking about, he was on the verge of getting the follow-up scoop!

The images quickly flickered past his eyes, and if he hadn't been so attuned to finding his guy, he would have missed it.

There he is!

Quickly stopping the tape, he slowly rewound it until he saw the man clad in the navy polo shirt and jeans pause at the diner's front door, turn around . . .

His face!

. . . and slowly enter the diner.

Travis Everett had hit the jackpot once more. And he knew exactly what to do with the videotape, as soon as he smuggled it out of this convenience store. An old college roommate of his had been an expert with analog and digital video, and Travis was sure he could persuade him to enhance this image. At the moment, Travis was sure he could do just about anything.

Chapter Twenty-two

THE MAN PAID CASH for the train ticket at the window, then located a seat nearby in the waiting area. The Amtrak Silver Star didn't leave for another three hours, but he didn't have anywhere else to be, or go, at the moment. Sitting in the train station practically felt like home to him, anyway—he'd spent the greater part of his life passing time at bus depots and train stations. There was something nostalgic about riding the rails that always lured him back here.

His pop had been a porter working at both train stations and bus depots, and the best memories the man had of his childhood were sitting at the Ruston, Louisiana, bus station, watching the travelers arrive and depart. Birmingham. Jackson. Gulfport. Longview. The destination cities had been foreign, faraway places to his young mind, and his one recurring dream had been to board a bus with a one-way ticket to Anywhere, USA. Ironically, he now had the means to make that fantasy a reality, but he found no joy in that false freedom. The one place he longed to journey existed only in the past, and time travel was real only in the movies.

Leaning his head back on the wooden bench, he closed his eyes and longed once more for the one thing he knew he could never have again. The one person he knew he would never see again.

Nina . . .

• • •

THE OUTREACH EFFORT, given the ever-increasing healing testimonies, was an evangelist's biggest dream. Lynn had coordinated several revival services among churches in and around Richland and Sumter counties, and the expectancy level among the different congregations was growing by the week.

It was one thing, Lynn knew, to conduct mundane, church-as-usual services and then stamp "revival" on the program and make people think that's what they were having. But when blinded eyes were being opened, cancer cells drying up, deformed ankle bones being straightened, churches moved beyond ordinary services and began experiencing what could only be described as a move of God.

Lynn had been praying for something like this to happen, and seeing glimpses of it coming to pass radically charged her faith.

"Sister Lynn?" Brother Charles knocked on the door and peeked his head inside her office. Lynn looked up from her computer, where she'd been drafting yet another letter to send to these host churches.

"Yes?"

"Evangelist Barbara is ready to head back to Charlotte, but Mattie hasn't made it in yet to drive her to the station. Can you drive her back, in case Mattie doesn't show?"

Lynn smiled and shook her head. If only people realized the day-to-day drama of church operations. Evangelist Barbara Anderson had been helping teach a weeklong course at Faith Community, as she did every other month. Everyone loved her and looked forward to her coming, but Evangelist Barbara didn't care for flying, so she rode the train from Charlotte, North Carolina, to Columbia. Sister Mattie Hendricks regularly picked her up and served as chauffeur, but Sister Mattie had lately been having trouble with her eldest son, who was in and out of prison.

"Sure, I'll drive her," Lynn replied, stretching her fingers. A short break might do her good, anyway. The demand for Pastor Gentry and the outreach team to hold meetings around the area had been greater than usual, and Lynn had been the one charged with staying on top of everything.

Thirty minutes later, Brother Charles knocked on her door again. "Mattie's not going to make it. Today is visiting day at Manning Correctional, and her son . . ."

"I know," Lynn finished. The entire church had been praying for that boy for years now; his parole was coming up in two months and everyone was believing God for him to stay out this time for good.

"I'd be happy to take Evangelist Barbara to the station. Just let me get my keys."

• • •

"OH, GOD BLESS YOU, Sister Lynn," Evangelist Barbara gushed as Lynn pulled into the parking space. "Thank you for driving me. I'm telling you, it's been such a blessing talking to you. Your testimony of how God healed your eyes stirs my faith every time I think about it."

Lynn opened the car door for the evangelist, smiled, and hugged the elderly woman once more. She reached back in and retrieved the two garment bags from the backseat.

"I'm going to have you come up to our church in Charlotte and share that testimony with our members. I think it will be really special."

"I'd love that," Lynn replied as they walked together to the check-in counter.

"Good afternoon, Ms. Barbara!" the smiling lady behind the counter greeted them. "Did you enjoy your stay?"

"Always do, Loretta. I always do."

The two made small talk as Lynn handed the two garment bags to the porter, a man who tried to wink one too many times at Lynn.

If you tryin' to flirt with me, you better know Jesus, she thought.

"Your train's right on schedule, Ms. Barbara," Loretta said, checking her computer. "You gon' ahead and board when you're ready."

Evangelist Barbara thanked Loretta and turned to Lynn. "Sister Lynn—don't forget about coming up to Charlotte, when you find time in your schedule. I know Pastor Gentry keeps you busy as a bee with your work in outreach, but find a few days to squeeze us in, hear?"

Lynn smiled. "Of course, Evangelist Barbara."

Lynn waited until the evangelist was safely aboard the train before turning to leave.

"Excuse me, miss lady, but you sho' is looking fine today," the porter said, now sidling up to her and licking his lips. "Anybody ever tell ya that you look jus' like Natalie Cole?"

It was all Lynn could do to maintain her calm demeanor. Getting hit on was not necessarily new to her, but she never knew how to nicely tell a guy that she wasn't interested.

Better to go the Jesus route with this one . . . "I try to look my best every day," she responded, looking the man squarely in the eye and surprising him a little bit. He apparently hadn't expected her to be so forthright with her comeback.

"I try to look my best every day because I want to reflect the Jesus who lives in me." She paused for a beat. "Do you know Jesus, sir?"

"Um . . . ah . . . well, uh . . . yeah. Yeah, you know what I'm sayin'? I know God."

"Well, I pray you'll know Him better," she said, reaching into her purse, pulling out and then handing him a brochure for Faith Community Church. "You're more than welcome to come worship Him at Faith Community."

"Um . . . well . . . uh, yeah, yeah, I'll have to check y'all out sometime."

Smiling politely at him, Lynn stepped past him and walked toward the train station's front doors. She was halfway to the door when she happened to look down . . .

. . . and noticed yet another run down the front of her panty hose.

Lord, will I ever stop getting these?

She saw a ladies' room to her right, and she stopped in to change. Out of habit (and now, almost out of necessity) she'd begun carrying extra pairs in her purse. What she *needed* to do, however, was spring for the more expensive kinds than the generic brand she normally wore. She'd rather not even wear the uncomfortable things, especially during the summer, but as the outreach director for one of the largest churches in the area, she knew the wisdom of looking her best at all times.

Five minutes later, wearing a fresh pair, she walked back out. Halfway to the exit, the sound of a man's voice made her slow her gait, and then stop altogether.

I . . . know that voice . . . I know that voice!

It was a voice that she'd never forget for as long as she lived.

"As I lay hands on my sister's eyes, I speak the healing power of Jesus Christ to manifest with her eyes being . . ."

Unmistakably, it was the voice of the man who laid hands over her eyes the evening of the healing crusade in Sumter.

She quickly looked around her, determining the location of the voice. It was coming from a bank of pay phones by the wall a few feet away. She walked over until she was two phones away, then picked up the phone and pretended to use it.

What am I, a spy now? Lynn Harper, 007?

But what was she *supposed* to do? Standing merely yards away from her was a man God had used to restore her sight. Apparently, God had used him to heal others as well, though nobody seemed to know who he was.

"I'm glad you're doing well, Pop," Lynn overheard the voice saying. "When am I coming home? I . . . I don't know. I thought I'd give it some more time. What? Yeah, yeah, I know it's been two years. But it still feels like yesterday to me."

"If you would like to make a call, please deposit—" Lynn blinked and replaced her own phone receiver on its base. Then in a burst of inspiration, she pulled out two quarters from her purse, fed the pay phone, and dialed a number. A few seconds later, Pastor Gentry's voice mail beeped into her ear.

He must be out of the office . . . I should try his cell number . . .

She fished two more quarters from her purse, but before she could deposit them she heard the mystery man hanging up his phone and quickly walking away.

No!

She'd wanted to call Pastor Gentry, explain her situation, and ask his advice. Should she introduce herself?

But now, she had no choice but to follow the fast-walking man, watching as he boarded the Silver Star train. Lynn glanced at the electronic arrivals/departures board and saw that the Silver Star was headed for Savannah, Georgia. She still hadn't gotten a look at the man's face, and to be this close to him . . . well, she just *had* to know what he looked like! Of course, there was one way to do that . . .

That's crazy . . .

"All aboard! All aboard! Silver Star Express to

Savannah will be leaving in five minutes," came the announcement over the public-address system.

In seconds, Lynn made her decision. It was crazy, but she was absolutely positive she knew that voice. When she had been blind, her heightened sense of hearing had enabled her not only to hear voices better, but also to hear the rise, fall, and pitch of the human voice better. She knew the same man who had laid hands on her eyes was now on that train.

"May I help you?" Loretta asked, peering at her with curious eyes. No doubt it was because she'd seen Lynn at this ticket counter with Evangelist Barbara only moments earlier.

"Yes," Lynn replied, reaching into her purse and retrieving her Visa card. "I'd like to purchase a ticket for the Silver Star."

"O-kaay," Loretta said, still looking at her curiously. "You want to take a round trip to Savannah?"

Oh, God . . . this is crazy . . . Lynn thought, hesitating for a moment. But then she remembered the wonderful feeling of being outside Hope Springs Church, finally able to see after being blind for seven weeks. And it was because *this* man had helped her.

"Yes," she finally breathed. "That's exactly what I want to do."

Chapter Twenty-three

THE MAN GAZED OUT the train's small window and let out a long sigh. Summer was giving way to autumn, as the leaves began changing colors and the sun now cast longer shadows earlier in the evening. He faintly heard the last call for passengers to board over the public-address system, but his mind was a million miles away.

Nina . . .

She had loved the outdoors as much as he had, if not even more. Their ranch house had been spread out over ten acres of northern Louisiana real estate, nestled among grass and trees stretching as far as the eye could see. And though the property had been constructed with a design suited for raising animals, neither he, Pop, nor Nina was especially fond of cattle-raising.

"This land is just God's gift to our family," she was now saying in his dreams, sipping a glass of lemonade outside on their deck, watching the sun dip down in the western sky. "A place for you, me, and all the children we're going to have."

"Are you ready for that?" he asked. "Motherhood, I mean."

Nina turned to face him. The backlit glow from the sunset beautifully framed her features and figure in an angelic glow. "Oh, yes. I've been thinking about being a mother for a long time. There's nothing more that I want than to raise a family here, with you."

In his mind, he could see her, touch her, taste her. At that moment, he could almost *smell* her, given how real she was to him. He leaned his head back against the headrest, not wanting this dream to end.

However he instantly became aware that someone was standing over him. *A fellow passenger*, he thought with irritation, because it meant he would have to prematurely end his dream with Nina. Opening his eyes, he nearly fainted, as none other than Nina stood there, smiling at him.

Oh my God . . .

"Um . . . excuse me, sir?" Nina was saying. "I'm sorry to trouble you, but . . ."

He blinked. Why didn't Nina know who he was?

And then it hit him—the face was the same, but the voice was different. It was a voice he'd heard somewhere before. It was the voice belonging to the woman he'd prayed for outside Hope Springs Church at that healing crusade.

". . . as I was saying, I'm sorry to trouble you, but I saw you—well, actually I heard your voice—in the station, and . . ."

"Wait a minute," he said, rubbing his eyes. "You followed me onto the *train*?"

"Well no, well . . . yes, but I just . . ." Lynn looked away for a second, her fingers fidgeting with the leather strap on her purse. "I . . . just wanted to meet you.

What you did at Hope Springs was . . . well, you changed my life. But you just vanished afterward, without anybody knowing who you were. When I heard your voice talking on that pay phone a few minutes ago, I . . . well, I know it sounds crazy, but I had to meet you. Do you have any idea what it feels like to be blind for seven weeks?"

The man looked away for a moment, shaking his head. Comprehending the craziness of all this was too much for him. "No, I don't know what it feels like to be blind for seven weeks. But you probably don't know what it feels like to be dead for two years."

"I'm sorry?"

He waved his hand dismissively. "Forget I said that." He sighed. "It doesn't matter anymore." He looked in her eyes, the eyes of a woman he'd once pledged undying love to. *How can this not be Nina standing in front of me?*

"So . . . you just *bought* a ticket to Savannah? Just to meet me?"

Lynn smiled sheepishly. "That's what my Visa statement is going to say."

"But you're looking at a four-hour round trip . . . What are you going . . ." His words trailed off as he noticed her looking at the empty seat next to him.

"Do you mind?" Lynn asked.

He shook his head.

Lynn sat down. A final whistle sounded as the train's wheels began turning along the tracks.

"Why don't you want anyone to know who you are?" Lynn asked.

He continued staring out the window. As the train

increased speed, the multicolored leaves on the trees and the buildings merged, forming one big blur.

"It's just better that way," he finally said. "Sometimes, things that are dead should stay buried."

• • •

LYNN HAD COUNSELED many as a full-time minister, yet she'd never encountered anyone as vague and seemingly complex as this man, for whom she *still* didn't have a name. She took it as a good sign that he hadn't objected to her sitting beside him, or even boarding the train in the first place. But what was she supposed to do over the next two hours?

Lord, help me to minister to him with Your love and compassion . . .

"Can I ask your name?" she ventured, figuring this to be as good a starting place as any. The man continued staring out his window, either ignoring her or choosing not to answer.

"Um . . . listen, if you're uncomfortable talking with me, or if I've offended you in any way, just—"

"Chance," he interrupted.

"I-I'm sorry?"

"No, that's my name. Chance Howard."

"Oh. Oh, well, Chance . . . it's nice to finally meet you. I'd just like you to know how grateful I am that you prayed over me at that healing crusade. Thank you."

"You're welcome," he replied, turning away from the window and looking into her eyes.

Lynn blinked. "You've prayed for many people to be healed of all sorts of things. Where do you get that kind of faith?"

Chance looked back out the window. "I just do what the Bible says I can do. It's more a principle of obedience than faith."

"Obedience? As in God . . . has *instructed* you to do this?"

"Something like that."

"I always hear of Christians talking of having the same power that raised Jesus Christ from the dead living inside them, but not many seem to be walking in the fullness of that power. I get the feeling that you're different."

Chance was quiet for nearly a minute. "Salvation is free," he finally replied, "but everything else in God comes with a price—the level of anointing a believer operates in is equal to the level he or she has sacrificed for it. A price has to be paid."

Lynn was about to ask something else, but she sensed that Chance was not yet through talking.

"When you start talking about possessing that power," he continued, "having what the disciples had in the book of Acts—you have to realize that those disciples gave their *lives* for Christ. Not only did they forsake all to follow Jesus around for three years, but virtually everyone became a martyr for the early church. A sacrifice on that level . . . well, it's no wonder that sick people were healed just passing by Peter's shadow."

"You're absolutely right," Lynn agreed. "That makes me think about the dynamic the apostle Paul writes of in the third chapter of Philippians—knowing Christ not only in the power of His resurrection, but in the fellowship of His sufferings. You're . . . um . . .

you're saying that you've paid a price to have that healing anointing?"

Chance, still looking out his window, nodded. Lynn opened her mouth to ask what that price had been, before having second thoughts about prying into his personal life.

What am I doing here, Lord?

Not that she needed to ask God such a question. She was here because she, too, wanted to possess a level of anointing or faith or healing or *whatever* it was Chance had that she didn't. And why shouldn't she? She had heard what Dr. Winthrop and all those other medical experts had said—that she would never see again. But look at God!

"Chance, would I be prying too much if I asked what that sacrifice was that you paid?"

"Yes," he answered.

"Oh. Oh . . . I'm sorry. I just thought—"

"But that doesn't mean I won't answer the question." He turned from the window to look directly at Lynn. "The more important question is this—are *you* ready to hear what I have to tell you?"

Chapter Twenty-four

"TRAVIS, WHADDYA GOT?"

For once, Travis didn't care about Ryman Wells's gruff voice as he proudly strutted up to his editor's desk. With a flourish, he whipped out a five-by-eight-inch photograph from his folder and slid it across the desk's glass surface. His old college roommate had done an excellent job enhancing the video image of the mystery man.

"What's this?" Ryman barked.

The cover of tomorrow's newspaper, you arrogant, little . . . "The mystery man who's been linked to those Sumter healings," Travis answered.

"Is that right?" Ryman carefully studied the photograph through his squinty eyes. "How do you know?"

"Three solid eyewitnesses at Five Points Diner say it's him, as well as the pastor of that church where those healing services were held." Travis neglected to mention that his sister Andrea had also positively identified the man as the one who'd prayed for Eddie. In the first article, Eddie had only been mentioned as a "boy born deaf with deformed ankle bones." Travis wasn't sure if he was flirting with a conflict-of-interest issue by being so closely related to one of the people who'd been healed, but that wasn't the main point. The main point, at least from his perspective, was that he was no longer Ryman Wells's whipping boy.

Ryman abruptly cleared his throat. "Well, well. You've been doing some good work lately, Travis. Some real good work. Piersall's been telling me the feedback from the original article on this has been impressive. Seems all sorts of people want to know who this man is."

Ryman was speaking of Franklin Piersall, the editor in chief, and the main person to be in good graces with if one ever desired to move up the *State*'s pecking order.

"I assume you got a story to go with this picture?" Ryman asked.

Travis smiled and produced two pages from his folder. Ryman read over the article and nodded his head. "I don't know what you've been doing, Travis, but you keep it up. I'm sure we can get this picture on tomorrow's front page, with the story on Metro's front page. Real good work."

The large smile on Travis's face stayed put. If only his family could see the black sheep now.

• • •

THE OLD FRAMED PORTRAITS hanging along the wall were not arranged in any particular order. But Bennett Howard wasn't concerned about aesthetics or decoration. Instead, his attention was for the young boy posing in all the pictures. Gazing at them and wistfully longing for days gone by brought tears to the old man's eyes. They always did when he looked at these pictures.

The John Coltrane song playing on the eight-track transported Bennett back to the days when his family was still together. The last part of his family—the young boy in the portraits—had gotten older and left him two years ago, and with that departure the sobering reality of Bennett's world had come crashing down around him.

"Ain't nobody left in my life now," he muttered, the cadence of his words flowing from his mouth in perfect sync with Coltrane. "Ain't nobody but me."

The house was in total disarray. Empty beer cans and the cellophane wrappings of old TV dinners and snack chips littered the living room floor. The kitchen was in even worse shape, as was every room except for his son's old bedroom. That room remained clean due to the fact that Bennett refused to go in there. There were too many old memories in there. Too many haunting reminders of a dream that had cruelly morphed into a nightmare.

Steadying himself on his cane with his right hand, with his other hand Bennett reached for and carefully extracted one of the framed portraits from the wall. This was his favorite, by far.

The smiling, happy boy was ten years old and grinning from ear to ear, not caring at all about the huge gap in the middle of his teeth. In fact, that was the reason for his smile. Bennett remembered how proud the boy had been for pulling the tooth all by himself.

"Look, Pop!" he had said. "An' I dint need your help this time!"

"That's wonderful, son," Bennett had replied. "You gettin' to be a big man, just like your old man."

"Yeah. Just like my pop," the boy had whispered in return. He was always whispering to himself, like he had such important things to say that nobody else should be privileged to hear.

"You gon' be a great man someday, son."

"You think so, Pop?" Still whispering.

"Yeah. Yeah, son, I think so."

Bennett replaced the picture along the wall, not even noticing that his hands were now shaking. Nor did he notice the tears that, seemingly from out of nowhere, began streaming down his old, wrinkled cheeks.

Chapter Twenty-five

"NINA HARRIS WAS THE LOVE of my life," Chance began, speaking slowly while still gazing out the window. "She moved to Ruston with her mom from Trinidad right before our eighth-grade year. Talk about beautiful . . ." He closed his eyes and was silent for a full minute, visualizing Nina.

"She was the finest girl I'd ever seen in my life . . . spoke with this cute little island accent and everything. The next year, when we got to high school, all the guys were trying to go out with her. But she turned every last one of 'em down."

"And you, too?"

Chance shrugged. "She never turned me down. 'Course, she never got the chance—I was too shy to ask her out. Every time I got around her, my mouth would go dry and my brain just shut down. It was like that all the way through high school. Anyway, our senior year, there was this statewide contest for high school seniors to write a five-thousand-word essay on the American political system and how it affected our generation. The two students who were judged to have written the best articles got a chance to spend Spring

Break in Washington, D.C." He looked over at Lynn. "Guess who wrote the two best articles?"

"You and Nina? In the whole *state* of Louisiana?"

Chance nodded, smiling. "Not bad, huh? Our economics teacher, Mr. Jenkins, was very good, and under the circumstances, that's an understatement. I think it was the proudest moment of his life when two of his students were selected. I was more excited about spending time with Nina than going to Washington—our seats on the plane were next to each other and our hotel rooms were adjoining suites."

"And let me guess . . . your mouth stopped going dry and your brain remembered how to function again."

"Not really. Turns out I wasn't the only one who was shy."

"Nina, too?"

"No, but it was the craziest thing—Nina had liked *me* from the eighth grade, but she kept that to herself. Everyone thought she was stuck-up or something, since she was from Trinidad and her mom taught at Louisiana Tech, but it wasn't like that at all. She was just waiting for me to approach her."

"So I take it you both had a good Spring Break."

Chance sighed and leaned back in his seat. "Greatest week of my life. We were supposed to visit a set number of places every day—the Capitol, the White House, the Smithsonian Institution, the Mall, and all that, but Nina and I kept finding ways to cut those visits short and just spend time walking around, talking, and getting to know each other. We'd been living in the same town for four years, but all we knew was each other's name.

"When we got back to Ruston, we did everything together. You should have seen all the other guys' faces when I showed up with Nina as my date to the senior prom. They all wanted to know what I had that they didn't. And there was only one answer."

"And what was that?"

Chance smiled. "I had . . . Nina. And I was the happiest man alive. After graduation, she had the grades to apply to any college she wanted, but she got a four-year scholarship to Southern, in New Orleans."

"And what about you?"

"I needed to stay close to my pop—his health wasn't the greatest, and it was better that I went to Grambling, just a few minutes away from home. I visited Nina just about every other weekend, though. She came back every summer; those four years seemed like four weeks. Time flies, you know?"

"When you're having fun," Lynn finished.

"Yeah. After graduation, I took her to this antebellum estate in Natchez, a big ol' house like right out of *Gone With the Wind*. I had rented the house from a guy I knew in New Orleans, just for us to have the whole weekend. That Friday night, swinging in a hammock right at sunset, I popped the question. She said yes, and we got married a few months later."

"You didn't waste any time."

"Didn't need to. We'd known we were in love and supposed to be together, I think ever since that Spring Break of our senior year. After the wedding, we moved into a house just outside Ruston—a big ranch set on ten acres of land that I inherited from my mother, Jacqueline. My pop lives on the same land now."

"Inherited? Your mother . . ."

"She died when I was ten," he answered quietly. "I think that was part of the reason my pop's health began failing—when she died, a part of him died, too. But things were going so great with Nina and me. We were planning to have our first child when . . . when we got the news."

"News?"

Chance blinked back the tears welling up at the corners of his eyes. He refused to cry in front of this woman.

"Nina had just landed a job as a legal assistant for a law firm in Shreveport, and she was going in for a routine checkup, something she needed to do before she started the job. The doctors discovered a tumor on her liver." He bit his lip and stared directly out his window.

"Oh, Chance."

He nodded again, and a tear that he could not stop rolled down his cheek. He quickly wiped it away. "She was just twenty-five years old," he said, also unable to control the trembling in his voice. "I kept saying to myself, how can she have this disease *so young*? It wasn't fair! Not to me and certainly not to her!" He blinked back another tear that threatened to fall down his cheek. "And . . . and you bet I made sure God knew that, too.

"But we had to face this, so we prepared ourselves and got ready to deal with the chemotherapy, radiation, whatever it took. We were going to see this through because we were both fighters and we weren't about to let this take us out. We went ahead and scheduled the preliminary tests. But a few weeks before she was scheduled to start the chemo, she heard about a Floyd Waters meeting down in Lake Charles."

"Wait a minute, did you say a *Floyd Waters* meeting?"

"Yeah. You've heard of him, right?"

"Of course I've heard of him! He prayed for—um, I mean, yes . . . I've heard of him. I see him on television all the time, conducting healing crusades."

"Yeah, that's the guy. I really didn't want to go, because I'd heard some negative things about the man's ministry, but . . . but it was the strangest thing—Nina started believing that God was going to heal her through this man. She'd wake up in the middle of the night, saying how she'd had a vision of Floyd Waters laying hands on her and healing her. She could be really stubborn when she wanted to, so there was no way I could tell her anything different. I mean, sure, more than anything I wanted God to heal her, but I didn't . . . well, we didn't grow up believing in all that supernatural, blow-on-folks and be instantly healed stuff, you know? Our church didn't teach that either, but . . . but Nina kept urging me to take her, practically begging me to . . ." He bit his bottom lip, forcing himself to keep his roller-coaster emotions in check as he remembered how desperate his beautiful bride had been. How many times had he agonizingly wished that he could somehow trade places with her; wished that *he* had been the one sick instead of her? He would have willingly taken on any affliction, disease, or pain for her sake without even thinking twice about it. God, how he'd loved her!

I . . . I would have died for her . . . and in a way, I have . . .

"So without telling her family or our church, we went down there, and on that first night, Waters called for everyone believing to be healed from cancer to come to the stage. Nina just looked at me with those desperate, baby brown eyes . . . She . . . she was believing to be healed *so bad* . . . what else could I do? So I told her to go ahead and go up there.

"When it's her turn to stand before Waters, the man suddenly stops the music and the choir and tells everyone to be quiet. He asks Nina where her husband is. When she answers that I'm in the audience, he then asks for the husband—me—to come join them onstage. I . . . I *really* didn't want to go up there, but the whole stadium is *so* quiet, waiting for me, I didn't have a choice. And I figure if I didn't go, Nina would've been crushed."

Lynn opened her mouth, as if she might say something, but Chance continued on.

"So I'm up there, in front of hundreds of people, and Nina's up there trembling and shaking and then . . . then I hear her begin to speak in tongues. We weren't raised Pentecostal and I . . . I didn't even *know* she could speak in tongues. And . . . and all the time, Floyd Waters is just staring at me, looking at me with eyes so clear and piercing it was like he was seeing right through me. I'd never seen anything like it before. Then he puts his hand on my head and announces that I've been chosen by God to bring healing to the nations of the world, that through my hands many shall be healed and testify to God's healing power."

Chance took a deep breath, remembering everything as clearly as if it had happened yesterday. "Then he said that if I would but lay hands on my wife, she would be healed." Another tear trickled down his cheek, but this time he didn't bother to wipe it away. "Nina's just standing there, shaking and trembling like she's having a seizure or something. I didn't think . . . I didn't know what to do, but Waters tells me again to lay hands on my wife. So I did. When I touched her head, she fell backwards and onto the stage floor, and then everybody started shouting, the music started playing again, and Waters raises his hands and gives God praise for another healing."

"So . . . so she was healed?"

Chance did a cross between a nod and a shrug. *She certainly thought so* . . . "She told me that when I touched her, a lightning-like sensation ran through her body, and she knew instantly that she had been healed.

"After we got back home, Nina started telling everyone that she was miraculously healed, and that I had God's healing power in my hands. At first, I didn't want her to say anything because nobody knew where we had gone, but she was so . . . so *happy.* I'd never seen her so happy in all the time I'd known her. So I said fine, if you want to go around testifying, at least go to the doctor and have this healing confirmed, but she wouldn't accept that. Said it was a lack of faith on her part to do that; that she *certainly* was healed and she would never set foot in a doctor's office again. Our church thought she was crazy, and so did her mother, Jucinda." He whistled and shook his head. "Everyone knew Jucinda had a real bad anger problem, and that just about set her over the edge. But Nina didn't care, and after a while I didn't either. I mean, she was feeling more energetic, more alive, and more *happy* than she ever had. So who cared *what* people thought as long as she kept living and being healthy, right?"

He paused for a moment.

"But then . . . she died," he whispered.

"Oh, Chance . . ."

"My beautiful bride, my beautiful Nina . . . died. She just passed away one night while she slept—I took small comfort in knowing that at least she didn't feel any pain. Jucinda was outraged, and she demanded an autopsy be performed. The autopsy showed . . . that in fact Nina's cancer *had not* been healed; instead, it had gotten worse after she stopped taking medication. The real miracle was that Nina didn't feel the pain of the cancer, or if she did, she didn't let on."

"Oh, Chance, I'm so sorry."

He didn't say anything for a minute. "Jucinda never accepted the fact that Nina refused medical treatment. She thought it was my fault for taking her down to Lake Charles in the first place. She not only blamed me for brainwashing Nina about this divine healing stuff, but through her large circle of influence she made me the town outcast. Said she was going to make sure I paid for what I did to Nina, and if you knew Jucinda, you knew not to take her threats lightly. Everywhere I'd go, I'd get all kinds of whispers and dirty looks. When you're living in a small town, everybody knows everybody, and I just couldn't take it anymore. I got on the first train out of there and spent some time in Longview, then back east toward Gulfport and Birmingham."

"You just knocked around in those places? I mean, you didn't get a job?"

Chance shook his head. "The same inheritance fund that had given me the house allowed me to kick back for a while. My family tree on my mother's side dates back to a wealthy slave owner years ago. For whatever reason, this man willed his land and most of his assets to my great-great-grandmother, and it's been passed down the family line ever since. What I was doing in those small towns was continuing my ongoing argument with God—I couldn't deal with how He just allowed her . . . just allowed her to die."

"Chance, you can't just—"

"I know. I know, but that season of my life was hell to get through. And sometimes all you want is someone to blame, even if it *is* God. One day I came across one of Nina's diaries, though. She had been so deep into this divine healing stuff during the time she was diagnosed with cancer, and she'd written about how she had visions of me laying hands on people in wheelchairs and seeing them walk, stuff like that. And I couldn't shake what Floyd Waters had prophesied to me either."

Or what my mother had been telling me all my life, that God was going to whisper such special things to my life . . .

"So for six months, I focused on praying and studying what the Bible said about healing. Then I started attending some tent revivals and small church services, looking to put into action the things I'd learned."

"You just went up to people and started randomly praying for them?"

"No. It was . . . Well, let me explain it this way. I just

felt led by the Holy Spirit to ask certain people—whether they were walking with a crutch, or in a wheelchair—if I could pray for them. And I didn't meet anyone who refused prayer, especially after the prayers I was praying . . . began to work."

"What happened?"

"Well, the first time, I was at a small church in Vicksburg, Mississippi. There was an old man whose back was so bent over he was constantly looking at the ground. He'd been in that condition for years, but he still prayed daily for God to heal him. Other than Nina, I had never seen someone with faith as strong as his. I prayed the Word of God over him, laying hands on his back and commanding his spinal cord to come in line with how God created it, in Jesus's name. As soon as I lifted my hands, he starts shouting and jumps in the air three times. When he landed that third time . . . his back had completely straightened out."

"My God . . ." Lynn whispered.

"Yeah. To actually see that with my own eyes . . ." Chance just shook his head. "I felt a little like what Peter must have felt like, walking on the water. I stayed in Vicksburg for a while, but the word of mouth and attention got too much for me. I didn't want to be some kind of sideshow attraction. And when some people I prayed for didn't get immediately healed like that old man, they got upset and started calling me *everything* but a child of God. I got out of Vicksburg quick, taking the train east and just stopping in various small towns."

"What God is doing through you is awesome, Chance. But you just can't keep avoiding whatever it is in your past that you're running away from."

Chance shook his head. "Every time I think about that night in Lake Charles, when I laid hands on Nina . . . and *nothing* happened, I start going through that hell all over again. Why wasn't she healed? How come I can lay hands on perfect strangers—people I will only meet once in my lifetime—and *they* get healed? How am I supposed to live with that irony?"

"Chance . . . I know that has to be hard for you, and I don't have an answer as to why Nina wasn't healed. All I know is that God is using you right now to do things that make an unbelievable difference in people's lives. My doctor told me I might never see again, and to have that fear weighing on your heart every single night . . . *that's* going through hell, too. And what about that little boy who can now hear and walk? Or Pastor Smallwood? Or God knows how many others who have healing testimonies because you prayed for them?"

"I'm real happy for you, Lynn . . . and for those others, too. But I don't know that it takes the place of the joy I felt being married to Nina."

"Chance, you said you weren't raised in a Pentecostal church. When you were married to Nina, did you have any thoughts of having such a healing ministry?"

He shook his head. "Furthest thing from my mind."

"Okay . . . and this is just a small place to start, but if that night in Lake Charles never happened, I may have still been blind today. And Pastor Smallwood may have been dead of a heart attack. And little Eddie Everett is still deaf and handicapped. All throughout the Bible, God used men who had not only incredible faith but incredible frailties, too. Moses stuttered and struggled with self-esteem issues, yet God chose him to be Israel's deliverer. King David was described as a man after God's own heart but he was also an adulterer, murderer, and a man who struggled with sexual lust his whole life. Elijah called down fire from heaven, but he also hid in a cave and wanted to die over a single threat from Jezebel. Jonah was disobedient and stubborn. Abraham and Isaac both lied about their marital status out of fear. Jacob was a—"

"I get the point," Chance cut in. "And I know what you're trying to say. But that doesn't mean *my* pain isn't less real. I didn't ask for this gift."

"I know you didn't. You know, Billy Graham once asked a question of the Lord. 'Why me?' he asked. 'Why did You choose a little boy from a farm in North Carolina to spread the gospel across the world?' Chance, we don't always know why God does what He does. But the fact remains—in spite of your questions and ponderings, He still chose . . . *you.*"

• • •

THE SILVER STAR pulled into Savannah at just past seven in the evening. Lynn stood and stretched her legs before looking at Chance, who was still gazing out his window. It seemed he had been looking out his window the whole trip.

"Are you getting off?" she asked.

He nodded. "Yeah. But I'm catching a connecting train to Jackson, Mississippi, and then on to Ruston. You're not going to follow me all the way *there*, are you?"

Lynn sensed that she was blushing, as she was still somewhat embarrassed at having purchased a ticket on a whim. But at least she'd met the mystery man, right? And at least she was in a better position to help him, if that was what God wanted her to do.

"No. I should be getting back home. We're organizing an important outreach effort this weekend, and I should be there. Chance, is there any way I can get in contact with you? I know you've told me you don't want any media attention, and it wouldn't be for anything like that. I just . . . well, I'd like to help you."

"Help me with what?"

"It's not good to carry that burden around without anyone to talk to, or pray with. You've been talking with me for the past two hours, and—"

"It's not like I had a choice," he interrupted with a faint smile.

"But you were willing to open up and share. And that's important."

"What's *important* is my privacy. How do I know you won't give out my name to that newspaper reporter you've already talked to? Or that you won't tell him what I've just been telling you?"

"Chance, what you've told me today was said in confidence—you have my word on that. The reporter called me late Monday night and asked some basic, general questions. Then he twisted my words around to make it sound like I said something I didn't."

They walked off the train and into the station, finding seats in the waiting area. While Chance excused himself to the restroom, Lynn went to the counter and checked on the departing time for return trips to

Columbia. The next train was scheduled to leave in one hour. She returned to find Chance not sitting down, but standing by a window.

"You have a fascination with the outdoors, huh?"

He shrugged. "Me and my pop . . . we used to go fishing every Saturday when I was younger. Never caught much of anything, but sometimes we'd take our boat out for miles on the river, surrounded by water and trees . . . just the two of us. I stopped doing that after Nina and I started hanging out. Pop asked me once to go out with him again on the river, but I told him I was too busy." He turned around from the window and Lynn was horrified to see he was on the verge of tears. How often did she see men cry?

"But you're going to see your father now, right?" she asked, wondering what she would do if he did start crying.

Chance shook his head. "It's not the same. Even though I was the one Nina's mother made to be the outcast, people think of Pop as the outcast's *father*. He ran a bait and tackle shop for years, but the business stopped when people stopped coming by. Now he barely even gets out of the house. And when he does, it's only to hobble on down to the liquor store."

Now Lynn felt like the one about to cry. "Chance, you shouldn't be going through this by yourself. Let me help you."

"Help me do what? What are *you* going to do? You know what it's like to be me? You know what it's like to go places and see sick people, have a burden to lay hands on them and see them healed? All the while you're dying to have someone lay hands on you? How do you heal a broken heart? Can you answer that since you want to help so much? Maybe women know the answer better than men, because we're taught to be tough and don't show emotion, right? We're supposed to let problems bounce off us like rubber. But all that macho talk is a lie—all I know is, I had a great life. Love, happiness . . ." He turned away from Lynn, back to facing the window.

"But Chance, you can have a great life . . . *again*. I don't know why you had to go through what you did, but neither did Job. You know the story—Job kept his faith and in the end God blessed him double for his trouble."

"Losing Nina was more than just *trouble*."

"But will you let me . . . uh, talk to you sometime? Or listen? I can just listen if you need an ear."

"You're asking for my phone number?"

"If you put it that way, yes. Yes, I suppose I am."

He shook his head as he looked around him, finally picking up a piece of scrap paper lying on the windowsill. He quickly scribbled ten digits on it and handed it over.

• • •

THE SILVER STAR'S RETURN TRIP to Columbia was taking forever, at least in Lynn's mind. She'd finally gotten her wish about knowing the mystery man's identity, but it was like that proverb her mom had always told her as a child: "Be careful what you wish for."

"God, I don't know what You had in mind here," Lynn said, gazing out the same window Chance had been staring out a few hours earlier. With darkness settling over the landscape and her compartment's reading light on, the window doubled as a reflecting glass.

"I just wanted to know who this man was," Lynn continued, praying to God in the best way she knew how—simply talking as if she were having a conversation with her best friend. For in many ways, that's exactly what she was doing.

"I prayed for someone with the faith to believe for my healing, and You answered my prayer with Chance. And I know it didn't make sense for me to get a ticket and follow him onto the train, but what else was I supposed to do? And after he confided in me the incredible things he's gone through, what am I supposed to do with that information?"

Even as she asked the question, she heard the quiet answer from the Lord resonating in her spirit.

Minister to him . . .

"But God, how am I supposed to minister to him?" It was a strange question coming from the outreach director of one of the largest churches in the Carolinas. As a full-time minister, her community involvement included daily counseling of pregnant teenage girls, praying with gang members, ministering to people in halfway-house transitions, and helping unemployed people finding work. And that was merely community ministry, which came *in addition* to her administrative duties at Faith Community. She'd been faced with a number of hopeless situations, yet seen the Lord work miracles time after time.

But through all the experiences in her ministry,

she'd never encountered someone like Chance—a man possessing such a great gift and yet in such great need of help.

"How am I supposed to minister to him, God?" she asked again, staring out the window but really staring at herself. She made a mental note to meet with Pastor Gentry—maybe as another man, he would know what to do.

Chapter Twenty-six

THE PHOTOGRAPH WAS SPLASHED on the *State*'s front page, on the left column below the fold. The tagline underneath read, "Mystery Healing Man Captured on Videotape." Travis had also wanted to be able to disclose the man's name, but he hadn't yet been able to uncover that information.

The mystery man had paid cash during all the times he'd stopped by the diner (which meant no credit card trail), and his picture hadn't turned up any matches at nearby motels or hotels. Travis theorized the man was from out of town; if he'd been a local, surely someone would have recognized his picture. But Travis wasn't worried about discovering the man's identity, since it was bound to come out sooner or later. The interest in the story was growing daily as several area churches announced they would be teaching on the subject of divine healing or holding special services for the sick.

Travis's stature was rising in the eyes of his fellow journalists as well. He was no longer thought of as a lazy reporter, since he had done all the legwork on a story now dominating the local news. He'd been approached by two colleagues, inquiring if they could do anything to help on the story, but had turned them away with a big smile. This was *his* byline. And Benny Dodson had been purposely avoiding him, not having anything to brag about. Benny had never had *his* name mentioned on the front page of the entire newspaper.

The red light on his phone began blinking, something it had never done before at eight o'clock in the morning, and he picked it up on the second ring.

"Everett speaking."

"Travis, what do you think you're proving by getting a picture of this man in the paper?" He instantly recognized his sister's voice.

"Andrea, I'm just doing some follow-up reporting. The people of South Carolina need to know—"

"Travis, I've heard your 'the people need to know' spiel. But what the people *really* need to know is that the Lord Jesus is the one deserving of the glory for all these miraculous healings. Your wild-goose-chase search for a man who's only *serving* Christ is placing the attention on the wrong person."

Travis rolled his eyes and had a notion to hang up the phone. But he was already on Andrea's bad side—why make it worse? And why wouldn't Andrea just let him have his moment in the sun? Was it so hard for her to be happy about him becoming an important person in the local news scene?

"Travis, did you hear what I said?"

"Yeah, but what difference does it make? My only responsibility is to report the facts. And the *fact* is, this man was spotted several times at Five Points Diner, and

I was lucky enough to get a picture of him. Since everyone's talking about this guy, the editor deemed it important enough to place the picture on the front page."

"Well, another *fact* is that many area churches are now holding special healing services for the sick, Travis. Since you're holding so strongly to this 'reporting the facts' shtick, you should come to one of these services. As a matter of fact, we're going to the one at Faith Community Church on Sunday night. Consider yourself invited."

"Uh . . . I don't know," Travis began, racking his brain for an excuse.

"Maynard's flying in from Boston, too, since he wants to see Eddie walk and talk with his own eyes. And afterwards, we're all going out to eat at Damon's Clubhouse."

Travis bit down on his lower lip. His sister *knew* Damon's was his weak spot. A stack of all-he-could-eat, honey-glazed ribs? And with big brother Maynard footing the bill, no less? An offer like that was not to be easily turned down.

"I'll have to . . . um, I'll have to think about that . . . especially if Maynard's flying in. But I could just meet y'all afterwards at Damon's."

"No. This is important, Travis. Eddie is going to say a short speech at this service, and as his uncle, I think you should be there."

"So now you're using both Eddie *and* a plate of ribs against me, huh? You're killing me, Andrea."

"I'm doing no such thing. I'm giving you a chance to see your nephew *speak* in front of a crowd for the first time in his life. And I'm giving you a chance to see another side to this healing story."

"Oh yeah? And what side's that?"

"The side that . . . *believes.*"

Chapter Twenty-seven

"PASTOR, DO YOU HAVE A MINUTE?"

Pastor Gentry looked up from his large study Bible and removed his reading glasses. "Sure."

Lynn walked inside the spacious office, which had been designed in much the same way as a corporate executive's suite—plush, but understated. She was always amazed at the sheer volume of books, commentaries, and concordances lining the wall-to-wall mahogany bookshelves. She'd once thought Pastor Gentry couldn't *possibly* have read all these books, and so she used to randomly select books from the shelves and ask what they were about. Without fail, however, her pastor had given an exhaustive description on the subject and content of each book. Lynn was still looking for a Christian book he'd neither read nor knew anything about.

"What's on your mind, Sister Lynn?"

Lynn took a deep breath. Where to begin? She started by explaining how she had run into the mystery man at the train station, and then subsequently purchased a train ticket to Savannah to follow him. Emphasizing that some parts of her conversation with

Chance had been confidential, she retold how situations from his past had contributed to his conflicting psyche.

"That man has gone through a lot," Pastor Gentry agreed after she was finished. "You know, when I accepted my call to the ministry, I'd heard about the trials and tribulations that ministers of the gospel have to endure, but experiencing them firsthand almost shook my faith completely. There were times I felt like closing up this Bible and forgetting about preaching. But the love of Christ constrained me, and I think Chance is experiencing the same thing. Even though he's gone through a lot, he's been blessed with a gift that he can't ignore. To whom much is given, much is required."

"But shouldn't all Christians be walking in the healing power of God to lay hands on the sick and see them recover? There's a scripture that says as much."

"Mark 16:18," Pastor Gentry said, nodding his head. "God has given gifts to the body of Christ, as it's written in 1 Corinthians 12, and among those are the gift of healing. Some Christians are graced to operate more fully in one gift than another, but that's what makes us all a body. There are diversities of gifts, but the same Spirit. There are many members, but one body. Chance is certainly not the only person who can lay hands on a sick person and by faith see God heal that person—throughout the history of the church, there have been some highly anointed faith healers." He gestured to the bookshelf on his right. "Could you get that book for me? Right there—the blue hardback right there on the edge."

"*God's Generals*," Lynn read from the spine, pulling the book off the shelf. "Written by Roberts Liardon—I think I've heard of him."

"You've probably heard about many of those generals, too. Roberts Liardon received a mandate from God to preserve the heritage and history of many of the church's great leaders."

Lynn pondered that statement for a moment. "You think Chance could be . . ."

"A modern-day *general*?" Pastor Gentry leaned back in his chair. "With what you've described and the gifting he appears to operate in, it's possible. You see, what you have to realize about truly anointed—and I mean *truly* anointed—people is that, in addition to their gift, they also have incredible flaws. Just take some of the generals in that book, for instance.

"Many people consider William Seymour to be the catalyst of the Pentecostal movement in the twentieth century, based on how God used him in the Azusa Street revival. But though he was highly anointed, he was also blind in his left eye. John Alexander Dowie was a great healing apostle in the early days of his ministry, but he eventually became sidetracked from God's plan for his life and he started believing he was the prophet Elijah. William Branham possessed an incredible healing gift, but was semiliterate, had very little Bible knowledge, and as such became a walking disaster concerning healing doctrine. At the height of John G. Lake's ministry in the early 1900s in Spokane, Washington, so many people were healed under his ministry that the government declared Spokane the healthiest city in America. Yet his passion to see people healed was partly born out of seeing eight of his brothers and sisters killed by a strange digestive disease."

Gentry leaned even farther back in his chair and crossed his legs. "So you see, possessing a healing gift alone does not make a man immune to heartache, adversity, or controversy. In fact, I believe it does exactly the opposite."

"I agree. Chance seemed so . . . lost, so shaken up by the tragedy of losing his wife. I wish there was something I could do to help him, to minister to him."

"You know, the more I think about it, the more I wonder about your meeting him at the train station. The Bible says that our steps are ordered by the Lord. God may be up to something."

"You think so?"

"Oh yes," Pastor Gentry responded, nodding slowly. "Oh yes."

Chapter Twenty-eight

RUSTON, LOUISIANA, situated seventy miles east of Shreveport and thirty-five miles south of the Arkansas border, was the only home Chance had ever known, which explained his mixed memories as he stepped off the Greyhound bus. It had only been two years since his exile, but those two years had felt like twice as long. Stuffing his hands into his pockets, he headed south down Trenton Road, a path he'd walked countless times as a child. Nothing about the road—from the towering tree branches blocking highway signs, to the beer bottles and random paper debris littering the grassy shoulder, to the scent of freshly chopped firewood heavy in the air—had changed.

He'd never imagined he would ever leave Ruston—and be *forced* to leave, at that. He knew the flavor and pulse of this town intimately, the way a veteran mechanic knows the varied sputters of a classic automobile. Not that there was a great deal to know—life here was slow and steady, with many of the twenty thousand or so residents well into their golden years. Louisiana Tech, the local college, helped infuse the town with a fresh supply of young people, but Chance always thought of the students as four-year tourists. The people who called Ruston home were the ones who'd always called it home—those whose families had land here, had grown up here, and would eventually depart from here to enter their final resting place.

"Hiya!"

Chance turned at the voice and waved back at the elderly man sitting in a rocking chair on a porch. He recognized him as Ol' Man Rollie and recalled that Rollie was always out here on his porch, waving at passersby. Rollie hadn't recognized him (the old man's eyes, along with his hearing, had been bad for as long as Chance could remember), but Chance knew that if he stayed here long enough, *somebody* would recognize him sooner or later. He hadn't wanted to return in the first place, but he really didn't have a choice. He had to come back . . . for Pop.

Bennett Howard had returned from Vietnam disabled and disillusioned by what the remainder of his life held for him. His left leg, decimated by shrapnel, had been amputated at the knee, and he had been shot three times, with two of the bullets still lodged inside him. Though he'd been awarded the Purple Heart for his service, Bennett Howard didn't care about that. Chance had asked to see his pop's medals once and had been answered with enough curses to shame a sea-weary sailor. Now the man lived to spend the rest of his days fishing out on the river, especially after Chance's mother died. Who could blame him? Life had not been easy for Bennett, which only made the scandal surrounding Chance that much harder to deal with.

The screen door was locked but the front door open

when Chance finally walked up the steps to the house he'd called home as long as he could remember.

"Pop!" He rapped on the screen. "Pop, you awake?"

He waited for a few minutes, hearing nothing inside.

"Pop!"

After another minute of silence, Chance stepped off the porch and walked around to the back of the house. He had once hidden a spare key behind the old air-conditioning unit in the backyard, and he wasn't surprised to find it still there. He unlocked the back door and walked into the living room. The air smelled stale and sweaty; neither the air conditioner nor the fan had been used in weeks.

"Pop! You in here?" He walked to the bedroom and opened the door. In addition to the stale, sweaty odor, a strong liquor scent attacked his nose. His pop lay facedown on the bed, his hands splayed out on both sides like a human airplane. Several empty beer and vodka bottles decorated the floor next to the bed.

"Pop!"

Chance rolled the old man over on his back, tilted his head forward and gently pressed on his father's eyelids.

"Pop!"

"Ungghh . . ." Slowly coming to, Bennett started coughing and wheezing, spittle and foam flying from his mouth and dripping down the front of his T-shirt.

"You messing with this stuff again?" It was more of a statement than a question.

"Ungghh . . ."

"Pop, wake up! You hear me?"

Bennett groaned again. "Dat you, Chance? You back?"

"Yeah, I'm back."

"For good? 'Cause Jucinda ain't have no business spreadin' that bull—"

"Pop, I don't know how long I'm back," Chance interrupted, taking a handkerchief from his back pocket and wiping his father's mouth. "How much have you had to drink, Pop?"

"Who you now, the liquor police? I ain't had but a couple beers."

"You've had more than a couple of beers. A couple of beers ain't nothing for you anymore. You're just killing yourself, you know that?"

Bennett coughed, a wheezing, racking noise that caused Chance to wince.

"Already dead, son. Going to 'Nam killed me long time ago."

Chance shook his head, not wanting to get into another discussion about Vietnam. "C'mon, Pop. Let's get you in the bathtub." Gently, he lifted his father's frail body from the bed and carried him to the bathroom. He set him down on the toilet stool, reached over, and turned the tub's faucets on.

"Ungghh . . . don't make that water too hot, Chance. I . . . can't . . . don't like it . . . when the . . . hot."

"I know, Pop. I know."

• • •

"When we going back out on the river, Chance?"

Chance looked over at his father, washed and dressed and lazily swinging in the hammock. He had sobered up at last and was now finishing off the last of the chicken drumsticks Chance had gotten from KFC.

"I don't know, Pop."

"Well, you better figure it out quick. I'm gettin' too old . . . gettin' too weak to be handlin' that boat by myself."

"You could always get one of those Williams boys to go out on the river with you."

Pop laughed. "Hell gon' freeze over 'fore I ask one of them sorry, no-good—"

"Alright, Pop. So you still can't forgive and forget. I'm just saying, you shouldn't be going out there on the river by yourself."

"But now, I ain't got to. 'Cause *you* back! And I know you back for good. Jucinda can't do nothing to you no more."

Chance wasn't sure of that, because Jucinda Harris had never been one for idle threats. But he would let Pop think what he wanted—as stubborn as the old man could be, it was better to keep things that way.

Chapter Twenty-nine

THE SANCTUARY BEGAN FILLING hours before the healing service's scheduled start, as South Carolinians from all over made their pilgrimage to Faith Community Church. Television crews from three Columbia stations, WIS-NBC, WOLO-ABC, and WLTX-CBS, were on hand with their reporters covering the events on the church's front lawn. The outreach team had organized a massive effort urging sick people to come to the house of God for prayer, an effort that coincided with the printing of the mystery-man newspaper articles. The combined effect of both fostered expectation among Christians and curiosity among non-Christians.

"God has given us a tremendous opportunity." Pastor Gentry spoke to the guest ministers and altar workers, addressing them in the conference room a half hour before the service's start. "I'm told there are several television camera crews here as well as newspaper reporters from as far away as Charleston. Now, they may be here for the hype, but we are here for the manifestation of God's healing power. We've all been fasting and praying, believing God to pour out His Spirit tonight, and like never before, I believe the season for healing is *now*. People are genuinely concerned about rising health care costs, the spread of AIDS and other terminal illnesses, and it is imperative that our faith and trust must be in Christ. Now, God may work through doctors, the government, and other means, but what would happen if the church returned to an old-fashioned outpouring of the Holy Spirit like in the book of Acts? What if people got a hold of faith and started laying hands on their children daily, anointing them with oil and speaking the Word of God over them?

"For whatever reason, we have been blessed with a great opportunity. The testimonies of Sister Lynn and others have shown that God is moving by His Spirit here in South Carolina, as He is doing all over the world. If revival is to begin at the house of God, then let it begin with us."

• • •

"CHURCH, ARE YOU READY to board that train for glory?" T. R. Smallwood had been invited to the healing service as Pastor Gentry's special guest, and the standing-room-only crowd filling the five-thousand-seat sanctuary of Faith Community Church responded enthusiastically. On cue, the praise team took their places at the front and began singing an uptempo worship song.

"Jesus, we worship and we praise Your name . . ."

Sitting four rows from the front, Travis squirmed in his seat as he silently cursed having been *tricked* into coming to church yet again by his sister. And Andrea had come with both barrels shooting this time, using his nephew and a free dinner at Damon's as bait. But maybe the service wouldn't be so bad—two hours at the most, perhaps—and with all the news coverage tonight, it wasn't such a bad idea to be present. His older brother, Maynard, was seated to his left, clapping his hands and looking at ease amidst all the people worshipping Jesus.

Figures as much, Travis thought. *Maynard fits in anywhere he goes . . .*

To his right sat his nephew, Eddie, and Travis *still* could not grasp how a boy deaf and disabled for the first seven years of life could be so . . . instantly healed. It was enough to make Travis wonder about the reality of God.

"And now we lift our hands . . . and now we lift our hearts," the praise team sang.

Officially, Travis was agnostic, not an atheist. He accepted there might be a higher power of some sort; surely human beings (with all their shortcomings and limited knowledge) couldn't be the highest life-form. But that this higher form was Andrea's neatly packaged "Jesus as the Son of God" ideology was not something he could believe.

Twenty minutes later, the praise and worship period ended and Pastor Gentry approached the center pulpit.

"Good evening, everyone, and welcome to Faith Community Church, where faith is increasing every day. And faith is certainly increasing here for God to heal the sick, to open the blinded eyes, and to cause the lame to walk! Amen?"

The congregation responded with another enthusiastic shout.

"The Bible tells us in Revelation 12:11 that we overcome the devil by the blood of the Lamb and by the word of our testimony. With that in mind, let's create an atmosphere of faith and expectancy by hearing a few testimonies of God's healing power. First, I'd like to introduce you to a young boy who was born deaf and with ectrodactylism, a birth defect that made him unable to walk. His doctors had been resigned to the fact that he would be in such a condition for the rest of his life. But how many of you know that with God, *nothing* is impossible?"

"Amen!" someone shouted. "Hallelujah!"

"God healed little Eddie Everett's body, and he's now a living, breathing testimony to what the Lord can do. I'd like you all to put your hands together and give a great big Faith Community welcome to Eddie as he comes and shares his story!"

Everyone stood and clapped as Eddie walked up the aisle and to the center podium. Pastor Gentry warmly hugged the boy, then released the microphone from its holder and handed it to him.

"H-hello. My name is Eddie Everett. I was born deaf and my two legs never worked right. I was always in a wheelchair and I couldn't hear anything. My mom and dad taught me sign language and helped me and stuff, but . . . but it was still hard. It was hard to watch baseball games on TV and know that I'd never get a chance to hit a home run and run around the bases. My mom and dad talked to me about Jesus every day. They taught me to pray to Jesus every night . . . and . . . Jesus would help me hear and walk. And that's what Jesus did! After mom and dad and the nice man we met at the restaurant prayed for me, we were at this church . . . and all of a sudden, I felt my legs tingling . . . they were gettin' stronger . . . and then I heard people talking. I never heard people talking before—that was awesome!"

"Glory to God!" someone shouted.

"Mom and Dad praise Jesus every day for helping me hear and walk. And I do, too. And you know what? Yesterday, my dad signed me up for T-ball. And the first thing I'm gonna do when I hit my home run is look up to Jesus and tell Him thanks!"

There was not a dry eye in the place as people began standing and clapping. Even Travis couldn't deny his nephew's moving testimony. He was genuinely happy for Eddie—it seemed only right that the kid should be able to play baseball and enjoy the carefree days of one's youth.

"Wasn't that tremendous?" Pastor Gentry asked, now speaking again into the microphone. *"And a little child shall lead them . . ."*

• • •

THE EVERETTS LEFT Faith Community Church almost three hours after the service began, although many people were still at the altar, praying to receive their healing. Due to the late hour, Andrea and Maynard decided to postpone dinner at Damon's until the following day.

"You mean I came out here for nothing?" Travis

asked Andrea, pulling her to the side and out of earshot of anyone else. He didn't know whether he could hide his irritation and anger. To waste an entire evening and not even get a barbecue sandwich for his troubles?

"How can you even *say* that?" Andrea retorted. She forcibly removed her brother's hand from her arm. "That's a horrible thing to say. You heard Eddie's testimony, as well as the testimonies of so many others. Are you telling me you weren't moved by that?"

Travis reluctantly admitted that Eddie's testimony was moving. "But you didn't tell me I was going to be in that church almost three hours!"

"There's no time limit on the move of God. You think the people in there getting healed of cancer are complaining about how long the service is lasting?"

"You really believe in this stuff, huh?"

"Yes, and you should, too. Especially now. You can try and write Jesus off, but you know James and I have been praying for Eddie ever since we took him home from the hospital. We kept the faith, and now Jesus has healed our son."

Travis shrugged. He couldn't stop Andrea from believing what she wanted to believe. He admitted he had no explanation for what happened to Eddie, but that didn't necessarily mean Jesus was responsible. Didn't things like this happen on that television show *Unsolved Mysteries*? Unexplained phenomena, UFOs, and all that?

"You're joining us for dinner tomorrow, right?"

Travis cracked a sheepish smile. "If Maynard's still buying, yeah. I'll be there with bells on."

After settling for a half dozen tacos from Taco Bell

to slake his late-night hunger cravings, Travis returned home thirty minutes later. Switching on his living room light, he headed straight for the La-Z-Boy, kicking away discarded T-shirts and magazines cluttering the floor. He'd been meaning to clean up for some time now, but he knew such an activity would be pointless—why go to all the trouble? He lived by himself and couldn't remember the last time he had company over. The way he figured it, the only company he needed was his big-screen TV and a cupboard full of snacks. And tonight, the half-eaten bag of Doritos on the coffee table would be his snack while he caught the midnight *SportsCenter* edition.

Before turning on the television, though, he noticed the red light flashing on his answering machine. That in and of itself was rare, because not only did he not usually have company over, but there weren't too many people who bothered calling him. And even fewer who would leave a message on his answering machine. He walked over and pressed the button.

"Hey, Travis, this is Stu."

Stu Frazier was a friend that Travis had asked to do a little extra digging on their mystery man. Though Stu was now a detective with the local police department, he had grown up with the Everett family, and had even dated Andrea for a while during high school. But that relationship hadn't worked out because Stu, like Travis, hadn't been keen on having organized religion as a priority in his life. And Andrea, committed Christian that she was, wasn't about to be involved with someone who couldn't share Jesus with her. Still, Travis and Stu had remained close over the years, and Travis had always longed to work on a story where having a trusted source in the police department would come in handy.

"We found something," Stu's voice continued talking. "One of the cameras at the train station picked up your guy, talking on a pay phone. In one shot, the camera showed him placing his full palm on the side of the phone. Nobody else had smudged that print by the time my guy looked at it, so I had him lift a nice extraction. After running that through my contact at CPD, we got a match. Your mystery man . . . well, he's no longer a mystery. We've got a name."

Chapter Thirty

THE BROOK'S SLOW-MOVING CURRENT produced a calming effect on Chance as he skipped tiny pebbles across the water's surface. The tip of the sun peeking over the tops of the pine trees was a beautiful sight to awaken his sleepy eyes, though it also brought back many memories. He used to come to this secluded spot in the mornings with Nina, where they would sit and hold each other, watching the sun rise over the horizon. Sometimes they would even strip down to their birthday suits and take a dip in the brook, the kind of romantic thing people did in the movies all the time. Chance didn't think skinny-dipping was so romantic in real life, but it was worth it because they almost always ended up making love.

"God, I just don't know what You want me to do," he now spoke aloud, still skipping pebbles. His best tosses sometimes got five bounces from the tiny pebbles across the water.

The nagging theme of purpose weighed on his mind heavily from time to time, and though his personal purpose in life should have been clear (given the gift God had blessed him with), that wasn't always the case.

A preacher in Birmingham, Alabama, once prophesied that Chance was to bring God's divine healing to the church through signs and wonders, ushering in a great end-time revival. And of course, there was the Floyd Waters prophecy, that he was "chosen by God to bring healing to the nations of the world and that through his hands many shall be healed and testify to God's healing power." And then of course, the healings. The old man with the bent-over back in Vicksburg. The lady with carpal tunnel syndrome in Auburn. The mother of two in Marietta whose cancerous tumor had disappeared while he prayed for her. The teenage boy in Starkville, paralyzed from the waist down from a motorcycle accident. The young boy in Aiken who'd been diagnosed with leukemia. Pastor T. R. Smallwood. Eddie Everett. Lynn Harper. So many people . . . so many families and lives changed. So many churches who now prayed for their sick and shut-in members not merely as a formality, but with a fervent faith that *believed* God could heal them. All because some stranger had stopped by their church, prayed over someone with an impossible-seeming condition, and had gotten results similar to the miracles in the book of Acts.

"God, I just want to love again," Chance whispered. "I just want to stop running from my past . . ."

My grace is sufficient for You . . .

It was the same answer the apostle Paul had been given to his persistent question asked of God in 2 Corinthians 12:8, but the power of the response was momentarily lost on Chance. The past few days had produced too much pain—first with the newspaper article in South Carolina, then running into that strange woman on the train who looked just like Nina, and finally coming home to find his pop drunk.

"I'm tired of the pain, God. I'm tired . . ."

He fired another pebble across the brook's surface, but this time the tiny rock didn't skip across the surface. Instead, it sunk directly to the water's bottom.

• • •

TRAVIS HAD NOT BEEN ABLE to sleep, so anxious was he to meet with Stu after hearing Stu's message. He couldn't remember the last time he'd been so excited. Then again, up until now his life hadn't produced much to be excited about.

He walked into IHOP at 8 a.m. and found Stu seated in a corner booth, his plate piled high with pancakes and syrup. Even though the man was of a slender build, if there was anyone capable of putting away more food than Travis, it was Stu.

Travis slid into the seat opposite his friend and nodded a hello. "You got the stuff?"

Stu laughed. "Stuff? Who am I, Deep Throat? Relax, man. This ain't Watergate. Just the name of some guy who's picture made the front page of a South Carolina newspaper. In my line of work, we call that small potatoes."

"Yeah, well those small potatoes are about to put more money in my pocket. If I land this guy's name, that's a surefire raise for me."

"Good. 'Cause I might have to charge you for this info. I had to pull some strings to get access to the fingerprint database."

"Wait a sec—isn't that a *criminal* database? You're saying our mystery man did hard time somewhere?" This was much better news than Travis had expected. In journalism, nothing was more valued than a piece of scandalous news.

Stu shook his head as he dipped a large pancake morsel into a round of syrup. "No, nothing like that. Your man's name is Chance Howard. Born and raised in Ruston, Louisiana. His prints got on file after a disturbance at a bar in Shreveport when he was nineteen. Seems he got into a fight with one of the locals over something his father said. His father was drunk, rowdy, causing a scene—you know, typical bar fight. Chance paid a small fine, but his prints stayed on record."

"Ruston, *Louisiana*? What's he doing here?"

Stu shook his head again. "Can't figure that out. His wife died two years ago, and it seems he's just been wandering around small towns all over the South. He's been making a name for himself over this healing business, though. There was a story in the *Vicksburg Post* about a man who supposedly healed a seventy-year-old man with scoliosis of the spine for forty years. Just laid his hands on this old guy and the vertebrae straightened out."

"The *Vicksburg Post*? You don't waste time gathering your information, do you?"

Stu smiled. "I've got very good sources at the department."

"Yeah, well . . . let's get back to the tape. Anything else interesting on it?"

"As a matter of fact, there was." Stu slid a manila folder across the table. "The camera shows a woman two pay phones down from Chance. Right after he hangs up, she follows him to the trains. Then she purchases a ticket to the same destination Chance was headed—Savannah. You recognize her?"

Travis's eyes widened as he stared at the grainy black-and-white photo stills inside the folder. He'd seen this woman just *yesterday* at that church service! She'd gotten up right after Eddie's speech to give her own healing testimony.

"Th-this is Lynn Harper, the woman who claims Chance healed her from blindness. I used some of her quotes in my first article."

"I thought you said that blind woman didn't know who the mystery man was."

Travis's ears started burning. "Th-that's what she told me, too! She knows this guy? What if they got a scam working?" He started nodding as he pieced it all together in his mind. "Yeah, I bet they prey on gullible church people and make it *look* like people are getting healed, but it's all fake. Steve Martin did a movie on that years back, didn't he?"

Stu nodded. "*Leap of Faith*. Funny movie."

"Yeah, this has *gotta* be a scam!"

"But why? Where's your motive?"

"I don't know." He also didn't know how his nephew fit into this scenario, because whatever argument he tried to make, it was beyond his intellect how Eddie could now hear and walk. That healing was *certainly* not fake.

"I think I need to have another talk with this Lynn Harper woman. My gut tells me she's hiding something."

Chapter Thirty-one

AS THE HEALING SERVICE'S new testimonies continued piling in, Lynn's team worked double time to make sure all the testimonies were documented. Every person who had gotten healed at the altar received periodic prayer calls, ensuring that they "hold on" to their healings. Pastor Gentry had stressed the importance of these prayer calls, reminding them the devil often brought seeds of doubt to the minds of those who'd been healed.

"Walking in divine *health* should be the primary aim after a miracle healing service," Gentry had said to the outreach team. "It's wonderful to see someone healed of cancer, but not if that cancer comes back after a one-year remission. We need to arm those testifying of their healings with God's Word so they can daily confess the divine health that God desires they walk in."

In addition to the prayer calls, initiatives were also set up to provide healthy-living alternatives. The reasoning behind such effects were sound—those healed of high blood pressure–related problems, diabetes, or heart problems needed to modify their daily eating and exercise habits with positive alternatives. Pastor T. R.

Smallwood had been the first to enroll in Faith Community's new senior-citizen aerobics class, making it widely known that it was now his *personal* responsibility to maintain the healthy heart God had blessed him with.

Lynn heard a knock on her door and looked up to Arlene's smiling face. "You doing alright today, Lynn?"

Lynn smiled back at her friend. "I'm doing great. Busier than I've ever been in recent memory, but great."

"Well, ask and you shall receive, right? How many healings have been documented so far from the service?"

"Fifteen, so far. Everything from arthritis to chest pains, chronic migraines to heart conditions. God is so awesome, Arlene! And the faith of the congregation for divine healings is growing by leaps and bounds."

"I know *my* faith is growing in the area of healing. My nephew was sick with the flu this morning, so I stopped by his house to lay hands on him and pray the Word of God over him." She smiled. "Of course, I'm also believing God to work through that TheraFlu medicine and chicken noodle soup, but I know that God can touch his body."

"That's absolutely right. You know, during those weeks that I was blind, I sometimes wondered where God was. Why did He allow my car window to explode right into my eyes? It seemed so unfair, and I couldn't understand why a loving God would allow that to happen to me. But now that my sight is restored, it's like my faith has gone to another level. I was praying for this woman at the altar who was dealing with the early stages of Alzheimer's. And even though my rational mind *knows* there's no known cure for the disease, my faith didn't care! I mean, I was blind for seven weeks with virtually no chance to recover full sight! But what the doctors couldn't do, God did! And now my 20/20 vision has been restored, and I'm beginning to understand why God allowed me to go through those seven weeks. Because in order to go from strength to strength, you first have to go through weakness. In order to go from glory to glory, you have to endure some . . . Well, for lack of a better word . . . you have to endure some *hell.*"

"Lynn, you're preaching now! And you are so right. I watched you go through that devastating season, and seeing how you kept confessing the Word for your healing stirred something up in me."

Lynn was about to reply when her phone started ringing.

Arlene shook her head knowingly and headed for the door. "No rest for the weary, huh?"

"Apparently not. Talk to you later, girl." Lynn picked up her receiver. "Faith Community Church, Minister Harper speaking."

"Lynn? Travis Everett, the *State*. You got a moment?"

Lynn's first response was to give this lying reporter a good piece of her mind, but that wouldn't be right. It would've felt good, but . . . it wouldn't have been right.

"Do I have a moment to *talk*? About what? You want to use my name to support your half-truths and unfounded theories once again?"

"Miss Harper, in no way did I intend to—"

"Whatever your *intentions* were doesn't matter to me. What does matter, however, is the good faith on which I spoke with you concerning this man God is using in a mighty way."

"Good faith? You want to talk about good faith, Miss Harper? If I remember correctly, you told me you had no idea who this man was."

"Yes, and what I told you was the truth. What you wrote, however, was nothing but sensationalism and lies. I never said this man claimed to be Je—"

"Pardon me, Miss Harper, but you're hardly in a position to lecture me on the subject of lying."

What! Was she hearing this man correctly? Who in the world did he think he was? He was on the verge of harassing her, and if he wasn't careful, he was going to be staring at a lawsuit. Saved woman of God or not, she wasn't one to play the fool.

"You listen to me carefully, Mr. Everett. I don't know who you think you are, but—"

"Let me tell you *exactly* who I am. I'm a reporter with the scoop on the most talked-about story in South Carolina. And before you say something else that you might regret, I should probably inform you that I'm in possession of a videotape showing you and our infamous mystery man boarding a train to Savannah, Georgia, five days ago. Oh, and he's not such a mystery man anymore. His name, as you well know, is *Chance Howard.*"

Lynn's mouth fell open. *He knows Chance's name . . . he has a videotape . . .*

"I'm *also* in possession of a videotape showing you

and Mr. Howard talking rather candidly in that Savannah train station. Now, would you care to retract your previous statement about not knowing who this man is?"

"I . . . I . . . um . . . you can't . . ."

"Oh, I most certainly can, Miss Harper. You see, as a newspaper reporter, I believe in the freedom of speech and freedom of the press, which is protected by the First Amendment of our great Constitution. So I have every right to publish this information whether you like it or not. Cat still got your tongue?"

The . . . nerve! The nerve of this man! "Mr. Everett, I . . . I can explain everything."

"I'm sure you can, Miss Harper. But you see, I have quite an important story to write—one based on facts and not the lies of someone who claims to be a minister of the gospel."

What! "Mr. Everett, you are way out of line! I haven't said anything to you that was not true. At the time we spoke, I had no idea who this man was."

"Rii-iight. So I suppose you just *happened* to run into him at that train station."

"Well . . . yes," Lynn replied, knowing how unrealistic that sounded. "Yes, that is exactly what happened."

Travis started laughing. "You expect me to believe that? You expect the 115,000 daily subscribers to the *State* to believe that?"

"B-but . . . but surely you don't plan to reveal this man's identity!"

"I most certainly do. As a matter of fact, I have a flight to catch to Louisiana to obtain a quote from

Chance Howard himself. Seems I can't track down his phone number, but being the diligent reporter I am, I understand the importance of allowing all involved parties an opportunity to be quoted. You've had your opportunity, and I've got to say, I'm a little disappointed in you. But no matter—it will make a better story if I get a quote straight from the horse's mouth."

"You know about *Louisiana*?" Lynn could not believe what she was hearing. After Chance had confided in her how much he respected his privacy, and how she had sensed the extent of his personal pain, how could she let this headline-seeking reporter just go traipsing off to Louisiana! Making matters worse, she felt guilty about the whole affair, like she had somehow personally led Travis to Chance.

"Mr. Everett, you don't understand," she started pleading once more, but she quickly realized that saying anything else was a waste of breath. The hollow, empty ringing of a dial tone on the other end of the phone signaled that Travis Everett had ended this conversation.

Chapter Thirty-two

I'*VE GOT TO WARN* CHANCE . . .

This immediate thought raced through Lynn's mind as she hung up her phone with now-trembling hands. Forgotten were all the wonderful healing testimonies she'd just documented on a spreadsheet just ten minutes earlier, and in their place was a world of worries.

What was she supposed to tell Chance, assuming she now called him? The conversation she imagined in her mind was downright foolish-sounding.

"Hello, Chance?" she might say. "Um . . . I know how much you value your privacy, but there's a reporter headed your way wanting to do a surprise interview with you. What? How did he find out where you live? Well, he must have tracked security tapes at different Amtrak stations after he spotted me with you. What? Yes, he spotted you with me. Why was he following me? Now that's . . . a good question."

Chance Howard did *not* need the misguided publicity of a headline-seeking reporter prying into his personal life under the guise of "the people's right to know." And why was Chance Howard's identity such a big deal to Travis Everett anyway? Not only was this reporter way out of line to initially write such lies about Chance, but he was still missing the most important story angle—that *God*, not man, was working all these miracles. Lynn had even reminded her outreach and altar workers team not to get caught up by one person possessing a gift of healing. It was the same principle written about in Acts 5:13, where the people esteemed the disciples highly, as the disciples healed all manner of sicknesses and diseases. It was easy to become distracted by the men you *saw* perform the healings in place of God, who alone possesses the power to heal.

Wait a minute, Lynn thought, mentally processing a piece of information she'd missed before.

Everett . . . Everett . . . Earlier, she'd been typing the names of those healed at the altar into her database, and there was something familiar about the last name Everett. She quickly pulled up her alphabetical list and scanned for the E's.

Everett, Eddie.

It was the name of the little boy who had had his hearing restored and been given strength to his ankle bones. In the column underneath Eddie's name, Lynn had listed all family members who were living in the area. Eddie's mother and father, Andrea and James, lived in Columbia. And Eddie also had an uncle in Columbia by the name of . . . *Travis.*

"No, it can't possibly be . . ." Lynn dialed the phone number listed by Eddie's name.

"Hello?" a woman's voice answered on the third ring.

"Hello. Is this Andrea Everett?"

"Yes, it is. May I ask who's speaking?"

"Oh, I'm sorry. Lynn Harper from Faith Community Church."

"Oh, hello! So great to hear your voice! How are you?"

"Blessed, thank you. Um, listen, I was just running through the list of everyone who spoke during our healing service, and I had a quick question for you. It's really nothing . . . I was just curious—Travis Everett is Eddie's uncle, correct?"

"Yes. Travis is my brother. If you're asking about our last names, it's a funny thing, but we're all Everetts. James, my husband, also has the last name Everett. I had to make sure we weren't cousins when we started dating!"

"I just had a question about Travis. Does he work as a reporter for the *State*?"

There was a definitive pause on the other end of the line. "He . . . well, yes. Yes, Travis is a reporter with the newspaper. Are you asking that because of what he's writing on the mystery-man story?"

This is *the same Travis!* "Sort of. Travis called me as a reference on the first story, but I'm afraid he took my words completely out of context."

"Oh, Miss Harper, I'm so sorry. I've been trying to talk to him about not writing this story, or at least to stop being so skeptical about God's role in these healings."

"But I don't understand. As Eddie's uncle, Travis must have seen that remarkable miracle up close."

"He did! But Travis can be so . . . stubborn sometimes. He's never believed in Christ, you see, and even though the *proof* of God's power is right before him, he still won't believe. But I'm still praying for him. The Bible says that God is not willing for any man to perish, and the effectual, fervent prayers of the righteous avail much."

"That's certainly true," Lynn agreed. More than anything else right now, she held fast to the truth of that scripture.

• • •

"WE CERTAINLY HAVE a situation here," Pastor Gentry remarked after Lynn filled him in on her conversation with both Travis and Andrea Everett. "If Chance is as guarded as you say . . ."

"He is."

". . . then I believe he should be forewarned about Mr. Everett showing up in Louisiana."

Lynn nodded. "I know. When Chance told me how the people in his hometown treated him and how he still blames himself for his wife's death . . . the *last* thing he needs is for a reporter lusting after publicity to show up on his doorstep. What should I do?"

Pastor Gentry leaned forward and steepled his fingertips together underneath his chin. "You have his phone number?"

Lynn nodded.

"Well, I suppose you could call him, or . . ." He arched an eyebrow.

"Or . . . what?" Lynn had been mulling over the idea since Travis had told her he was heading to Louisiana, but the thought was even crazier than purchasing a last-minute train ticket to Savannah. She wondered where these newfound radical thoughts were coming from. Well, the man had been so instrumental in healing her of blindness, so what else was she to do?

"Well, you could fly to Louisiana like this reporter is doing," Pastor Gentry said, confirming Lynn's crazy idea. "Remember what I said to you earlier? How nothing happens to us by coincidence and how our steps are ordered by God? You may have thought it merely an impulse to buy that train ticket, but doing so gave you an opportunity to spend meaningful ministry time with Chance. And after how God used him to open your blinded eyes, it's only reasonable to grasp some sort of connection between you and him."

"I was thinking the *exact* thing myself."

Chapter Thirty-three

"POP, TODAY I'M GONNA FIX you a real breakfast," Chance yelled out over his shoulder, while the egg whites fried in the skillet. He was once famous for his mouthwatering egg-and-cheese omelets, but it had been years since he'd last stood in front of a stove. Still, he was discovering that he hadn't lost his touch; it was just like riding a bicycle—once you knew how to do it, you didn't forget. He used to make Nina breakfast in bed from time to time, knowing that the only thing better than preparing a delicious meal was having someone to prepare it *for.*

"What you say about breakfast?" Bennett asked, hobbling into the kitchen.

Chance turned around, wiped his hands on his apron, and grinned. "I said I'm gonna fix you a real breakfast, one of my omelet delights."

"You aim to put a hurtin' on an old man? My body can't take all that cholesterol."

No, your body can't take all that alcohol, Chance wanted to respond. "I've modified my recipe, Pop. I make 'em low in cholesterol now, but the taste stays the same. It's just what the doctor ordered."

"Well, alright. If you say so."

A few minutes later, Chance carried two plates over to the table and watched with faint amusement as his pop attacked his omelet with gusto.

"Hungry, huh?"

"Mmm . . . starving is more like it. I ain't had something this good since you left, son."

Since I left . . .

"You not leavin' me again, is you?" Bennett asked, seemingly reading Chance's mind.

"I don't know, Pop. Everything was so messed up before, you know? And I just needed some . . . some time. I had to get away for a while."

"I know you did. But Jucinda ain't talking about you no more."

"That's because she hasn't *seen* me in two years. But Nina was her only daughter. And Jucinda resented me for what she thought I did like a black man resents the Ku Klux Klan. I just . . . I don't know that I'm ready to come back and face all that. I don't know if I'll ever be ready."

Bennett snorted. "Jucinda jus' needs to wake up and smell the coffee. You didn't take her baby away. Cancer did. It's a hard fact of life, but there ain't nothing nobody can do about it."

Chance nodded. "I don't think that's true, Pop. God can heal any disease."

Bennett snorted again. "God can do whatever He wants to, but that don't change the facts of what happened."

Chance fingered the rim of his glass, staying silent about his gift of healing. He had never felt led by the

Spirit to approach his father and ask if he could lay hands on him; he supposed it just wasn't in God's perfect timing yet.

Bennett finished the last of his omelet and smacked his lips together. "That was good, son! When a man fills his stomach like that, it makes him ready for God's greatest leisure activity. You ready to take the boat out on the lake?"

Chance took another bite of his omelet, chewing slowly as he gazed out the kitchen window. Going fishing with Pop was the chief reason he'd come back here. Chance knew, like all children instinctively know as their parents get older, that the time he had left with his father should be valued and cherished. Pop's health was getting worse, though the old man refused to see a doctor. And because Chance didn't know the *specific* nature of his pop's ailments, he could only pray a prayer of general health over him. He longed to lay hands on Pop and command every organ, cell, and tissue in the old man's body to line up with the Word of God, but he knew Pop didn't believe in that. He'd been against Chance taking Nina to see Floyd Waters, too.

"Chance?"

Chance blinked and came back to the present. "Huh?"

"I asked if we going out on the river today."

Chance nodded. "You bet."

• • •

THE SPORT OF FISHING, according to Pop, was all about mastering the art of patience.

"Them fish got all day under the water to watch that bait," Pop had always said when Chance was a little boy. "And if you keep jerkin' that bait in and out of the water, they gon' know that ain't natural. Them fish is smart critters. So me and you—we gotta be smarter than them. We gotta wait them out. And when they can't wait any longer, bam! When you see that lure bobbing like crazy, that's when you got 'em."

Chance had never really liked fishing, even though he'd always respected what Pop had been talking about concerning patience. What he *had* always liked was being outdoors, surrounded by nothing but trees, the sky, and water. And since Pop had gone fishing on his boat nearly every weekend, Chance would tag along, as the perfect opportunity to get lost in nature anytime he wanted.

And he was now back to that place he'd been so many times growing up—tagging along behind Pop. He watched now as Pop baited the hooks of three fishing poles, a delicate procedure given the hooks' sharp edges, but something that Pop could've probably done in his sleep. Pop noticed his son watching and smiled—a big grin that seemed to spread over his whole face.

"Jus' like old times, eh? You, me, fishin' and the great outdoors."

"Yeah," Chance answered, struggling to spear the squirming earthworm in his hand around his own hook without pricking his finger in the process. "Just like old times."

Except it wasn't just as it had been years before. Two of the most important women in his life—his mother, Jacqueline, and his wife, Nina—were gone. In Chance's mind, they had been taken from this world much too soon. Complicating matters even more, he was now a veritable outcast in his hometown and alcohol had reduced his pop to just a shell of the man he'd once been. Nothing would ever be the same as it had once been.

But you have to try to make things right, he thought, finally getting the earthworm onto the hook. Seconds later, he cast the line out into the lake. *You have to try. For Pop.*

• • •

EITHER TRAVIS WAS BECOMING more skilled as a reporter or the people of Ruston were simply too talkative, because getting Chance Howard's address turned out to be easier than downing a half-gallon container of ice cream during the first quarter of a football game.

He had started by going to the local post office, inquiring about obtaining the address of his long-lost friend Chance Howard.

"Oh, I'm sorry, sir," the kind, white-haired old lady at the desk responded. "I'd love to help you out, but I'm not allowed to give out addresses. Perhaps you have a phone number?"

Travis shook his head, thinking he would have to find another way to get Chance's address. Just then, though, a man filling out a green certified-mail slip for an envelope looked up at him.

"Asking about Chance Howard get you in trouble round these parts," the man said.

Travis pounced at the bait. "You know Chance Howard?" he asked, walking closer.

"Sorry to say I do." The man narrowed his eyes. "He a friend of yours?"

Travis noted the man's sudden hostility and decided to drop the "long-lost friend" bit.

"I'm actually a reporter, trying to get more information on Chance Howard for a story."

"Oh, yeah? What kind of story? He ain't leadin' more gullible people on with that crazy healing talk, is he?"

Bingo! Travis thought. He had to hand it to the small-town mentality of people talking too much. "Well, he may be. I'm from Columbia, South Carolina, and he may have done some . . . *things* up there that are causing people to ask questions."

"Oh, yeah? Did somebody else have to die, like that poor young girl?"

Have to die? "Um, I'm trying to do what I can to prevent that, sir. Do you know where Chance Howard lives?"

"Yeah, I know where he stays. But he ain't been back here for a couple of years. And he *won't* be back here, if he knows what's good for him."

Travis nodded his head, as if he understood. "Okay, but I still need to know where he stays. Can you tell me that?"

The man shrugged and proceeded to give directions. Travis almost physically patted himself on the back. There wasn't anything to this detective business after all.

• • •

THE MAN'S DIRECTIONS TOOK Travis to a dirt road just off Interstate 20. Here the homes' yards were more like pastures, as cows and horses grazed on the grass or lounged in the sun. A bull stared menacingly at Travis as he drove along, making him uneasy in his rental truck. The old Ford pickup was the cheapest vehicle available for rental, and the way it had been driving, it wouldn't stand a chance on this dirt road against this bull.

The road wound and twisted its way for a half mile through thick shrubbery and foliage. In some places, it was only wide enough for one car to pass at a time. After a few minutes of tedious navigating, Travis came to a clearing. A two-story brick house sat nestled between a large barn and a structure that looked like an oversized greenhouse. This had to be the place, although Travis couldn't help but feel confused. A house like this—on so many acres of land—had to cost a fortune. Which of course prompted the question: how could someone like Chance afford this?

Has to be that moneymaking scheme, he thought, now feeling even more resolve to get the scoop on this story. He thought about parking underneath a large pine tree at the edge of the clearing and then walking up to the house on foot (which seemed like the detective thing to do), but that meant at least seventy to eighty yards of walking.

Ain't no way . . . Never one for exercise anyway, he instead drove to within a few yards of the front door before killing the sputtering engine. He looped his camera around his neck, got out, and walked to the front door. The place looked deserted, but well-kept.

Travis rang the doorbell, not really expecting Chance to open the door and give him that easy a photo opportunity. After he'd rung the bell a few times more and after several minutes of waiting, he figured he'd just sit in the back of his truck and wait Chance out. All signs indicated that Chance had taken the train back here, so sooner or later he would have to show. And when he did, Travis would be right here, ready to add to the story that was going to launch his career.

Chapter Thirty-four

THE 2:45 P.M. FLIGHT TO MONROE, Louisiana, had taken just under four hours, but by the time Lynn had retrieved her luggage, sorted out which rental car service best fit her needs, and driven the thirty miles west to Ruston, dusk was approaching. She had been talking to herself on the plane and in the car—repeatedly telling herself how foolish and impulsive her actions were. Buying a train ticket for a two-hour trip to Savannah was one thing, since people took trips like that all the time for shopping or for an afternoon getaway. But *flying* almost halfway across the country for no apparent reason? She tried convincing herself she just wanted to warn Chance, but couldn't she have made a phone call and done that?

No, the truth of the matter was that the whole situation had become too personal. Chance Howard was not just a mystery man whose picture should be displayed on a newspaper's front page like a wanted fugitive. He had been the special person, like an angel, that God had used to lay hands on her blinded eyes and heal her. And while anyone with the faith to believe God like that could've theoretically done the same, it had been *Chance*. Why had *he* happened to be outside Hope Springs Church at the exact moment Lynn found herself locked out of the restroom? And why had *she* happened to be just two pay phones away from him at a train station she never frequented? If it hadn't been for Evangelist Barbara needing a ride and Sister Mattie unable to provide one, Lynn would've never even been there. Mere coincidence? Lynn didn't think so, and apparently neither did Pastor Gentry.

Once she entered the Ruston town limits, Lynn pulled into a convenience store parking lot and pulled out the slip of paper on which Chance had written his phone number.

I'm probably too late, she thought dejectedly. If Travis had caught a flight before she had, chances were good that he had already located Chance. Still, she hadn't come all this way just to let her fears get the best of her. She took out her cell phone and dialed the number. Thinking she would probably just get voice mail, she wasn't expecting anyone to answer, least of all Chance. So when he did answer, his voice jolted her, just like it had at the train station.

"Hello?"

"Chance? Oh, I'm sorry . . . I didn't think anyone would pick up."

"Is that what you normally assume when you make a phone call?"

"Well, no. It's just that people think you're so hard to get a hold of."

"People think what they want, Lynn. You asked for a number to call me at, and I provided one. Doesn't get much simpler than that."

"I guess you're right. I was calling to warn you about a potential problem . . . well, it's more like a nuisance, that's headed your way. Some of this might be my fault, so I apologize in advance, but you know that reporter who's writing those articles about you in the *State*?"

"Remember? How could I forget? Those articles were the main reason I left."

Lynn winced. "Uh . . . right. Well then, you should know that he's headed your way."

"What, exactly, is that supposed to mean?"

"That reporter—Travis Everett—is headed to Ruston, probably to take another picture of you and get some more material for his story."

"He's headed to *Ruston*?"

"Yeah. He's probably already here."

"What? I can't believe that a—" His voice broke off as Lynn winced some more, feeling even more guilty about putting him through this added pain. For a man as guarded about both his privacy and past as Chance was, his defensive walls were surely now crumbling down around him like the collapse of the Berlin Wall.

"Wait a minute," Chance finally said. "You said he's probably already *here*? Why do you say 'here'? You're in Columbia, right?"

Surprise again . . . "Uh, well . . . no. Actually, I'm in Ruston, too."

Chance was silent for a few seconds. "You're making a habit out of following me, Miss Harper."

"I know. Is that good or bad?"

"I don't know. That's what has me worried."

• • •

JUCINDA HARRIS HAD WORKED at Louisiana Tech in various roles over the past twenty-five years, primarily in the College of Liberal Arts. The past two years she had been on a type of administrative leave, directly attributed to the painful loss of her only daughter, Nina. People had always said Nina was the spitting image of Jucinda—tall, long black hair, curvaceous physique, and free-spirited. Jucinda had moved here with Nina from Trinidad because of the chance to provide her daughter with a better education. Nina had certainly been on her way, too. The scholarship to Southern had been a fantastic start, and Jucinda envisioned Nina attending graduate school somewhere back East. The plan had been working perfectly until that boy . . . *Chance* ruined everything.

In retrospect, Jucinda knew she should've taken a more active role in her daughter's relationships, but in truth, there were none until Nina and Chance were selected to go to Washington, D.C., in the spring of their senior year.

Nina hadn't really dated anyone all throughout her junior high and high school years, which, of course, had made Mama proud. As beautiful as Nina was, there were many would-be suitors, but Jucinda had always stressed to her daughter the importance of an education above all else.

"What you have in between those ears is the only thing that matters," she constantly reminded Nina. But something happened between her daughter and Chance during that Spring Break trip that Jucinda could never understand.

"What on earth do you see in that boy?" she'd asked Nina.

"I don't know, Mama. He's so sweet . . . and he carries on the most interesting conversations. I never knew he was like that."

Jucinda had nothing against the boy being nice and carrying on interesting conversations. What she *didn't* like, however, was that Chance was a country boy who would always live in the country. Jucinda had learned Chance had inherited a large tract of land just north of town from his late mother, meaning he would be settling here . . . *forever.* Jucinda couldn't bear the thought of her educated, independent, free-spirited daughter living on a *farm* with cows and chickens.

Adding insult to injury, not only had Nina gotten involved with Chance, but she'd also gotten involved with some charismatic church while she was in college—a church that believed in speaking in tongues, prophesying, and casting out demons. She'd come back from college pronouncing herself born-again and Spirit-filled.

"Mama, they got the Holy Ghost," Nina had argued to her mother one night. "And I wanted what they had. So I went down to the front of the church to receive salvation and the baptism of the Holy Ghost. Mama, it was so wonderful! God just filled me up and—"

"Stop that nonsense!" Jucinda had cried out, unable to take any more. "I will have none of that crazy talk in my house, you hear me? The nice Catholic church we attend is all the religion we need."

Of course, this rift in their relationship had pushed

Nina further away, infuriating Jucinda. All that she'd worked for and planned for her daughter was going down the drain in the name of misguided affection and spiritual emotionalism.

Years later, Nina's discovery that she had liver cancer had initially devastated Jucinda, but she soon thought of it as something that might bring them back closer together. She had gone online and researched all the facts—how the success rate for beating cancer was much higher when it was detected early, and how the M. D. Anderson Cancer Center in nearby Houston housed the country's foremost cancer research hospitals.

But Nina, to Jucinda's horror, would hear none of her mother's careful research.

"I have faith, Mama. God is going to supernaturally heal me."

"God's going to do *what*? Honey, have you lost your mind? This is not the time to bring up your prophecies or Holy Ghost language or whatever it is you're always talking about! Cancer is real, honey. But we're going to be fine, because I'm going to make sure you're seen by the best doctors in the country."

"But Mama, one of the ladies at my church was diagnosed with cancer until this awesome man of God named Floyd Waters laid hands on her and declared her healed in the name of Jesus! She went back to the hospital, and the doctors couldn't find the tumor! And you know what? Floyd Waters is coming to Lake Charles next month. It's a divine setup! I'm going to be supernaturally healed, and then you'll see how great God is!"

Jucinda didn't doubt the greatness of God, but her daughter was clearly delusional. Unfortunately, she was also as stubborn as her mother and couldn't be talked out of going to that healing meeting.

And then Jucinda's worst nightmare came true—her only daughter, her pride and joy . . . *died.*

After Nina's passing, with the autopsy clearly showing that the cancer cells had spread all throughout her body, Jucinda didn't care about who'd been right or wrong. What good was there in saying, "I told you so," if her baby girl was gone forever? The only person she could direct her anger and frustration on was Chance Howard—the one person Jucinda felt directly responsible for this mess. If Nina had never met Chance, then she would've been in grad school somewhere back East, away from all this foolish talk about supernatural healings and the Holy Ghost.

The two years since she'd run Chance out of this town had done nothing to ease Jucinda's pain, and today, as she walked into the post office to mail a care package back to her aunt in Trinidad, that old wound reared its ugly head once more.

"Jucinda, there was a reporter in here today asking about Chance Howard," Betty, the old postmistress, said as Jucinda set her box on the counter.

"What!"

"Yep. Came right up here and asked me if I knew where Chance lived. I didn't tell him, but ol' Walter DuBose did. That reporter got up out of here quick after that. I wonder what that was all about—do you think Chance is coming back?"

Jucinda was still speechless, in shock. If she as much

as *saw* the man responsible for her daughter's death, she swore she'd put her hands around his countrified, chicken-chasin' neck and strangle him to death.

"You know, his old man's not doing so well," Betty continued. "Flora says Bennett's bound to croak any day now. Chance probably came back to—"

"That's *enough*, Betty! Not another word of this, you hear me?"

Betty nodded and finished metering Jucinda's care package.

"If that boy is dumb enough to show his face here after how he treated Nina," Jucinda continued, "then I'll make sure the next time he leaves this town, he'll only be headed one place—six feet under."

Betty's eyes went wide with shock. No doubt this was good gossip to start spreading around town.

Chapter Thirty-five

CHANCE HAD INSTRUCTED LYNN to meet him before dawn at a docking point on the banks of Caddo Lake, a popular fishing and recreational spot seventeen miles north of Shreveport. Lynn wasn't thrilled about boarding a *boat* and getting out on the water, though she wasn't going to let that fear be known to Chance. The fifty-foot sport fishing boat with the word *Jacqueline* painted on the bow, however, was quite different from what she had expected.

"Who is Jacqueline?" she asked, indicating the boat's name.

"My mother," Chance explained as he helped her onto the deck. "Pop and I decided to name it after her, though if she were still alive, she'd probably kill us both. She hated fishing."

"It's . . . nice," Lynn commented, far from an expert on what a nice boat should look like. Still, it seemed like the right thing to say.

"She's just another boat to me, but she's my pop's pride and joy. Come on, I'll introduce you." He led her to the starboard side, where an elderly man was untangling a mass of fishing line.

"Pop, I'd like you to meet Lynn Harper. Lynn, my father."

The man flashed a near-toothless grin and extended his hand. "Name's Bennett, but you can call me Pop, too."

"It's a pleasure to meet you."

"A pleasure? Ha! Wait till you get to *know* me!" He started laughing.

"C'mon, Pop," Chance said, gently leading him away. "Why don't you get this baby started and let's get around to Big Cypress River. The fish will be biting there at dawn."

"Aye-aye, Cap'n!"

"Your father's . . . quite a character," Lynn remarked as Pop hobbled over to the boat's controls.

"He hasn't been the same ever since Mom died. He has his good days and bad days . . . although probably not many more. He's got some medical problem, but I'm not sure what."

"Hasn't he been to a doctor?"

Chance shook his head. "He's like a stubborn mule with bad legs. He refuses to go to a doctor, and I can't make him, either." He walked toward the stern. "I'm coping with it, though."

Lynn walked up next to him, resisting the urge to place a hand on his shoulder. "Seems to me like you're coping with a lot more than you should have to."

Chance shrugged. "That's life, right?"

"No, that's *not* life. God brings people into our lives to help share burdens. The Bible says that two are better than one, because if one falls the other is there to help him up."

Chance nodded, but said nothing.

An awkward silence between them ensued, as Pop got the motor started and the *Jacqueline* chugged out to deeper waters. Sunrise was still an hour away, and the moon's reflection cast silvery-white shadows across the water's surface.

"Have you heard from Travis Everett yet?" Lynn asked, more to interrupt the silence than anything else.

"No. And if he's able to find me out here on the river, I might start thinking you're working with him."

What? "But . . . you couldn't think . . . that I'm—"

"I don't know *what* to think anymore. You want me to check off the reasons? How about this—the only woman who ever meant anything to me is gone and I can't bring her back. My mother-in-law ran me out of the only town I ever lived in, and swore to hurt me if she ever saw me again. My father is in denial about his drinking problem, which probably won't matter since he doesn't have a whole lot of time left to live. Some crazy reporter is chasing me around like Tommy Lee Jones in *The Fugitive*, so apparently I now have to keep looking over my shoulder everywhere I go. Should I continue?"

"That's not very encouraging," Lynn admitted, "but here's what I *know*—God has blessed you with a wonderful gift that can touch the lives of so many. Alright, you tell me this—if your life is as messed up as you just described it, then why did you go to all those church services, looking for people you could pray for?"

"I don't know. I was just trying to—" The words seemed to catch in his throat. "Nina *died* believing

God had healed her through my hands! You know what kind of a guilt trip that will put you on?"

"Hold on a minute. You've said that it takes *faith* to believe God for divine healing."

"Faith activates the hand of God, sure. But God can do anything He wants to—there are aspects to Him that we'll never figure out, no matter how many seminaries we attend or Bible classes we take. That first healing God did through me—the man with the bent-over back in Vicksburg—I don't really believe my faith had anything to do with it. Like I said, that old man had more faith in God for the miraculous than anyone I'd ever met. After that healing, when I started studying the Word more and praying for more people . . . my personal faith for divine healing became stronger."

"Well, *however* your gift developed, the truth is that you now have it. You have it like the disciples in the book of Acts had it. And the Bible says that when just two of those disciples went to a city, they turned that city upside down! Look what you did to Columbia and Sumter—and you were only there for a few weeks!"

"Yeah, but it was different back in the biblical days," Chance said, gazing out over the water. "The church was in its infancy then, and the signs and wonders the disciples performed helped in adding new converts to the movement. But the culture here in America is different. Now performing signs and wonders will get you the front page of a newspaper and tabloid media coverage instead of new converts. Plus, you're competing with psychics, black magicians, tarot card readers, Yoruba followers, and New Age spirituality. People aren't moved anymore by walking on water, because they've probably seen it on David Copperfield."

"Do you honestly think Eddie Everett wasn't *moved*? Or Pastor Smallwood? Or *me*? Chance, what you did by faith in God forever changed our lives and the lives of those who witnessed it! The difference between some street magician doing tricks and the power of God is so huge; the two can't even be compared."

"That may be true, but the facts of my life haven't changed. I didn't ask for—"

"You didn't ask for this gift," Lynn finished for him. "Yes, I know that. But to whom much is given, much is required."

"You sound like you're speaking from experience."

Lynn looked away for a second. "God called me into the ministry when I was just a teenager."

Chance's expression lightened a bit. "Tell me about that."

"Tell you about what?"

"What it was like to hear the call . . . learning to make decisions based on the Spirit of God . . . the whole nine yards."

Lynn recognized this as her golden ministry opportunity, especially since Chance had now turned completely around to face her. She had his undivided attention.

"Well, growing up, I was sort of a loner. Not shy, just quiet. I would rather read a book than do much of anything else. I always had these questions, you know? Normal questions like why is the sky blue? If a tree falls in the forest, and there's nobody around to hear it . . ."

She stopped when she saw Chance smiling. "What? What's so funny?"

"Nothing. It's just that those aren't normal questions for a kid to ask."

Lynn felt herself blushing. "Th-they are, too!"

"Fine, fine," Chance responded, showing the palms of his hands. "If you say so."

Lynn cleared her throat. "Like I was *saying*, I had all these questions, especially at church. One of my Sunday school teachers, Sister Imogene, took time every Sunday not only to answer them for me but also to share God's love with me. Of course my parents did that, too, but there was something about the *way* Sister Imogene talked about God—it was like talking to someone who knew God as a best friend. I can remember getting saved and baptized when I was eight, and a few years after that . . . I had a dream."

"A dream?"

Lynn nodded. "I was in a small room, surrounded by fifteen or twenty people singing my favorite worship song at that time, "Oh Come Let Us Adore Him." The way the people were singing, and the small, intimate confines of the room—it was all just so . . . breathtaking. It was like Jesus Himself was in the room, giving each of us a great big hug. There was so much love in that room—more love than I could've ever imagined, and I remember thinking, *If only everybody else could experience this kind of love*. And that's when I heard Jesus's voice—it was no louder than a whisper, but even now, when I recall it, chills run up and down my spine. What does the book of Revelation say about His voice? That it's the sound of many waters? That description using plain old English doesn't do it justice. Anyway, He whispered to me, ***I want everyone to experience this kind of love. Will you be my voice to share it with them?*** Right when I said yes, I woke up. My radio alarm clock was on, playing 'Oh Come Let Us Adore Him.' Now, you have to understand—I'd *never* heard that song played on that particular FM station. So either someone called in and requested it, or . . ."

"Or your dream meant something much more," Chance finished for her, softly whistling. "That's . . . that's some call to the ministry."

Lynn nodded. "It was that and so much more. It affirmed who I was, and more importantly, who I was supposed to be. And I needed that affirmation, because there weren't any other women around whom I could emulate in my own ministry calling."

"What about Sister Imogene?"

Lynn looked away, shaking her head. "She became sick during my first year of high school and was sent away to live with her eldest son in Florida. I never saw her again . . . She went home to be with the Lord a few years later."

Chance was quiet, watching the sun slowly rise on the distant horizon. Lynn was watching the sunrise, too, remembering how not long ago, she was unable to behold such a beautiful sight. And then, a revelation of how she might reach Chance opened up in her spirit.

"Chance, you know that Nina, like Sister Imogene, is home with the Lord now, right?"

He nodded. "Her faith defined every aspect of her life. People might've thought she was crazy, but if there was one thing I know for sure—that woman loved the Lord."

"In no way am I trying to diminish your loss, even after two years, but if she *has* gone home to be with the Lord, isn't that . . . better for her? I mean, when a believer goes home to be with the Lord, it's cause for a celebration. Here on earth, we can only imagine what it must be like to be in heaven, in the wonderful presence of the Lord forever. There's no cancer there. No sorrow. No tears."

"It *is* better for her," Chance admitted after a few minutes. "And maybe I'm too selfish to let go of her, but that's not what keeps me up at night."

"What is it that keeps you up at night, Chance?"

"If God is using my hands to heal, then why didn't they work for Nina? Why didn't they work for the one person who believed with every bit of faith in her—even against the opinions of everyone else—that God would heal her of cancer?"

"But God . . . *did* heal her of cancer," Lynn said quietly, the words coming from her mouth without her realizing what she was saying.

"What?"

Oh my God, what did I say? "Well, He did heal her. You said it yourself. She's in heaven right now. There's no cancer there; only peace and love. So . . . much . . . love."

Chance shook his head. "But that's not what Floyd Waters prophesied. He said . . . he said . . ."

"He said *what*, Chance? He said that if you laid hands on Nina, she would be healed, right? And he also said that many people shall be healed and testify to God's healing power through your hands."

"You've got a good memory," Chance muttered, still looking at the sunrise.

"I'm just saying that Floyd Waters didn't prophesy anything that didn't come true. Many people *are* testifying to God's healings through your hands. And Nina was healed, just not how you or anyone else expected it. Perhaps it was . . . her time. We don't know why God does what He does—His ways are higher than ours. But we have to trust in His sovereignty. We have to trust that His perfect will comes to pass every time."

"Why are you defending Floyd Waters all of a sudden?"

"I'm not defending him. But from personal experience, I . . . well, I do know that he's a man of God, and not the con artist some portray him to be."

"Personal experience, huh? Like what?"

Lynn proceeded to tell him about the time she contracted pneumonia when she was nineteen months old, and how Floyd Waters had been contacted to come pray for her. Though the doctors had given up on her, saying her immune system was too weak to fight off the disease, the man of God had prayed for her and she was miraculously healed.

"I haven't been sick a day in my life since," she said in conclusion. "Now, you tell me—after an experience like that, what am I supposed to think about Floyd Waters?"

"I don't know; you can think what you want. But God must have something special for you to do. He's miraculously healed you *twice* after doctors had given up on you."

"Chance, God has something special for you, too."

Chapter Thirty-six

By daybreak, Travis had grown as restless as a milk-deprived newborn. His initial excitement over getting another picture of Chance Howard had transformed into anxiety as the one o'clock deadline neared for e-mailing the story to Ryman Wells. He wasn't panicking, though—even if he couldn't get a picture or a quote from Chance, he still possessed a fantastic story. He had connected enough pieces of the mystery together that the readers of the *State* would soon know exactly who Chance Howard was.

Travis had concluded that South Carolina's mystery man was nothing more than a religious phony. While there were some unexplainable healings surrounding this man, most notably that of his nephew Eddie, there were equally enough questions and deaths surrounding him to cast a gloomy pall over the scope of Chance's overall activities. The one documented death of Nina Howard had left a distraught, vengeful mother who'd driven Chance out of town. Who knew how many other people's lives Chance had damaged, but they just hadn't come forward yet?

Tired and starving after a night of only a dozen stale

doughnuts to snack on, Travis climbed back in the rental truck and steered back down the path. Halfway along the trail, he saw a Jeep coming in his direction, sending out a plume of dirt and dust in its wake. Though his stomach was growling and he longed for his comfortable waterbed back home, his reporting instincts quickly kicked in—was this . . . *Chance*?

The Jeep pulled over into the weeds and grass, presumably to let Travis's truck pass, but Travis had no intention of passing. He killed the truck's engine, got out, and started walking toward the Jeep.

"Hello! Hey there!" he called out.

The Jeep's door opened and a middle-aged man in overalls stepped out. Travis's heart sank just a bit when he realized the lone occupant of the Jeep was not his mystery man.

"Whatsa matter?" the man called out.

"Do you know Chance Howard, the man who lives in that house?" Travis asked, pointing back down the trail.

"Yep."

"You know where I can find him?"

The man shook his head. "Mr. Howard don't like nobody askin' about him."

"I can understand that. But I just flew in from . . . from . . ." Travis racked his brain, trying to think of an excuse, though in the end he settled once again for the truth.

"I just flew in from South Carolina, and I was hoping to speak with Mr. Howard before noon today. I'm a reporter, and I need to get a few quotes from him on an important story."

The man continued shaking his head. "Only way you gon' talk with Mr. Howard today before noon is if you a fisherman."

"Why is that?"

"Ain't really s'posed to tell. Mr. Howard don't like nobody ask—"

"I understand that. But this is really important. Listen, Mr. . . . ?"

"Name's Telfair. I cut the grass round here."

"Uh, Telfair, listen, are you *sure* you can't tell me where Mr. Howard is right now? I can make it worth your while."

Telfair dug his hands into his pockets and spit on the ground. Travis could see he was chewing a wad of tobacco. "How you gon' do that?"

Travis grinned. "Name your price."

Telfair grinned right back at Travis. "A hunnerd bucks."

"How many—oh, you mean a *hundred* bucks?"

"That's what I said. A hunnerd bucks."

A hundred dollars was all the spare money Travis had on him. But he didn't hesitate to reach in his pocket and part with it, since he was convinced he was getting the better end of the deal.

Chapter Thirty-seven

REEL HIM IN, POP! That's gotta be a six-pounder, at least!"

As Chance and Lynn watched, Pop began reeling in the line, periodically pulling back on his pole for leverage against the weight of whatever was hooked underwater. Within seconds, the telltale thrashing of a fish's tail broke the water's surface.

"That's it, Pop!" Chance yelled again. "Bring him on home, now."

When the ensnared fish was a few feet from the boat, Pop planted his one good foot firmly against a water cooler and yanked backwards on the line, bringing aboard a two-foot-long largemouth bass.

"Whoo-ha!" Pop shouted. "Whoo-hee! Bass like that'll bite like crazy this time of morning." He picked up the flopping fish by its gills and proudly raised it up like a trophy.

"Pop's like a fish magnet in these waters," Chance explained to Lynn. "He'll bag seven or eight of these before the sun gets high in the sky."

"Bass fish are just like humans when the temperature gets too warm," Pop added. "In warm water, they won't so much as nibble even if the bait is right in front of 'em." He gestured with his free hand. "Come over here, Nina, and have a look at this beauty."

Chance's body immediately stiffened, and a confused expression darkened Lynn's face. Pop didn't recognize that he'd done something wrong. "Well, what are you waiting for?" he asked.

"Um . . . Chance," Lynn whispered. "Did your . . . father call me . . . what I think he did?"

Chance nodded. "Pop, this is *Lynn*, remember? Her name is Lynn."

"I know that," Pop responded. "You just introduced me to her. I mean, I know that she looks just like Nina, but—" Pop's eyes widened. "Oh, God. I called her . . . *Nina*, didn't I? I'm sorry, son. Didn't mean no harm by that."

Lynn shot a curious glance at Chance. "You never mentioned that I look just like her. Oh, I'm sorry, too, if I've caused you any—"

"It's nothing," Chance said, holding up a hand. "Don't even worry about it. Uh, excuse me for a second," he added, walking toward the other end of the boat.

Pop shrugged his shoulders. "He just can't let go of the past, Lynn. What's done is done and there ain't nothing anybody can do about it."

"Does . . . does he ever talk about her? About Nina, I mean?"

Pop shook his head. "Not without crying like she just passed yesterday. That Nina was a good woman, I'll give her that. But it ain't natural to carry on like this two years after her death. Chance always was a sensitive one, though."

"He mentioned once that everybody in town blamed him for Nina's passing. Is that true?"

"Yep. It's a shame, too. *Nina* was the one wanting to go to that healing meeting, not my boy. Guess it was easier for Jucinda to blame Chance rather than admit maybe her daughter was misguided."

"Misguided?"

"Well, yeah. Everyone knows there ain't nothing to that instant healing business. Nina should've known better."

Lynn instinctively reached for her eyes. There wasn't anything to this healing business? She would still be blind today if that were true!

"Mr. Howard, I—"

"Pop. You can call me Pop, too."

"Okay . . . Pop. So, you don't have any idea what your son has been doing for the last two years?"

"He ain't been doin' much of nothing, far as I'm concerned. I guess he been trying to cope with Nina's death and trying to find himself. Don't look like he's done either one."

"Would you excuse me, Mr. . . . uh, I mean, Pop?" Lynn turned around and walked to the other end of the boat. She saw Chance leaning against the rail, staring out into the water.

"Chance, how come your father doesn't know about your gift of healing?"

Chance shrugged. "I've never been led to tell him."

"But . . . this is your *father* we're talking about. Don't you think he should know? Your gift . . . it's so—"

"Lynn, I don't think he needs to know, alright? Pop doesn't have a whole lot of time left, and for the time he does have left, I want to be the son that's always made him proud, not some weird traveling sideshow that nobody understands."

"Chance, you are *not* a weird traveling sideshow. I know that I can't imagine all that you've gone through, but I'm here to listen . . . and to try to understand. A life devoted to the ministry is not easy—believe me, I know that. But I've also learned that it helps having a few people in your corner."

"And that's where you want to be, huh? In my corner?"

"I just want you to know that I *care.*"

The sounds of nature filled in the relaxed silence—the small cresting waves gently lapping against the side of the boat, the cawing of geese flying overhead, and the occasional duck calls. Lynn stared out at the water, amazed at how . . . endless it seemed. She had been on a boat in the middle of the water only one other time in her life. Four of her study partners from her college history class had rented a boat and water-ski equipment, then had driven to Hilton Head the Spring Break of her sophomore year. Lynn hadn't been thrilled about going, but she'd been praying for an opportunity to witness to the study group, all of whom thought she never had fun because she was a born-again Christian. Well, she'd had fun all right, and by the week's end, everyone in the group had given their lives to Jesus Christ.

"You . . . *do* look like her, you know," Chance said, finally breaking the silence. He pulled out his wallet and slid out a photograph, which he handed to Lynn.

Lynn almost gasped when she looked at the picture, because it was almost like looking in a mirror. The woman's hair in the photograph was cut differently from hers (although Lynn had once sported the same 'do), but they had the same skin tone and smile.

"Didn't know you had a twin, did you?" Chance asked, now looking back at the water.

"Well . . . our eyes are a little different."

"Yeah, but not much."

"Chance, I can't even fathom how hard this has to be for you, me resembling Nina like I do and following you around like I have."

"Don't beat yourself up about it. Actually, it's been kind of nice having you . . . I mean, I know you're not her . . . and I wouldn't want you to be . . . but it's been nice. For your information, it's not how you look that reminds me so much of her, anyway."

"Oh?"

"Nina had . . . and you have that unshakable faith in God, the kind that believes in Him no matter *what.*"

Lynn managed a smile. "Well, let me tell you—literally having your blinded eyes opened can do wonders for your faith."

"I imagine so. Let me ask you something—because I've wondered about this after I lay hands on someone and that person *doesn't* get healed. Is it all about having faith? I mean, what if there had been no change after I laid hands on your eyes and prayed for you? Would that have changed your faith in God?"

"That's a tough question, Chance. If I were still blind today, would I still have faith that God is a healer? My heart tells me that I would, because I've lived most of my life walking by faith . . . and not by sight—uh, no pun intended. But I also think back to something the three Hebrew boys—Shadrach, Meshach, and Abednego—said before King Nebuchadnezzar threatened to throw them into the fiery furnace. They said, *'God is able to deliver us from the burning fiery furnace . . . but if not, then let it be known that we do not serve your false gods nor worship your golden image.'* To me, that is a level of faith that most people don't have—knowing that even if God *does not* deliver you, that doesn't mean that He *can't*. That was my thought process during those seven weeks that I was blind. I did have faith to believe that God would heal me, because I believed that it was His will."

"But isn't it God's will that all of His children be healed? Didn't Jesus's death, burial, and resurrection give all believers access to that divine benefit?"

"We *do* have benefits because of the work of the cross," Lynn agreed. "Psalm 103 tells us that."

"But I would go to some churches and lay hands on people, and nothing would happen," Chance countered. "Is that solely because those people had a lack of faith?"

Lynn could read between the lines and sense what Chance was really asking. Did his beloved Nina somehow have a lack of faith? Or did *he*?

"No man can completely know the mind of God, Chance. I mean, by and large we're quoting passages of scripture authored by the apostle Paul, who himself wrote that he had not arrived at the full knowledge of God, and that he was still pressing toward the mark of the prize of the high calling of God in Christ. Ultimately, I believe that the *will* of God is paramount—if it's His will that someone be healed here on earth, then by faith it will happen. I stress *by faith* because it's clearly seen throughout scripture that Jesus healed according to a person's faith. Remember the woman with the issue of blood who touched the hem of Jesus's garments? Jesus told her that her faith made her whole. Or the centurion who asked Jesus only to speak a word and his sick servant would be made whole? Jesus not only healed that centurion's servant, but exclaimed that he had not found such great faith in all of Israel! And how can we forget the Canaanite woman with a sick daughter, whom the disciples rejected and Jesus practically ignored until she began to worship Him out of sheer faith. Jesus declared that her great faith made her daughter whole."

Chance smiled. "You're like a . . . a walking Bible, aren't you?"

Lynn smiled back at him. "Isn't that what believers are *supposed* to be? Living epistles read by all men?"

"That's not what I meant. I was—"

"I know, Chance," Lynn cut in, still smiling. "I know."

From the other end of the boat, they both heard Pop shout, "Whoo-hee!"

"Another one?" Lynn asked.

Chance nodded. "Told you he was a fish magnet in these waters."

Chapter Thirty-eight

THE BUSTLING ACTIVITY surprised Travis as he pulled up to the dock's office just after eight o'clock.

Don't people sleep in late anymore?

Dozens of people carrying fishing poles and tackle buckets hurried past his pickup truck, while a smaller number closer to the lake fiddled with surfboards and water-skiing and diving apparatus. Travis got out of the truck, feeling out of place among all these fishermen, sportsmen, and fun-loving exercise fanatics. It was not that he didn't like exercising; he just employed different methods for working up a sweat.

Hand-to-remote, one-two-three, turn-television-on, one-two-three, hand-to-mouth, one-two-three, feed-my-face, one-two-three . . .

A weathered-looking man with his deeply tanned face buried in a *Field & Stream* magazine sat behind the counter as Travis walked up.

"Can I help you, partner? Whaddya need—bait, fishing license, boat rental?"

Travis quickly sized up his options. All he wanted was more information, but what was the best way to get it? The truth? Telfair had told him that Chance had come here to Caddo Lake to go fishing with his father, but he hadn't known the name of the boat.

"Sure, you can help me," Travis replied in his best southern accent. "I'm s'posed to meet a longtime friend to go fishing, but doggone it if I didn't oversleep! He's probably already out on the water, but I forgot the name of the boat he's using."

"Well . . . we've already got fourteen boats out there, most of them fishing boats. What's your friend's name?"

"Chance Howard."

"Chance Howard?" The man's face scrunched up as he visibly tried to place the name. "No, I don't believe I know a Chance How— Oh, wait now. I believe that's ol' Bennett's son you talking about. Haven't seen Chance for a couple years now, but if he's here, and he's with Bennett, then they been out there for hours. Bennett wakes up with the owls when it's time to go fishing."

Yeah, yeah, whatever . . . "So you know the name of the boat?"

"Sure I do. Bennett fishes in the *Jacqueline*, named after his late wife."

Travis made a mental note of the boat's name. "And how long does Bennett usually stay out on the water?"

The man laughed. "Bennett could stay out on that water all day, if he wanted! But he don't like it much when it gets hot around noon. Plus, since he's got company aboard his boat, I imagine he'll be docking in at a little before noon."

Travis checked his watch. It was not yet eight-thirty. His deadline for sending his story was one o'clock eastern time, twelve o'clock Louisiana time. He would be cutting it close, but he figured he could get his story ready, leaving a few blank spaces for Chance's quotes. What really mattered was another picture, though. One more picture of the mystery man and Travis was golden.

• • •

MUCH TO JUCINDA'S GROWING DISPLEASURE, more people were confirming they'd seen Chance back in town. First, Ol' Man Rollie, who sat outside on his porch all day and thus saw everything, said he'd seen Chance walking past his house, and had even spoken briefly with him.

"Did he say why he'd come back here?" Jucinda had asked, speaking slowly and loudly because Ol' Man Rollie was hard of hearing.

"Naw . . . he dint say that. He just . . . come walkin' down the road."

Next, Jucinda had called Telfair Williams, the handyman who took care of many yards for the elderly. Telfair had been cutting Bennett Howard's grass for years, since Bennett didn't move around so well on his prosthesis.

"Yep, I seen Chance come back to his pop's house a few days ago," he answered over the phone. "Bennett was real happy to see him."

"So he's still at Bennett's house? Right now?"

"Naw, not right now. They gon' fishin' up at the lake, jus' like they always used to do."

Jucinda could not believe the *nerve* of Chance,

coming back to town and going fishing, like everything had returned to normal. Didn't he know he was not welcome here? Didn't he know that he'd ruined her own life and disgraced the memory of one of the town's most promising young women? Well, if he had somehow forgotten that in two years' time, then Jucinda would be delighted to give him a jarring reminder.

"Telfair, thank you for the information. I—"

"Oh yeah—one more thing, Jucinda. Some guy I never seen before came down here askin' questions about Chance, too."

"He was asking *questions*? Like a policeman or something?"

"Naw. Reckon more like a reporter. He asked me if I knew where Chance was, and I told him."

You did what? "Telfair, why didn't you just tell him you didn't know where Chance was? Or tell that reporter to come talk to me?"

"Jucinda, for a hunnerd bucks I'da told that man anything he wanted," Telfair replied, laughing.

Jucinda silently cursed as she hung up the phone. Not only was Chance back in town, but apparently he was attracting a lot of attention as well. Grabbing her car keys from the hook next to the door, she hurried out of her house, aiming to take care of this problem the way she should've taken care of it two years ago—*permanently*.

Chapter Thirty-nine

AS THE MORNING HOURS PASSED, the sun rose higher in the sky, and just as Pop predicted, the bass began biting less and less. Pop had already snared five large-mouth bass, two catfish, and a handful of small brim that he'd thrown back into the lake.

"They too small to keep," he explained to Lynn. Lynn had tried her hand at casting a few lines into the water, but she had much to learn about the sport. Three times she'd reeled her line back in, only to find the bait missing from the hook.

"You jus' feeding the fish, child!" Pop had exclaimed, laughing. "There's an art form to fishing. You feel a gentle tug first, not even enough to make the line ripple. But that tells you the fish is there, jus' circling the bait. You might want to dangle the line a lil' bit, make the fish think it's a live worm—gets 'em every time, if you do it right. Then, right when you sense that fish coming in to take the bait, you jerk back on the pole, let the hook get 'em right in the gills. After that, you just reel him in. Easy pickings, I tell ya. Easy pickings."

"My goodness," Lynn replied, overwhelmed. "I didn't realize so much effort went into this."

"Oh, don't take Pop so seriously," Chance piped up from where he had been watching his two fishing lines. "Pop can—and *will*—compare everything in life to fishing."

"That's right," Pop agreed. "Fishin' is the perfect metaphor for life."

Chance looked at his watch. "Uh, Pop, before you launch into your spiel on how fishing should be taught to every child in America, you think maybe we should head back? The bass aren't biting as much, now that it's warming up."

Pop nodded. "Yeah, this is probably gon' do it for today. Wasn't great, but not bad, either."

Chance reeled in his two lines, then walked back to the steering wheel. In seconds, *Jacqueline* was skimming through the water back to the land. Lynn walked up behind Chance and tapped him on his shoulder. "What are you going to do about Travis Everett?"

"I don't plan to do *anything*," Chance replied after a pause. "I'm . . . I'm tired of running. If this guy's here and he wants to talk to me, fine. I don't care anymore. Everything can be on the record except what happened here two years ago."

"But what if that's *precisely* what he wants to talk about?"

"Then he'll get a bunch of 'no comments,' won't he?"

While Lynn went back to help Pop on the other side of the boat, Chance slowly navigated *Jacqueline* into the docks, which were now not as full with most of the boats still out on the lake. He steered the craft into the registered spot and anchored her.

He was about to hop onto the pier when he noticed her. She was leaning against the "No Running" signpost, smoking a cigarette and staring in his direction with a gaze that smoldered even at ten yards.

Jucinda.

Chance instinctively froze, not because he hadn't seen this woman for two years, but because her last words to him burned in his memory.

"If I ever see you here again, I swear to God I'll kill you . . ."

Her threat was more than displaced anger, he knew. Jucinda's temper had been one of the things Nina had never liked about her mother, though Jucinda had gotten better over the years with anger management classes. But when Nina died, and Jucinda had blamed Chance for not taking her to get medical help, all those lessons Jucinda had learned fell to the wayside.

"I thought I told you never to come back," Jucinda began, through clenched teeth. She tossed her cigarette down and squished it with her shoe.

"Jucinda, let's be adults and talk about this," Chance replied, not moving from his spot on the boat. He could hear Pop and Lynn on the other side, putting away their fishing poles.

"Ain't nothing more to talk about. You're the source of all my problems. Always have been, ever since you ruined my baby's life."

"Nina *chose* to be with me, Jucinda. You never accepted that, but that's the truth."

"How *dare* you tell me that was the truth! That was *not* the truth. Nina was going places . . . she was going to move away from here and make a real life for herself.

But you wouldn't let her, would you? You had to control her life, didn't you?"

"Jucinda, if you believe that, then that shows how much you really knew about your daughter. Nina was a strong person; she wasn't about to be controlled by anyone. What we had together was . . . love. We loved each other."

"Hey, who's that you're talking to about love?" Lynn asked, walking around to where Chance stood.

"Now, who's that!" Jucinda spat, pointing a trembling finger at Lynn. "Uh-huh . . . I knew it. I figured you must've had another woman. That's why you brainwashed Nina's mind, so you could get rid of her and—"

"Jucinda, now that's enough. Talk like that is crazy."

"No," Jucinda retorted. "*Talk* is crazy, and I'm through talking with you. Kneeling down, she opened a backpack at her feet. When she stood back up, a compact 9 mm pistol rested in her trembling hands. And it was pointed directly at Chance.

Chapter Forty

TRAVIS HAD CLEARED OUT a stakeout spot in some thick shrubbery to the right of the space where *Jacqueline* was kept moored. He'd learned from talking with a local fisherman that every boat had a registered spot, and that Bennett Howard had "parked" his boat in the first spot for a number of years, since he usually was the earliest out on the water.

That's perfect, Travis had thought, downright giddy because it meant that he was now certain to get Chance's picture.

He'd been waiting in the bushes ever since half past ten, so he'd seen the middle-aged woman who'd walked right up to *Jacqueline*'s registered spot and started pacing back and forth for ten minutes before finally leaning against a signpost. Travis had thought her behavior strange, especially after she'd smoked through a half pack of cigarettes and checked her watch every few minutes. He'd taken a few pictures of her, just for good measure. No telling what interesting angle she would provide for his story.

The *Jacqueline* appeared around a bend in the water a few minutes after eleven, its golden-yellow hull shimmering and sparkling in the sunlight. Travis pulled his cap down lower on his head to shield his eyes from glare and steadied his camera. His right index finger twitched spasmodically over the camera's red button, like a gunslinger's finger might twitch against a trigger during showdown at high noon.

Showtime, mystery man . . . you're gonna make me a star . . .

Chance Howard stood alone at the steering wheel, guiding the boat into its spot. Travis furiously worked his tiny digital camera, like he was orchestrating a silent photo shoot.

You're making me a star! I'm gonna be a star . . .

And that's when the nervous-acting woman began talking, and Travis quickly realized just how *big* a star he was about to become.

Chapter **Forty-one**

"JUCINDA, THERE'S NO NEED for that," Chance began calmly, raising his hands defensively, the way most people react when staring down the barrel of a gun.

"You ain't in any position to tell me what I need or don't need to do," Jucinda retorted, her hands still trembling around the gun.

"Oh my God," Lynn whispered, slowly retreating to the other side of the boat.

"No, you stay right there!" Jucinda ordered. Lynn immediately froze.

"Jucinda, will you think about what you're doing?" Chance asked. "It's broad daylight and you're standing there with a gun for the entire world to see."

"You think I care? Didn't I tell you not to come back here, Chance Howard? Didn't I warn you what would happen if I *ever* saw you back in this town?"

"Jucinda, be reasonable. My pop is sick, and I—"

"My daughter was sick, too!" Jucinda cried. "She was sick, and she needed help. But you . . ." She pointed a trembling finger at Chance. "You wouldn't help her, you country son of a—"

"Jucinda, I tried to help her. Couldn't you *see* how

much I loved your daughter? Couldn't you see how I'd have gladly traded my life for hers? I told her several times to listen to the doctor's advice and undergo the chemotherapy."

Jucinda shook her head back and forth wildly. "I don't believe you—you just saying whatever you want to now to shift the blame, just like you did two years ago."

"Jucinda, I know you're still upset over Nina's death. I'm upset, too . . . and I will be for the rest of my life. But what is shooting me going to prove? How is that going to help anything?"

"It's my justice . . . it's my only justice. I had dreams for my beautiful Nina. She was so smart—she was ten times smarter than you—and she had such a future to live for."

"I know that, Jucinda. I—"

"Liar! You shut up and let me talk!" She waved the gun around in her still trembling hands. "You just let *me* do all the talking now. You see, I knew you were no good for Nina . . . I used to have bad dreams about you, but I couldn't do anything about them because Nina blocked me out of that part of her life."

"That's because . . ." Chance began, before quickly closing his mouth as Jucinda raised the gun and took a step toward him. It was then that he became aware of movement to his right, in the shrubbery. The glare of the sun off the boat's hull partially blinded his view, but he could make out what looked like a moving . . . paw?

Jucinda began talking again, verbally attacking his character once more, but Chance's attention was now diverted by the movement to his right. The paw moved again, and this time Chance could see that it was not a real animal paw. It was an orange paw plastered on the white background canvas of a . . . baseball cap. But what kind of cap had an orange paw on a—

And then he remembered. He'd been at that train station in Columbia and seen a similar type cap, worn by a teenage boy. The boy had been wearing a matching T-shirt that read, "Clemson Tigers." So the person in the bushes was wearing a Clemson Tigers cap. Which meant he or she was probably from South Carolina. But who else from there besides Lynn knew about—

It's the reporter, he thought, in a sudden burst of realization. But why wasn't this guy doing anything to help him? Couldn't he tell that this woman was crazy? Couldn't he see that she was bound to hurt somebody?

". . . gonna make sure you get what's coming to you," Jucinda was now saying. From the way she was handling the gun, Chance was fairly confident she wasn't steady with her aim. And knowing that, he would've tried ducking underneath the steering wheel or diving into the water, if not for Lynn standing in harm's way beside him.

Stay calm . . . keep your cool . . . "Jucinda, if you shoot me, what's going to happen to *you*? Have you thought about that? You can't plead self-defense or temporary insanity. If you kill me, you're looking at a premeditated murder rap. And this isn't Ruston, where you think you have so much influence. We're in Shreveport. The police here don't—"

"I said, shut up!" Jucinda screamed. "You are not in

control, here! Do you understand? I—am—in—control!"

The next few surreal seconds unfolded in slow motion for Chance, as if in a dream. A tree branch snapped loudly, diverting Jucinda's attention away from him. In that split second, he knew what he had to do.

Spinning on his heel, he pushed Lynn hard to the deck. She cried out in surprise, causing Jucinda to turn back toward Chance, who was now clambering atop the boat's railing and preparing to jump overboard.

The 9 mm pistol fired once, twice.

Still perceiving everything in slow motion, Chance could almost see the first bullet flying toward him.

I must be dreaming . . .

He did not feel that first slug pierce his shoulder, twisting his body further sideways. Neither did he feel the next bullet slam into his lower back, sending him toppling over the boat's railing. He did, however, feel the warm Louisiana water as it enveloped him, slowly swallowing him within its murky depths. The last thought in his mind made no sense to him whatsoever.

Why is the water . . . so . . . red?

Chapter Forty-two

THE SENSATION OF WEIGHTLESSNESS was horrifying, and yet wonderful at the same time. Floating in a bluish darkness where everything was so serene, Chance tried to move his head and body, but it felt like he was not in a body at all.

This is it . . . I'm dying . . .

He wasn't sure if he was still underwater, because the darkness clouded his visibility. In the distance, he could see faint lights, or at least he imagined that he could.

There's supposed to be bright lights, right? Because I'm dying, right?

It was more of a thought to convince himself of this reality than a prayer to God. Of course he was dying. He'd been shot by Jucinda, he had fallen overboard, and he'd hit his head against a rock. These kinds of tragic incidents usually preceded the termination of life. But if there was any comfort, it was that he knew Jesus Christ as his Savior, and therefore had the peace to know he would forever spend eternity with Him.

And Nina, too! I'll soon see Nina again!

Death, then, was a comforting thought, and he welcomed it as one embraces a long-lost friend. Still, something nagged at him.

This is my life? Twenty-eight years of living, blessed with a wonderful wife but a disappointingly short marriage? To be given an incredible gift of healing but always be unable to help the people I loved most? That's all the life I'm ever going to know?

He half expected God to answer him, being so close to death and all. But amidst the silence, there was no answer. Chance wasn't sure how much time had elapsed since he'd hit his head against that rock and now, but . . . shouldn't something be happening? Shouldn't there be angels escorting him to Jesus, who would then welcome him into the joy of the Father?

Maybe this isn't it . . . maybe I'm not dying . . .

Chapter Forty-three

TRAVIS HAD NOT WANTED to stand, but his legs had been severely cramping. He'd thought he could stand and quickly stretch them without Chance and the gun-toting woman noticing him, but he'd grossly underestimated the pressure of his 250-pound frame easing off the tree branch. When the branch had snapped, he'd quickly ducked back down again, but not before he'd been spotted by both Chance and Jucinda. Five seconds later, as he was scrambling back through the bushes, as far away from the *Jacqueline* as his large feet could take him, he heard two loud gunshots.

My God—has she shot him?

He wanted to stop and turn around—but a quick glance at his watch showed that he had only ten minutes to e-mail his story, complete with corresponding picture, back to Ryman Wells. There was no time to go back and see what had happened. At his pickup truck now, he opened his backpack and booted up his laptop. Scrolling through the seventeen pictures stored in his digital camera, he finally settled on a close headshot of Chance in which Chance appeared to be directly staring into the camera.

Perfect . . . I'm gonna be the number one newspaper reporter in South Carolina . . .

He uploaded the file as an attachment to his eight-hundred-word follow-up story on the mystery healing man and clicked the send button.

• • •

LYNN HAD CRAWLED BEHIND the steering column for cover once she'd heard the gunshots, and now she slowly peered from around it, ready to bolt at the sign of more trouble. But Jucinda was nowhere to be seen.

Chance! Oh my God . . .

The images of the two bullets tearing into Chance's flesh and how he'd toppled overboard would forever be burned in her mind.

"Lynn, you alright?" she heard Pop calling out behind her, but she ignored him as she scrambled to the spot where Chance had fallen overboard.

She had never been much of a swimmer; her mom had enrolled her in a swimming class when she was five, but Lynn had lasted all of a week there. Her greatest fear then and now was of being completely submerged. Her swim instructor had been patient with her, repeatedly assuring her that putting one's head underwater was as natural as breathing. But Lynn had kicked, screamed, and practically *dared* someone to put her head under the water.

But this was not the time for fear. By her estimation, Chance had been underwater for at least thirty seconds—and he surely had been in no shape to hold his breath.

God has not given me a spirit of fear, but of love, power, and of a sound mind, she thought, kicking off her shoes and stepping onto the boat's railing. The blue water was tainted with streaks of red—Chance's blood—and if she had needed any more motivation for diving in after him, that was it. After all, this was the man whose faith (coupled with hers) had touched heaven and opened her blinded eyes. She took a deep breath and dived into the warm water. It stung at her eyes, and she blinked rapidly to adjust to the murky darkness as she swam toward the bottom of the lake.

Chance, where are you? Lord Jesus, help me . . .

Frantically, she looked to her right and left, but saw nothing except inky blackness the farther down she traveled from the surface. She could not believe how . . . dark . . . everything seemed. Once she felt her feet touch the bottom, she tentatively took one weightless step, then another. After a few seconds, not only could she not see anything, but her lungs were beginning to burn. How far was it back to the surface? And more important, could she *make* it back to the surface?

Feeling like crying after being unable to find Chance, she began scissor-kicking her feet, pushing upward. After what seemed like forever, her head finally broke through.

"Lynn!" she heard Pop calling from the boat, about twenty feet to her right. "Lynn, are you alright? I've called for help—help is on the way!"

For a few seconds, Lynn treaded water with her legs, sucking in precious mouthfuls of air. Air had never . . . *tasted* so good in her life. She was glad that Pop had called for help, but with each passing second, Chance was down there . . . dying.

Oh, God . . . oh, Jesus . . . no!

She had to try one more time. She gave a thumbs-up sign to Pop and inhaled deeply. Then, pushing every childhood fear of being submerged underwater to the far corners of her brain, she went back under. This time, she adjusted quickly to the darkness as she swam downward. After she remembered where the boat had been docked, her orientation was much better now. She kicked her legs furiously and stroked with her arms, swimming faster now. Her heart leaped when she saw what looked like a white tennis shoe resting on the lake's bottom.

That's Chance's shoe!

She swam over to see Chance's body wedged in between two rocks, then wrapped her arms around his torso, attempting to wrest him out. But he was like a dead weight, and Lynn's lungs were beginning to burn again.

No! God, help me!

Straining with every muscle in her body, she tugged on Chance's upper body once more. His waist suddenly twisted, and he was soon free from the rocks.

Yes!

Lynn's joy was short-lived, however. The exertion of freeing Chance from the rocks had sapped virtually all of her energy, causing her lungs to strain against her chest. She didn't know if she had the strength to swim to the surface *herself*, much less carry the body of a man weighing roughly 180 pounds.

It's not supposed to end like this, she thought, feeling

an overwhelming sense of despair. Had God not healed her blinded eyes to be a testimony to His power? Had He not spoken awesome prophecies into her spirit that should now go unfulfilled? And what about Chance Howard—a man in whom God had vested a healing gift the likes of which most Christians had never before witnessed? Was he supposed to die like this, too?

God, are we supposed to die here? Alone at the bottom of some lake? That can't be . . . Your will . . ."

If there was an answer from God, Lynn was not in a position to hear it. Her lungs felt like they would collapse any second. Slumping forward, she rested her head on Chance's chest, ready to let her spirit slip away to heaven.

Suddenly, she felt two arms powerfully encircle her and begin to lift her up.

Too little, too late, she thought, just before everything went black.

Chapter Forty-four

THE FINAL REHEARSAL for Faith Community's fall choral concert was a rousing success for all those blessed to be in attendance. Choir representatives from churches throughout the area and from as far away as Charleston came to finalize color arrangements, discuss song selection changes, and deal with any last-minute glitches. The hired video production crew from Raleigh had also come down to coordinate lighting and camera placement and to work alongside the church's audio technicians. The concert would be recorded live, in digital format, with the CD and DVD sets to be available just in time for the upcoming holiday season.

Arlene had walked through the entire program with Pastor Gentry, who was duly impressed with the scope of planning and preparation. He agreed this would be the finest fall concert yet.

"Sister Arlene, you simply amaze me," Pastor Gentry now said as they sat in the sanctuary, listening to a guest soloist from Winston-Salem sing "Mercy Said No." "Your anointing for directing is so strong, you could probably take four off-key cats sitting on a fence and form a first-rate quartet."

Arlene laughed. "Is that a special request? Songs in the key of *meow*?"

Pastor Gentry laughed along with her. "The Bible *does* say, let everything that has breath praise the Lord, right? No, seriously, what you've done in the past few years with the choir has been nothing short of tremendous. God has always designed music to be an integral component of worship, and you've always embraced that revelation. That makes pastoring so much easier, let me tell you."

"Thank you, Pastor. And it's blessed me so much to be under leadership that doesn't stifle the creative flow of the music ministry."

"It's a two-way street, isn't it?"

"Amen to that!"

As the guest soloist finished her selection, Sister Margie hurriedly burst through the sanctuary's side doors, making a beeline toward her pastor.

"Pastor Gentry," she began, nearly out of breath. "Three of us—on the intercessory team—we've all just had the same vision."

Pastor Gentry straightened up in the pew, sensing Sister Margie's alarm. He'd long since learned to take the combined visions of his intercessory team seriously. Charged with praying for Faith Community's members, they prayed six to eight hours a day and walked in a heightened level of sensitivity to the Holy Spirit.

"What is it, Sister Margie?"

"It's Sister Lynn, and that man she went to Louisiana to meet. They're in serious danger—right *now*. Oh, my sweet Jesus . . ."

Nothing more needed to be said. Pastor Gentry

immediately grabbed the hands of both Sister Arlene and Sister Margie and began fervently praying in the Spirit.

• • •

JEANNETTE HARPER LOVINGLY STARED at the framed picture of Lynn, a picture taken when her daughter had graduated from Sumter High. She squirted some glass cleaner on the frame and gently wiped the glass surface with an old cloth until it sparkled in the afternoon light. Jeannette took great pride in cleaning her house, and what she loved most of all was cleaning the countless pictures that hung in every room.

"Pictures paint the story line of families," she would always say to anyone who thought her numerous picture frames were cluttering the house. "And the story line of this family begins and ends with Lynn . . ."

Jeannette and Leonard had wanted more children—maybe four or five kids. But a medical condition had prevented Jeannette from having another child; the doctors thought it a miracle that she was even able to carry Lynn to term.

"Yes, you were . . . and you will *always* be a miracle," Jeannette now said, setting the graduation picture back on the mantel and picking up the next one. "*My* miracle." It was a candid shot of a much younger Lynn and Leonard, playing around at Myrtle Beach. Even though the picture had been taken more than twenty years earlier, Jeannette remembered it like it had been yesterday.

"No, Daddy!" Lynn had been screaming playfully,

as Leonard swung her by her arms, around and around. Leonard had been getting closer to the ocean's edge, and Lynn had been terrified of water.

"It's alright, baby," Leonard had reassured her. "I won't let anything happen to you."

Jeannette had snapped the picture just as Leonard had pulled Lynn closer to his chest—both of them laughing, wet, frolicking, and enjoying the special daddy-daughter bond they had always shared. Just above their shoulders, the purplish-red sun was peeking through gray-and-white clouds over the Atlantic Ocean. It was Jeannette's favorite picture because it beautifully highlighted the two people she loved most. She smiled as she recalled again how afraid Lynn had been (and still was, to this day) of the water.

"No, Daddy! You're getting too close to the water! Don't let me go under!"

"Relax, Lynn, I got you. I won't let anything happen to you."

Suddenly, the picture slipped from Jeannette's hands and crashed against the mantel's wooden surface, breaking the glass frame.

"Oh my God," Jeannette breathed, but for the moment all thoughts about her favorite picture had ceased. A new fear gripped her heart—the kind of terror that could only be linked with a mother's intuition. At that second, she *knew* that her child was in trouble—a mother's worst nightmare.

"Oh, my . . . *God*!" she screamed. The same horrible feeling had terrorized her at the exact moment Lynn had gotten into that car accident.

"Jeannette?" Leonard hurried into the living room.

"Are you alright? What happened?" He carefully steered her away from the broken glass around the fireplace, taking her over to the couch.

"It's Lynn . . . I feel . . . I *know* . . . something's wrong. She's in danger."

"Lynn? She's in Louisiana, right? She went to meet that man who healed her eyes."

Jeannette wriggled out of her husband's arms and picked up the cordless phone lying on the coffee table. She dialed Lynn's cell number, but the call went straight to voice mail.

"Her phone's not on . . . I told her to keep it on! She doesn't know anybody in Louisiana . . . anything can happen to her and we wouldn't—"

"Jeannette, that's enough now," Leonard said soothingly, taking his wife into his arms once more. "Getting hysterical is not going to help matters right now. We should pray—God has always protected Lynn, even when . . . and *especially* when we couldn't."

"But she's in trouble! I know—"

"Shh . . . Jeannette, come on, let's pray."

Jeannette nodded, convincing herself that Leonard was right. *"God, please help my baby . . ."*

Chapter Forty-five

TRAVIS HAD DRIVEN BACK to his motel room in pursuit of some well-deserved rest. The reporter in him wanted to return to the lake to find out what had transpired after the gunshots, but after camping out all night outside Chance Howard's home and then waiting all morning by the docks, his body was officially shutting down. Besides, he'd gotten what he came here for, so as far as he was concerned—*mission accomplished*.

The cheap motel room he'd gotten was not much for looks, but that was the least of his concerns as he flung his bag to the floor, kicked off his shoes, and tumbled onto the bed. The second his head touched the pillow, he was out cold.

He dreamed that he was sitting at a desk in a sprawling high-rise corner office overlooking Manhattan. Atop the mahogany desk lay that day's edition of the *New York Times*, with the right-corner headline displaying, "Travis Everett Captures Pulitzer Prize."

Travis picked up the newspaper, leaned back in his seat, and scanned through the first few paragraphs. He was now a celebrated writer at the *New Yorker* magazine and he'd apparently just won the Pulitzer for writing an article documenting the rebuilding project for the Ground Zero memorial. The article hailed his piece as a "courageous effort to capture the patriotism, courage, and honor shown by the heroes of the 9/11 tragedy." Travis was about to pat himself on the back when a stunning brunette appeared at his doorway. "Mr. Everett," she began in a voice dripping with pure honey, "you have a call on line one."

You must be my personal assistant, Travis thought, with a huge grin. He *had* moved up in the world.

"Thank you. Forward it to my phone."

When his line began ringing, he picked it up and answered. But there was no answer. The line continued to ring.

What the . . . ?

"Hello? Hello?" he spoke into the receiver, but the phone kept ringing. Why . . . was the phone still *ringing*? "Hello? Hello?"

And that's when he woke up to the real-life ringing of his cell phone on the table beside his bed. Still slightly disoriented from his dream, he rubbed his eyes and slowly reached out a hand and grabbed the tiny flip-phone. But the call had gone to voice mail.

Yawning loudly, he waited a few seconds, then entered his voice-mail password and pressed the phone back to his ear.

"Travis Everett, where the devil is my story!" Ryman Wells's voice barked in his ear with all the friendliness of a pissed-off drill sergeant addressing a truant basic trainee.

Wh-what?

"You told me you were going to have that story e-mailed to me by one o'clock. Well, I've been calling every hour since three o'clock, and this is my last call. Since you haven't checked in, you are now AWOL, soldier!"

Travis glanced at his watch and saw that the time was now 9 p.m. Had he been asleep *that* long?

"Do I have to remind you that you are using the *State*'s money to pay for those travel expenses?" Ryman continued ranting. "Do I have to remind you that I had to bend over backwards to get that expense report approved for you? And let me tell you something—if you hadn't written those two halfway decent stories on this mystery man, your lazy self wouldn't have gotten my approval to go to *Swan Lake*, much less Louisiana! You call me back pronto, Everett! You hear me? Pronto!"

"B-but . . . I *did* send the story to you," Travis sputtered, feeling the first signs of a massive headache beginning to form in the center of his forehead. He looked at the record of incoming phone calls and saw that Ryman had called a total of eight times since one o'clock.

"This . . . cannot be happening!" He tossed the phone down and reached for his laptop bag on the floor. He took out the laptop, booted up, and accessed his e-mail.

And there it was, a smoking gun mocking him like a horrible nightmare from which he could not awake. The message he'd sent to Ryman Wells had been returned as . . . *undeliverable.* Since Travis had not saved Ryman Wells's e-mail address in the laptop's personal address book, he'd had to actually type in the address. To his horror, he had misspelled his editor's name by one wrong keystroke, typing R-y-m-s-n in the address line. Of course, the e-mail server had automatically returned the message within seconds of its sending, but Travis had not seen that return message because he'd closed the laptop and had not opened it . . . until now.

"How could I have made such . . . a . . . *stupid* mistake!" he yelled, slamming his fist onto the laptop's keyboard. Misspelling his own editor's name and not returning phone calls were the mistakes of a rookie reporter, not someone on the fast track to becoming a star journalist!

I've gotta call Ryman . . . but what am I supposed to tell him?

He had both the pictures and the story now, but could he still submit them, given that he was now back in Ryman Wells's doghouse?

Knowing that Ryman was not in his office at the moment (and definitely not wanting to speak to his editor), Travis called his boss's voice mail and apologized for not checking and at the same time promised that he had a trump card to make up for the delay.

His "trump card" was locating Chance Howard and obtaining some exclusive quotes. Assuming, of course, the man was still alive.

Chapter Forty-six

A BEEPING NOISE, faint at first and then growing louder, continued ringing in his ears like the blaring of a never-ending alarm clock. Chance slowly opened his eyes, blinking quickly to adjust to the new light entering his world.

"Good afternoon, Mr. Howard," a voice to his right said. "It's good to see you finally awake."

"Where am I?" Chance's tongue felt like a piece of rubber.

"You're at Christus Schumpert Hospital, in Bossier City. My name is Dr. Peterson. You've had quite an ordeal—those two bullets passed close to some vital organs as well as your spinal cord. Thankfully there was no lasting damage, and we were able to cleanly remove the bullets. You did pick up a concussion."

The lake . . . Jucinda . . . gunshots . . . Pop . . . Lynn! The memory of everything that happened on the boat flooded his brain like a tidal wave crashing onshore. "Wh-what happened to Jucinda, the woman who shot me?" he blurted out. "And Lynn? And Pop? And that reporter—he was there, too, wasn't he?"

Dr. Peterson laid a hand on Chance's shoulder.

"Those questions will be answered soon enough. Right now, it's best if you rested some more. I believe *one* of those questions can be answered for you, however." He walked back to the doorway and made a motion with his hand. Seconds later, a nurse rolled a wheelchair in the room. The woman riding in it was . . . *Lynn*.

In spite of his injuries, Chance struggled to sit up in the bed. "Lynn, oh my God . . . you weren't *shot*, were you?"

Lynn shook her head. "No, I'm just a little sore from my . . . um, from my little swim."

"Miss Harper dived into the lake after you . . . *twice*," Dr. Peterson explained. "Here at Christus Schumpert, we've come to regard her as a hero."

Chance stared at Lynn, openmouthed and speechless.

"It wasn't so much heroic as it was foolish," Lynn said, faintly smiling. "I didn't know what I was thinking—I don't know how to swim! And all too late I realized that I didn't have the lungs or the energy to get us both back to the surface."

"Fortunately, rescue workers who were less than a quarter of a mile away heard your father's shouts," Dr. Peterson added. "They were able to pull both you and Lynn back to their boat and perform CPR to get you both breathing again. Your gunshot wounds posed a greater challenge, however. A helicopter was dispatched to pick you up and bring you here."

Chance finally discovered his voice. "Y-you *dived* in after me?" he asked Lynn incredulously.

Lynn shrugged, the faint smile still on her lips.

"Well, what was I supposed to do? Let a big fish swallow you like Jonah and then spit you up on dry land in three days?"

• • •

HOURS LATER, CHANCE AWOKE to see Lynn still in his room, now sitting by the window.

"I'm surprised Dr. Peterson let you in here," Chance began. "I'm supposed to be resting."

Lynn turned from the window and put a finger to her lips. "He didn't let me in here. I sort of . . . *snuck* in."

"You *what*?"

"Shh!" Lynn grinned. "I know it's crazy, but I just didn't feel like sleeping in some hotel room, and I didn't want to go back home with your father just yet."

"But . . . how did you get past security? And the doctors?"

"Well . . . I *am* the resident hero around here, remember? You can't begin to believe how many perks that affords me."

Chance was silent for a while. "Thank you. You know, for what you did at the lake and all. That took a lot of heart to dive in after me."

Lynn stood and moved the chair closer to his bed. "It took a lot of faith, too. I've always had a fear of putting my head completely underwater."

"Then why . . . why'd you do it?"

Lynn shrugged. "At the time, it was something that I just had to do. For one thing, I wanted to repay you for laying hands on my eyes. And I'd seen those bullets hit you, and how the water was so . . . was so . . ."

"Red," Chance finished. "I remember the water being so red."

"Right. So, I figured that even if you were a great swimmer, you were hurt and you needed some help."

"What happened to Jucinda?"

"The police caught her a few hours later and your father identified her as the shooter. She's at a correctional facility, awaiting formal charges to be brought against her."

Chance slowly shook his head. "I never thought she'd actually . . . I mean, I knew she had that anger problem, and that she was still upset over losing Nina and all, but I still can't believe she would do something like this. I think she needs prayer and psychiatric help more than what the criminal justice system has to offer. How's Pop doing?"

"He's doing okay, best as I can tell. He was up here throughout your surgery. The doctors told him to go home and get some rest, but he said he'll be back in the morning."

"And what about the reporter with the Clemson Tigers cap?"

"You are certainly full of questions, now that you're awake. You must be talking about Travis Everett—I saw him briefly at the docks. To tell you the truth, I'm surprised we haven't heard anything from or about him since. He clearly gave me the impression he was coming here *solely* to talk with you."

"Maybe what happened at the lake scared him off."

"Maybe. I seriously doubt that, though."

A page sounded over the hospital intercom system

then, requesting that a doctor come to the emergency room.

"This place never rests," Chance said, nodding toward his door. "Nurses come in at all hours, poking you with all kinds of needles and taking blood like vampires."

"You should be thankful you're still here for them to take your blood, Chance. You were almost a goner."

"A part of me . . . wanted to go. Did you know that? No, no, of course, you couldn't. But when I hit that lake bottom, and I felt the little air I had left in my lungs dissipating—I *wanted* to go. I remember praying to God that if it was my time, then I was ready. I was ready to spend eternity with Him. And . . . and with Nina."

"I thought it was my time to go, too, Chance. I saw you there—even tried pulling you up from those rocks, but I couldn't. And then I realized I didn't even have the strength to swim back to the surface. I remember laying my head on your chest and praying for my spirit to be with Jesus."

"Y-you wanted to go, too?"

"If it was the Lord's will, then yes, I did. Chance, it always goes back to the Lord's will. The Bible says in Hebrews chapter nine that it's appointed for man to die once, and after this the judgment. You see, the Lord knows our birth date, and He knows the date when He will call us back home to be with Him. If it had been our time to go, then we would have been in heaven right now.

"But it wasn't our time, don't you see? The two bullets Jucinda's gun put into you didn't kill you, and neither did hitting your head on that rock at the bottom of the lake. And I didn't drown in that lake, even though all the odds were stacked against me. God must still have a plan for both of our lives—there is unfinished Kingdom business that we must do!"

"Unfinished Kingdom business, huh?"

"You have to see this from God's perspective, Chance. The incredible healing gift God has given you—He intends for more lives to be changed for His glory! And it's because He can trust you with this gift—you are not someone who thinks that the power to heal is somehow of your own doing. You know that such a power only comes from God. And from what I can tell, every time you lay hands on someone and pray for the healing, you make it clear that God is the true Healer, and the only One worthy of the praise. The Bible says in 2 Corinthians that we have the treasure of God's glory in earthen vessels, that the excellency of the power may be of God, and not of us. You have a treasure inside of you, Chance Howard. And God is not finished unveiling that treasure."

"Unveiling that treasure to whom?"

"To the nations, Chance. To all nations of the world."

Chapter **Forty-seven**

TRAVIS'S PROMISE TO DELIVER quotes straight from the mystery man's mouth had bought him a little time from the *State*, although Ryman Wells clearly remained furious that he had waited so long to report back.

"You'd better write the best story of your career with this one, Everett!" Ryman had barked, after calling Travis early the following morning. "Or your career has just gone down the toilet!"

"It'll be my best story," Travis had promised, longing for the day when he would finally be free of his demanding editor's grip.

He had returned to the lake and quickly learned what happened from several eyewitnesses who'd seen the shooting. The most important information he learned, though, was that Chance had been flown to Bossier City's Christus Schumpert Hospital.

He arrived at the hospital at a quarter till noon and approached the front desk. "I'm here to see Chance Howard," he began, speaking to a nurse's assistant entering data on a computer keyboard. "He was admitted yesterday with gunshot wounds."

"Your name, please?"

"Travis Everett."

"Are you a family member?"

Travis racked his brain, searching for a way around this dilemma. What would Detective Columbo do?

"Sir?"

Travis blinked. "Yes?"

"Are you a family member?"

'Uh, no. Not exactly."

"Well, our standard policy would be to call Mr. Howard and inquire if he would like to receive you as a guest, but at the moment . . ." She tapped some more keys on her computer. "At the moment, I'm showing here that Mr. Howard is resting and is not to be disturbed."

Travis was fairly sure Detective Columbo would have come up with a clever way around this loophole.

"You are more than welcome to sit in our waiting area until Mr. Howard awakens," the nurse's assistant continued. "I can call then to determine if he wishes to receive you as a guest."

Travis mumbled his thanks and headed toward the waiting area. If Chance had done all he could to avoid Travis in South Carolina, why would he now want to receive him as a hospital guest?

But I've gotta get a quote . . . Ryman's gonna kill me if I don't . . .

What if he could find out Chance's room number and then somehow sneak in and conduct a surprise interview? Travis knew the chances of such a plan working were slim to none, but what other choice did he have?

At that very moment, however, he literally saw what

other choice he had. Seated in the waiting area, casually reading a magazine, was none other than Miss Lynn Harper.

Eat your heart out, Detective Columbo . . .

Chapter Forty-eight

"SEEMS THAT YOU and Chance Howard have this interesting habit of meeting by *coincidence.*"

Lynn recognized the voice before looking up from the magazine, though she was not completely surprised by Travis Everett's presence. It was inevitable that he would show up sooner or later, given his seemingly hell-bent approach to writing this story.

"And it seems *you* have this interesting habit of tracking me down," Lynn replied. "But I hardly think that's by coincidence."

"It's my job as a reporter to follow a story, wherever it may take me," Travis said, taking a seat opposite Lynn. "I'd like your assistance in something," he continued. "I'd like to ask Chance a few questions."

"Oh, really? Just like you asked *me* a few questions, then completely distorted and lied about what I said?"

"Now hold on a second—I didn't exactly *lie* about what you said."

"Yes, you did. You quoted me as saying this mystery man claimed he was Jesus Christ. That's a ludicrous statement, and one I'm quite sure I did not make."

"It was late at night when I was piecing that first

story together. Your name . . . may have inadvertently been attributed to a quote from someone else I interviewed, and for that I apologize."

"Do you really expect me to accept your apology? Not *once* in your articles have you included anything about Jesus Christ receiving the glory for these healings, a position that both I and your sister, Andrea, feel strongly about."

Travis was visibly taken aback. "You know about Andrea?"

Lynn nodded. "I've spoken with her several times, and I know she shares my disappointment that you've reported on this story from an exclusively skeptical standpoint. Didn't Eddie's incredible healing and testimony have any effect on you?"

Travis opened his mouth to respond, hesitated, and instead fiddled with the reporter's notebook in his hand.

"You witnessed Eddie being deaf and crippled for the first seven years of his life," Lynn continued, "and you knew that the doctors had virtually given up hope that he would ever hear or walk. You also knew that Andrea and James continued to pray and believe that God would heal their son.

"And that is precisely what happened. But instead of sharing such a powerful testimony of faith and answered prayer with your newspaper's readers, you write about some mysterious, delusional man claiming to be Jesus. Have you even *met* Jesus?"

Travis blinked a few times. "Th-that would be impossible, seeing how Jesus has been dead for over two thousand years."

"Once again, you exhibit the small scope of your knowledge. Since your profession is built around *facts*, what do you say to these factual statements: there has never been a record of Jesus's body being found after his burial, and over five hundred people witnessed him alive in the days following his crucifixion."

Travis was silent.

Looks like the cat's got your tongue, now . . . "It's because Jesus rose from the grave three days after His crucifixion, precisely as He had prophesied. And He continues to live today, at the right hand of God the Father and in the hearts of believers like your sister Andrea, Chance Howard, and myself."

"Y-you can't prove that," Travis stammered. "My profession is not only built around facts, but it's built around what can be *proven*."

"You're speaking as if this is a court of law, Travis. And God is not on trial here. But if you want to speak to Chance, then be my guest. You should be warned, though."

"Warned about what?"

"That you should be careful what you wish for." She went back to flipping through the pages in her magazine, although she wasn't reading anymore. Silently, she was praying for Travis Everett's soul.

• • •

A HALF HOUR LATER, the nurse's assistant walked into the waiting area. "Excuse me, Miss Harper? Mr. Howard is awake now, and he has asked to see you." The assistant glanced over at Travis. "I informed him that you were here as well, but he declined to speak with you at this time."

Travis shot a pleading glance toward Lynn.

"Just wait here, Travis. You'll get your interview. Just remember my friendly little warning."

Chance was sitting up in his bed and looking much better when Lynn entered his room.

"How're you doing?" he asked.

"Still a little sore," Lynn replied, walking over to him. "But I'll make it. How about you?"

"Tired, but fine. Shouldn't you be back home? I'm sure there are people in South Carolina who're missing you right about now."

Lynn smiled. "Let's just say I'm using this time as substitute time for the vacation I never really took in June. Really, though, I've called my parents and they're doing fine. I've also talked with the outreach team, and they're doing great. Those healings have really sparked revival all over the area."

"I'm glad to hear that."

"Listen, I just want you to know that I'm here to help you. I know it's not cool or popular for a guy to get help, much less from a woman, but I've never sided with the status quo."

"Lynn, you know how grateful I am that you dived in after me, alerting the rescue workers to where I was. But what kind of help do I need *now*?"

"Chance, have you thought about what you're going to do after you get out of the hospital?"

Chance scratched at the three-day-old stubble growing underneath his chin. "Well, with Jucinda not around to harass me, I can stay here with Pop."

"And do what? Go fishing every day? Chance, I'm not here to talk anymore about your gift—although the fact that my eyes see you will always bear testimony to it—but what if we were to organize your ministry?"

"What ministry?"

"Chance, for the past two years you've been going around to various churches, praying for people. And although you've changed many lives, think about what could happen if we were to arrange healing services all over the country, with financial support from local churches and partners?"

"You mean like what Floyd Waters is doing?"

"Yes and no. What God has given you is unique to you, Chance. There's no monopoly on healing ministries in the body of Christ. With all the sickness and disease out there, we need more men and women of God with the gift of healing to walk fully in that gift."

"Where did this 'we' talk come from?"

"I'm an outreach ministry director, Chance. It's what I do. And God's strength is made perfect in weakness. Who better to operate in a healing ministry than two people who understand what it is to need healing? I wouldn't want a pastor who's never gone through life's trials to preach to me about overcoming adversity; I wouldn't want a teacher explaining something to me that he doesn't really understand; I certainly wouldn't want someone praying for my healing who has never before experienced the healing power of God."

Chance stared out of the room's window. "Yeah, but I don't want the publicity. Nothing comes from that but scrutiny and criticism from both inside and outside of the church. For example, that reporter is here right now, isn't he?"

Lynn nodded. "He's in the waiting room."

"You see? That's what I'm talking about. Once you announce you have a ministry that heals blind eyes and makes the lame walk, you create this instant magnet of negative attention."

"That's because the devil doesn't want the world to see the true greatness of God's power, Chance. The Bible says that the devil has blinded the minds of people; that if our gospel be hid, it is hid to the lost. Yet the Bible also says that we are the light of the world. A city set on a hill that *cannot* be hidden."

Chance looked toward the window and sighed. "I just don't know, Lynn. I just don't know."

"Chance, there will always be haters in the world and in the church who will talk about God's vessels. But should that stop the light and the message of His love and power? What about the little Eddie Everetts of the world? What about the T. R. Smallwoods? What about all the people God has *ordained* for you to minister healing to? Are you just going to turn your back on them because you can't move beyond the events of the past? For the sake of God's call on our lives, Chance, we *must* move forward. Think about Nina for a second."

Chance shot her a look of both surprise and accusation. "I think about her every day."

"Okay, now think about how strongly she believed in divine healing, and how she believed God had given you that gift. If she could speak to you now, what do you think she would say about how you should use that gift?"

Slowly, Chance's expression softened. "She'd want me to lay hands on as many people as possible."

"Of course she would. But see, you have to remember the most important thing about gifts in the body of Christ—they're always for someone else. A gifted singer's purpose is to minister to the listeners, not to his or her own ears. Your healing gift is not for you. It was for me, and the countless others praying to be healed who will cross paths with you."

"You certainly don't lack for passion about this, do you?"

"That's because I was the one whom doctors said would never see again. I had to fight the fear of being dependent on someone else for the rest of my life, of having to feel objects with my hands to determine what they were, of . . ." Lynn wiped away a tear as the worst seven weeks of her life sprang to memory once again.

"I'm sorry," Chance gently cut in. "I . . . I didn't mean to make you cry."

Lynn sniffed, smiling. "You didn't make me cry. I just . . . well, I just get tears in my eyes every time I think about what God has done for me."

They were both silent for a while, remembering their own respective experiences of faith. After a few minutes had ticked off the clock, Chance looked into Lynn's eyes.

"God is so good," he breathed. "Listen, I know what to do about Travis Everett. I've always known what to do about him. He's still in the waiting area?"

"Yes."

"Well, you can go tell him I'm ready to talk now. He should have been careful what he wished for, though."

"That's funny. I told him the same thing myself."

Chapter **Forty-nine**

TRAVIS ENTERED THE ROOM behind Lynn, looking as wary as a rodent eyeing the cheese on a mousetrap. Chance quickly motioned for him to pull up a chair.

"I won't bite," Chance said, teasing. "Not unless you want me to."

"You two probably don't need an introduction," Lynn began, as she sat back down in her wheelchair. "But, Chance, this is Travis Everett. Travis, Chance Howard."

"You're a hard man to catch up with," Travis said as he flipped open his reporter's notebook. "Why so elusive?"

"I think of myself more as *private* rather than elusive," Chance replied. "There's a difference. Privacy is a freedom that everyone should be afforded."

"Everyone except public figures," Travis responded, scribbling something in his notebook. "Look, Mr. Howard, I don't intend to waste any of your time so let's get right to the point. A number of people claim that you touched them and healed them of various sicknesses or handicaps. Is that true?"

"Well, it's true that I laid hands on them, but only as a point of contact between believers and the Lord."

"Mm-hmm. So, in effect, you're saying you *did not* heal these people?"

Chance resisted the urge to roll his eyes. "Mr. Everett, I know what you're doing. You want me to say something that's already in agreement with your preconceived assumptions. You've probably already written your story, slanted in the extreme way you choose to frame it. My quotes are just gravy."

"That's not entirely true," Travis responded, shooting a quick glance toward Lynn. "I'm here to get your side of the story, in your own words."

"Oh, really? In my own words? Then why not print one of my statements, verbatim, in your article?"

"I couldn't do that; I'm only working within an eight-hundred-word limit."

"But that doesn't mean you can't reprint a person's statement verbatim, if the statement is short enough."

"*Theoretically*, that's true, but I don't write my stories in that manner. Like most reporters, I prefer using quotes within the context of my article."

"You've *never* done something like that? Really?" Chance narrowed his eyes. "Not even when you quoted, verbatim, a university researcher's statement on the proliferation of summertime gnats in greater Richland County?"

Travis's jaw dropped a few inches. "H-how did you . . . know about that?"

"I read the newspaper," Chance replied, winking. "Doesn't everybody?"

What Chance *didn't* say was that after sleeping outside at Congaree National Park (and after being inundated with swarms of gnats), he'd gone to the public library to do a little research. Specifically, he'd wanted to learn if the gnats were capable of biting or if they were just a nuisance. An online search had provided him with the information he'd sought (they were just a nuisance), and he'd printed out a few pages of a leading researcher's statement. Later that week, when he'd learned that Travis Everett was the reporter so diligently tracking him, he'd accessed the *State*'s Web site to find out some information on him. The first article he'd clicked on had been Travis's story on the proliferation of summertime gnats, of all things. The article, for the most part, had been an *exact* copy of what the university researcher had written, word for word.

Travis was now visibly uncomfortable with the knowledge that Chance knew about his past plagiarisms. He coughed a few times and tapped his pen on his notebook. Chance figured Travis *should* be uncomfortable—in light of news scandals still fresh in the public's mind involving journalists at two important national newspapers who had openly plagiarized articles, *every* reporter's worst nightmare was a plagiarism accusation.

"So, all you're wanting is one paragraph?" Travis asked.

Chance nodded. "A statement of mine that's copied verbatim and left completely unedited when it goes to print. I take it that you . . . do . . . know how to *copy* words verbatim, don't you, Travis?"

Travis coughed again before nodding.

Chance briefly glanced at Lynn, then took a deep breath. "Good. Well, here's my statement: I believe in God's power to heal using ordinary human hands because I've seen it happen many times . . . right under my own two hands. There's nothing fake about it—it's just the power of Almighty God flowing through the faith of His children. You can't manipulate, control, or direct this power any more than you can manipulate the wind. Because this *is* wind—a wind of the Holy Spirit sweeping through the hearts and souls of Christians praying to see God's power made manifest to this generation. To the believers, I want to encourage you to keep praying and keep speaking words of healing everywhere you go. Signs and wonders shall follow them that *believe.* When you do this, it won't matter what the world says about you. It will be as Jesus Himself said in Matthew 11:5—'*The blind see and the lame walk, the lepers are cleansed and the deaf hear; the dead are raised up and the poor have the gospel preached to them.*'"

Travis set his pen down. "Is . . . is that it? Is that your statement?"

Chance nodded. "It's not even two hundred words, so it's certainly short enough for your article."

"Matthew 11:5, huh?" Travis asked, scribbling something else in his reporter's notebook. "That's from the Bible, right?"

"The Word, yes."

Travis's hand paused atop the notebook. "The Word?"

"I call it the Word of God, you call it the Bible. It's the same book."

Travis scratched at a spot behind his ear, still visibly shaken from Chance's knowing about his plagiarized article. "Do you quote a lot of things from the Bi—from the Word, I mean?"

Chance shrugged. "It's not like I know it from cover to cover, but I try to learn as much as possible. I guess I'm just another brother who's trying to get direction from the Word."

"Sort of like . . . a . . . like Mr. Word, hmm? No, how's this for a name—Brother Word?" said Travis.

"That's a better name for him than you claiming he was calling himself Jesus Christ," Lynn cut in.

Travis coughed again.

"I'd have to agree with Lynn on that one," Chance said. "So, this story is going to be in Thursday's edition of the *State*?" he asked.

"Y-yes."

"Where? On the front page?"

Travis hesitated. "I-I think so." He took a quick glance at his watch. "I should be going . . . you know, if I want to finish this and send it back to Columbia."

"Good-bye, Mr. Everett," Chance said, a slight gleam in his eye. "It was a pleasure speaking with you."

As soon as Travis had left, Lynn stood from her chair and walked over to Chance. "Well, that was incredible! Brother Word, huh? I like it! Fits a man like you perfectly."

"It was like God . . . was giving me the words to say. All I had to do was open my mouth."

"And that's when you know that it's the Lord's will—that it's what He wants to say. Still, how can you be so sure Travis is going to include it, unedited, in his article?"

"Because it's the Lord's will, right? Besides, a little . . . gnat told me he would."

"A *gnat*?"

Chance shrugged, shook his head, and stared out the window. "It's a long story."

Chapter **Fifty**

THE FOLLOWING DAY, Dr. Peterson released Chance from the hospital. The swollen knot atop Chance's head would hurt for a few more days; likewise, the gunshot wounds in his shoulder and lower back would take time to heal completely, but his overall prognosis was encouraging.

"Just take it easy for a few days, then we'll get you doing some light physical therapy for two months, and you'll be as good as new," the doctor announced as he signed off on Chance's four prescriptions.

"That's what I like to hear," Chance replied, glancing at Lynn. She stood by the door, waiting with a wheelchair that he realized, all too late, was for *him*.

"Wait a minute, Doc," he began, protesting. "I can walk. I'm walking out of here on my own two feet."

"Not while you're still in my care, you won't," Dr. Peterson replied, not even bothering to look up from his clipboard. "This hospital can't risk a lawsuit if you were to fall down while walking out of here."

"It won't be so bad," Lynn piped up. "I'll even push you. Probably the only chance I'll ever have to *push* you around, anyway."

Dr. Peterson handed Lynn the prescriptions, then turned back to Chance. "I trust you'll follow my instructions and take care of yourself. To have experienced what you have in the past four days and emerge as strong as you are—I consider you highly fortunate."

"I consider him highly *blessed*," Lynn spoke up, wheeling the chair to his bed. "He's Brother Word, you know."

Chance swallowed his pride and took a seat in the wheelchair. With a final handshake from Dr. Peterson, they wheeled out of the room and down the hallway.

"Your flight back to South Carolina is today, right?"

Lynn nodded. "Tonight, actually. I leave at seven-thirty."

"Probably have a lot of work waiting for you at home, huh?"

"Not *work*—I think of it more as a labor of love. Pastor Gentry tells me the phones are ringing off the hook. And it's not just churches calling to ask our outreach team to conduct healing services—several nursing homes and hospitals have been calling, too. We're breaking through cultural, religious, and societal boundaries with the power of God's love—which is exactly what we've been called to do.

"And you played a role in this move of God, Chance. I'd like for you to come back, when you get stronger."

"Come *back*?"

"Yes, come back. Alright, so maybe your experience there wasn't as great as it could've been—"

"You don't say . . ."

Lynn playfully shoved the wheelchair in response to

his remark. "But think about all that can be done, *now*. You seem to have gotten Travis Everett's wild reporting antics under control, and our outreach team would be *so* inspired if you shared with them some experiences from your ministry. We're having special healing services at Faith Community now every Sunday night—people are flying in from all over the country and the testimonies of God's power are drawing people by the hundreds."

They were at Lynn's rental car now, and he stood and helped her first fold, then break down the wheelchair.

"Are you hungry?" Lynn asked, once she was behind the wheel. "I know that hospital food was absolutely delicious, but maybe you'd like to show me where the good Cajun restaurants are. This is my first time in Louisiana."

"Well, the best Cajun joints are in New Orleans, but I know somewhere we can get a good meal."

• • •

"IT'S CALLED A PO' BOY," Chance explained, watching Lynn's reaction as she took a bite of the shrimp sandwich. He'd taken her to Kelly's Po Boy, a popular restaurant on Milam Street in Shreveport. A tiny stream of mayonnaise dribbled down Lynn's chin and she quickly wiped it away with her napkin.

"I'm making such a mess," she said, laughing. "But this is delicious—I've never had one of these before. Why is it called a po' boy?"

"It's short for poor boy. These used to be the

cheapest way to get a solid meal. But the kicker is the bread—you've got to have that New Orleans French bread with the crunchy crust and light center."

"I'll remember that." She took another bite of the sandwich, smiling again when more mayonnaise dribbled down her chin.

Chance had been suppressing the fact that Lynn physically resembled Nina, but watching how she now politely dabbed her mouth with her napkin in the *same way* that Nina did was a new shock to his senses.

"Is my messy eating just too much for you?" Lynn asked, sensing his discomfort.

Chance shook his head. "No. It's not that at all. Nina used to do the same thing . . . I didn't realize how much you . . . how much she . . ." He fiddled with the straw in his soda. "You think you're going to be with one person for the rest of your life. I mean, I know how the divorce rates are climbing each year, but Nina and I . . . we were gonna be together forever."

"Chance . . ."

"Hmm?"

"I want to say this right, but forgive me if I don't. If you and I are still keeping in contact five years from now, will anything have changed? I don't mean to take away anything from the love you have for Nina, but . . ." She left the question dangling.

"You're asking if I'm ever going to be able to move on?"

Lynn nodded.

"I'd like to think that I would. If it had been me instead of her . . . I'd want her to continue living her life. I'd want the rest of her life to be *happy.*"

"What would it take to make *you* happy, Chance?"

"I don't know," he replied after a short pause.

"Love? A family? Money? Come on, there must be *something* that could make you happy."

He shrugged. "I've never been one to want a lot out of life. That's why what I had was so perfect—a wife, a house, land . . ." He looked at Lynn with a rueful expression. "I sometimes think I should've been born in the 1800s, because that was all a man needed then—a family and a place to hang his hat."

"Do you ever think that you could love again? Couldn't God give you someone else to share life's experiences with?"

"I haven't asked Him for someone else." He fingered his straw again, concentrating his attention on his glass to avoid Lynn's gaze. "Love is . . . an interesting thing. I can't imagine loving someone the way I loved Nina."

"Nina will always be special to you, Chance. No one will ever deny you that." She half shrugged. "Maybe I'm not understanding because I've never really had a strong love like that."

Chance saw a way to shift the conversation. "No boyfriends? No fiancés? Surely a life's calling to the gospel ministry isn't the same as a nun taking a vow of chastity."

"No, it certainly is not," she replied, laughing. "I've dated a few guys, but no serious suitors. The brothers I dated were all nice, but nobody was particularly interested about doing the work of ministry, even though they were Christians. I guess that was sort of a turnoff for me."

"Well, I'm sure God has somebody out there for you."

"Preaching to the choir, Chance. Yes, that's right." She finished her po' boy and looked at her watch. "Guess we should be going, huh? I want to get you back home, and maybe get some rest myself before going to the airport."

Chance looked at his watch, too. "I think we have time to make one quick stop before you take me home. Do you mind?"

"Absolutely not. In fact, I'm getting kind of used to this chauffeur job."

• • •

OAK GROVE CEMETERY was located near the town of Simsboro, a few miles west of Ruston on Highway 80. Chance could sense Lynn's hesitance as she pulled the car up to the front gate.

"I'm not going to be long," Chance began. "I haven't been by in two years, and—"

"I understand, Chance," Lynn cut in, resting her hand atop his. "No explanations needed."

"Would you mind walking with me? It would help having someone . . . having *you* . . . walk with me."

"Sure."

The weather was pleasant, in the low eighties with a slight breeze, as they navigated carefully around the headstones. Chance led the way, limping slightly as he walked.

"If you get too tired, just let me know," Lynn offered. "You can lean on my shoulder. Remember what Dr. Peterson said about resting for a few weeks—I don't want you hurting yourself on the same day as your hospital release."

"I'll let you know," Chance answered, his mind someplace else. The day of Nina's funeral two years ago had been bitterly cold and rainy. The inclement weather had been no match for the brewing storm between Jucinda and Chance, however. She had argued against him even showing up at the funeral, since in her mind he was squarely to blame for Nina's death. At the gravesite, he had sat as far from Jucinda as he could in the first row, although it was impossible to avoid the dagger-like glances she frequently shot at him. One week after her funeral, his exile from Ruston had begun with him taking the Greyhound bus to Vicksburg.

"Her grave is over there," he now said, stepping around one final tombstone and pointing to a red sandstone marble marker with an ornate flower design etched along the corners.

Nina Reneé Howard, the tombstone read. *You brought joy to all who knew you. Yours is a beautiful life that will be missed.*

"It's a beautiful stone and inscription," Lynn said.

"It was what Jucinda wanted on it. I wanted to place my own special message on it, but she was having no part of that."

"What would you have written on it? If you don't mind my asking."

Chance knelt down, eye level with the marker. *"An angel from heaven, now returned home,"* he whispered. He knelt there for a while, not even noticing Lynn silently retreat to give him some privacy.

The memories of Nina flooded his mind. Staying up every single night in Washington, D.C., that senior year Spring Break, excitedly discovering how much they had in common. Showing up with Nina at the senior prom, experiencing the unique pride of having the most beautiful girl in the room at your side. Going to the secluded brook behind his property for sunrise picnics and romantic skinny-dips. The rhapsodic sensation of making love to a wife as attuned to his needs as he was to hers. The way her belief in divine healing had forever changed his life. She had been his best friend, his lover, his soul mate, and his life partner. Only she'd left his life much too soon . . .

"Hey, baby," he said, gently caressing the headstone with his fingertips. "I've been wanting to come back here so much, but I guess you know how crazy it's been. I've tried to help your mother understand how . . . but I give up. I finally realize that I can't help her. Anyway, I didn't come here to talk about her."

His knees were beginning to hurt from being in a kneeling position for so long, so he took a seat on the grass next to her headstone.

"I can't believe it's already been two years. I mean, it just feels like yesterday when we were still waking up together. I remember how sometimes, when you woke up first, you would lie across from me and just watch me sleep. I never told you this, but a couple of times, I'd actually be awake, and through the slits of my eyes I would watch you watching me. I saw how you were praying over me and whispering aloud how much you loved me. That encouraged me so much, to know that you loved me like that.

"Everyone's telling me that I've had my time to grieve, and now it's time to move on with my life. But they weren't riding on buses and trains for the last two years, hiding and sleeping outdoors like a fugitive trapped in my own worst nightmare. I *couldn't* grieve over you, because I spent half the time *defending* myself against people who thought it was my fault you died.

"But I kept remembering the way you were looking at me that night in Lake Charles . . . how much you believed you were going to be healed the moment I laid hands on you. If *anybody* had faith for divine healing, it was you. And it was your faith that stirred me to get in the Word and discover for myself what God says about divine healing.

"I know that you're in heaven right now, with no more cancer and no more pain. And I know you've seen how God has healed people through my hands, just like you said. You always . . . *sensed* what God had in store for my life, even when I couldn't see it myself."

With his hand, he traced the etched outline of her name in the marble, hoping this action would cause him to feel something. But that notion was hopelessly nostalgic—he felt only cold, hard rock.

"Good-bye, Nina," he said, standing. "Love you . . . always."

Chapter Fifty-one

IN ADDITION TO FIVE DAUNTING PILES of paper arranged neatly on her desk, fifteen voice mails and thirty e-mails awaited Lynn when she returned to Faith Community the next day. The papers were either outreach-related expense reports she needed to sign off on or proposals needing her approval or rejection. Under normal circumstances, she would've been able to delegate most of the paperwork during a scheduled vacation break. However, her time in Louisiana had been both unscheduled and, due to her hospital stay, prolonged. And most of the members of her team who might've otherwise handled her paperwork had been so inundated with healing crusade calls that the paperwork accumulated even faster.

She quickly went through the paperwork, multitasking duties by both listening to her voice mails and periodically scanning her e-mails. By midday, the stack of papers had been cut in half, and Lynn was ready for a break. She stretched her neck, her fingers, and her back and went down the hall to Sister Arlene's office.

"You want to grab a bite to eat?" she asked, lightly

knocking on the door. Arlene was always good company for a lunch break.

Arlene nodded, still looking at her computer screen. "Just give me a minute. I'm putting the last touches on the fall choral concert."

"Take your time, girl. I've been drowning in paperwork all morning—it's been a tremendous blessing what the Lord is doing with the outreach effort, but that means double the work for us."

"Amen. But thank God for grace and the anointing."

"Mm-hmm." Lynn's eyes fell upon a folded copy of the *State* lying on Arlene's desk. "Is that yesterday's paper?" she asked.

"Yes. Sister Lynn, that article with the mystery man's statement was *nothing* but God. That reporter must have had a Damascus road experience, because *this* article was written for the glory of God."

Lynn picked up the newspaper. Not only hadn't she told anyone that Travis really had no choice but to write Chance's statement verbatim, but she'd also been so busy that she hadn't had time to read the article.

Travis had chronicled how he'd traveled to Louisiana and finally met the mystery man. He included a partial sidebar on Chance's history, not going into detail about his wife's death but explaining that her passing had sent Chance into a life on the road. During various stops in cities dotting the Deep South, he wrote, Chance apparently discovered God had given him a gift of healing. Travis ended the article with Chance's unedited statement, which no doubt had now been read by the 100,000-plus subscribers, since it was on the front page.

Glory to God, Lynn thought, setting down the paper. A better outreach tool *couldn't* have been created for any Christian in the area who was serious about evangelism and seeing the manifested power of God in this generation.

"Arlene, I'll meet you in ten minutes out front," she said, setting the paper back on the desk. "There's something I need to do."

Back at her desk, she quickly accessed the *State's* Web site and searched for the advertising contacts. She'd have to run the idea through Pastor Gentry, of course, but they both shared the same aggressive, yet practical view of evangelism. After a powerful front-page story like that, Faith Community needed to be buying advertising space to maximize this opportunity. Lynn knew that it was just as the Bible said—*"he who wins souls is wise."*

Her attitude concerning evangelism had always been based on a principle she felt most churches didn't quite grasp. The masses don't come to the church. It was the *church's* commission to go to the masses.

• • •

CHANCE'S LOWER BACK beat like a slow drum, awakening him with a jolt and causing him to grit his teeth in pain. Grimacing, he made his way to the dresser and popped in one of the pain pills Dr. Peterson had prescribed for him. He washed it down with a glass of water, pondering the dilemma of being unable to get rid of his present physical condition, despite his healing gift.

Two bullets, plus a slight concussion . . . what'd you expect?

He took another drink of water, and as he set the water glass down he noticed an envelope bearing his name lying on the dresser. He hadn't seen it before, although the previous evening another one of Dr. Peterson's pills had put him right to bed after Lynn had gone to the airport. It was a get-well Hallmark card Lynn had apparently left for him.

To Chance:

It's my prayer that God grant you not only a speedy recovery, but also the desires of your heart. I know it's difficult for you to think that way now, but remember that weeping only endures for the night. Joy comes in the morning. You've been a blessing to my life, and you've opened my eyes in more ways than just the obvious. Know that you'll always have a friend in South Carolina not only praying for you, but also thinking about you.

Many blessings,
Lynn

"She left that card for you yesterday," Pop said. Chance turned and saw his father leaning against his doorjamb. "Must've had it for a while, 'cause I didn't see her go to no store."

"The hospital had a gift shop," Chance said. "She probably got it there."

Pop hobbled into the room. "I ain't never been one

to tell you how to live your life, and I know how hard it's been for you to get over Nina, but it's been two years. And I *guarantee* you ain't never gon' meet someone like this Lynn gal for the rest of your lifetime."

"What makes you say that?"

"Is you blind or something? Boy, that girl dived in the water *twice*, tryin' to save your life! I saw the whole thing. And she wasn't playing when she said she was afraid to put her head underwater—her face was white as a ghost when she first got up on the rail of the boat. But she jumped in anyway. It don't take a rocket scientist to see that Lynn cares a whole lot about you. And you can't tell me she ain't pretty—she's a spittin' image of Nina."

"It's not about her being pretty . . . or even looking like Nina."

"What's it about, then?"

Among other things, *it* was the uncertainty of moving beyond the familiar and the fear of giving his heart away again to a woman, only to have it broken again. But Chance wasn't about to tell Pop that.

He finally shrugged. "I don't know, Pop."

"Well, you better figure it out soon. If you don't, you gon' live to regret it."

"Live to *regret* it? Who are you to tell me about regrets?" The words erupted from Chance's mouth before he had a moment to really think about what he was saying. Maybe it was a side effect from the medication he was taking, or the fact that Nina was gone forever and Lynn Harper might possibly take her place in his heart. More likely, it was all the years of watching Pop drink himself into an early grave.

"Now . . . you watch what you saying, Chance," Pop responded, steadying himself on his cane. "You probably ain't thinking straight and all . . . them painkillers done gone straight to your head. I'm gon' act like I didn't hear that."

"Then maybe I should say it again—who are you to talk to me about regret? If anyone's living in regret, it's you. You've been drinking your life away ever since Mom passed. Seems like you can't move past Mom's death any more than I could move past losing Nina."

"Chance, now that's enough outta you." Pop pointed a trembling finger at his son. "You talkin' about things you don't know nothing about. I ain't drinking 'cause Jacqueline died. Dying's a part of life—I've been over that for years."

"Yeah? Then why are you drinking, Pop? Why are you killing yourself?"

Bennett Howard fell back against the doorway. He looked away from his son as tears began welling up in the corners of his eyes.

"Killing myself?" He shook his head now as the tears began rolling down his face. "I ain't killing myself—I've been dead since '69, Chance."

"'69?"

"The year they shipped me to 'Nam." Pop buried his face in his hands as he began weeping loudly. His shoulders shook so violently that Chance feared he was in danger of hurting himself.

"I was jus' a kid, Chance. Didn't know nothin' about no Vietcong or what the government was tryin' to do over there. I had never been outside Louisiana, and here they were sending me to Fort Bragg and then over the ocean in the biggest airplane I'd ever seen."

"Pop, I—"

"No—this is your time for listenin' to what I got to say. You wanted to know why I drown my sorrows in the bottle, then you gon' know. I was eighteen, Chance. *Eighteen*. And I saw things . . . I did things . . ." His voice trailed off, creating a silence that lasted several moments.

". . . And then I came back home from that neverendin' nightmare, and I'm disrespected by everyone for going over there in the first place. It ain't like I had a choice—I was *drafted*.

"So, you happy now, Chance? You satisfied? You understand why I drink? I drink to forget the worst time of my life."

Chance wiped the tears that were now streaming down his face. Pop had never before spoken of Vietnam, never before spoken of the horrors he'd faced over there. And how was Chance supposed to respond to that? Closing his eyes to stem the flow of tears, he silently began praying. He prayed for the words that would reach that eighteen-year-old kid who'd been dropped off in the war-torn jungles of Vietnam and somehow reassure him that hope still remained for his life.

"Pop, I just want to say . . ." Chance began, opening his eyes. But Pop had left the room.

Chapter Fifty-two

THE NEXT DAY, THE HOUSE was quiet when Chance finally rolled out of bed and slowly made his way down the hallway. He assumed Pop had gone to the lake, or at least he hoped so. Pop's disability check had come in the mail yesterday, and his old man was good for spending most of it down at the liquor store.

With his injuries, it took Chance almost an hour to wash and dress. After dumping some cereal into a bowl and pouring a tall glass of orange juice, he walked outside onto the front porch. The ten acres of land his house sat on, passed down from Jacqueline, was privately nestled not far from the Arkansas state line. Chance had always relished the stillness and quiet of the land; the closest neighbors lived two miles away. It was a throwback to the post–Louisiana Purchase days, when folks settled on large property tracts and lived off the fruit of their land.

That's all I wanted to do, God . . . raise my family here and live out the rest of my days in peace and quiet . . .

A spiraling plume of dust caught his attention then, rising skyward just beyond a cluster of trees to his right. The dust meant a vehicle had turned off the road and was now headed his way. Chance hoped it might be Pop, and when the car came into the clearing and he saw the rooftop police lights, he was almost sure it was a police officer escorting his drunken father home.

But when the police car came closer, Chance recognized the driver to be Sergeant Boudreaux, one of the officers who'd been assigned the Jucinda Harris case. Boudreaux had twice visited Chance in the hospital, updating him on how the case was progressing.

"G'morning, Chance," Boudreaux said, stepping out of the car. He stretched his lanky, six-foot-four frame briefly, then made his way up the porch's steps.

"Good morning, Sergeant. Drove all the way from Shreveport, huh? If I'd known you were coming, I'd have fixed you one of my famous omelets."

Boudreaux shook his head and sat down in the chair beside Chance. "No need for all that trouble. I was just in the area, doing some more work on the case, and I'd thought I'd drop by. How ya feeling?"

"A little better. More good days than bad. Dr. Peterson says I'll be back to my old self in no time at all."

"Glad to hear that. Most cases like yours—taking two 9 mm shots to the body, then nearly splitting your head open on a rock—don't wind up with happy endings. Speakin' of happy endings, I got some good news on the case."

"Yeah?"

Boudreaux nodded. "Looks like Ms. Harris's lawyer is going to take the DA's plea bargain. Really didn't have a choice. The evidence against her is too strong—they've recovered the gun with her fingerprints all over it, plus the gun residue on her hands and the five eyewitnesses that saw her pull the trigger. It's pretty much open-and-shut."

"What's the DA's plea bargain look like?"

"I don't know all the particulars; they'll be contacting you soon, no doubt. But from what I gather, unless you want to pursue aggressive retribution, Ms. Harris will plead guilty to attempted murder and get anywhere from three to five, seeing as she's a first-time offender."

Chance nodded, drinking the last of his orange juice. "I don't really care about aggressive retribution; I've already told the DA that. I just want Jucinda to get some help." He set his glass down firmly. "And stay out of my life."

"I hear you loud and clear, Chance. I've talked to Chief Dobbs in Ruston. Seems Ms. Harris is well connected in that town, but Dobbs and I go way back. Even when she finally gets out of prison, she won't be causing any more problems for you down there."

• • •

TRAVIS FELT THE EYES of his coworkers locked onto him as he made his way to his cubicle. These were different stares than the ones he'd been receiving when he wrote the first mystery-man article. He'd rather liked that initial attention—the world of newspaper reporting was rife with jealousy and envy, and it had felt good to be the top dog for a while.

But Thursday's article, where he'd included Chance Howard's unedited statement at the conclusion of an unarguably pro-Christian article, had shifted those envious stares to looks of curiosity and concern, even pity. Ryman Wells had questioned the writing of such a radically Christian article, but Travis had debated (to his own surprise) the need to include the Christian slant as a precursor to his next story, which centered on the dramatic increase in the area's church attendance over the last month.

Travis, of course, wanted nothing to do with churches or articles covering church attendance, but what choice did he have? Even though Chance Howard had not openly threatened to expose his plagiarism on previous articles, the warning clearly had been implicit. And such an exposure would have ruined Travis's career, right as it was taking off. So if one or two pro-Christian articles were necessary to make Chance Howard go away, then so be it. But the stares from his coworkers . . . Writing such an article was almost as if Travis had declared that he, too, was a born-again Christian.

Objectivity in news reporting had subtly shifted to a liberal slant. While the industry outwardly applauded the idea of family values and Judeo-Christian ethics, such feel-good stories did not sell newspapers or garner high television ratings. The search for the next gripping national scandal like the O. J. Simpson trial or the Clinton-Lewinsky affair constantly lurked in the minds of everyone in the industry. While media figureheads outwardly deemed such scandals deplorable and shameful, inwardly they relished boosting their ratings with saturated coverage.

Travis's story about a delusional, mysterious man popping up in various small southern towns, "pretending" to heal people, had initially captured the interest of this news feeding frenzy, at least in South Carolina. But if in fact the story turned out to be nothing more than an honest Christian man believing God to heal diseases and periodically seeing miraculous results, where was the scandal in that?

As it was, Travis needed to write his story on the rising church attendance for Tuesday's paper, and he'd barely begun. His weekend had been spent, as usual, lounging on his couch with a remote control in one hand and a Doritos bag in the other. His intentions of attending a church service on Sunday morning to obtain a firsthand account of the increase in attendance were just that—intentions. More specifically, his body had screamed bloody murder at the thought of getting out of bed before noon on a weekend. So it was on to plan number two.

His fingers now danced atop the keyboard as he scoured the Internet search engines for anything on church attendance. There was usable data, of course, but nothing *specifically* highlighting Richland County. He needed a firsthand account, someone who went to church every Sunday in the area and could give him what he needed.

With a sigh, he reached for his telephone and dialed his sister Andrea's number. As the saying went, desperate people will do . . . *desperate* things.

• • •

ANDREA WAS HELPING Eddie read aloud from a primer when the phone rang.

"Keep on, Eddie—you're doing a great job," she said, patting him on the back as she reached for the phone.

"Andrea?"

"Travis?" She was surprised to hear her brother's voice on the other end. "Is everything alright?"

"Yeah. Why you ask?"

"How often do you call here, Travis? Usually, *I'm* the one having to call you. Anyway, I thought it was wonderful what you wrote in your last article. Bravo for Brother Word!"

"Yeah. Speaking of that story—I've got to do a follow-up on a related topic. People are saying there's been an increase in church attendance around Richland County over the past month, particularly at services where people are prayed over to receive healings."

"There *has* been an increase! Oh, it's been the most wonderful thing—James, Eddie, and I have started attending Faith Community Church, and every week the sanctuary is just overflowing with people. There's talk that the church might have to schedule another service in the afternoons just to accommodate the crowds. Plus, we've *personally* been invited to share in several healing crusades in the last three weeks. Churches and stadiums have been packed out, and Eddie's testimony has been—"

"Slow down, Andrea. You're talking faster than I can write."

"Faster than you can write? Are .you taking *notes*, Travis?"

"Well, you're giving me some good information here, and I figure I'd use it as deep background to my story."

"Oh, I get it now. So *that's* why you called. I knew there had to be some ulterior motive. Well, I won't let you use my quotes as your 'deep background,' baby brother. What's happening here in South Carolina is bigger than some newspaper story, and you of all people should know that."

"Andrea, it's not like I'm using you or anything. Didn't you once tell me I should also report this story from the side that *believes*? That's all I'm doing now—getting a firsthand account on church attendance from someone who should know."

"You want a firsthand account? Okay, you'll get one. James, Eddie, and I are going to Bible study tonight at Faith Community, and you're coming with us."

"*What*? I don't have time for—"

"Then I suggest you make time, Travis. You want to report on church attendance? Try reporting on one thousand people showing up on a Monday night for a Bible study on divine healing. I doubt that's ever happened around these parts, and if you're writing a story on it, I'd say you have an obligation to be there."

She heard Travis sigh audibly on the other end of the line. "We'll pick you up at five-thirty. Don't keep us waiting." She hung up the phone before Travis could protest.

Chapter Fifty-three

"So then faith comes by hearing, and hearing by the Word of God," Pastor Alonzo Gentry began, opening his Bible and looking out among the congregants. "Sister Dana, thank you for that wonderful solo. How many in here have tried Him and know Him?"

Bible study at Faith Community was held on Wednesday nights, but Gentry had started conducting special Bible study services to specifically address the growing questions people were raising concerning divine healing. It had come to Gentry's attention that all over the city people with infirmities, or in wheelchairs or otherwise handicapped, were being stopped on the street and prayed over. While he was encouraged by the believers' zeal, he wanted to ensure such fervor was balanced with a proper understanding of the scriptures concerning healing.

"I know that we've all been using Mark 16:18 as a foundational basis for laying hands on the sick and healing through faith in the Lord Jesus Christ. And, glory to God, we *are* seeing people healed, but I want to remind us to stay focused to the heartbeat of God, which has always been . . . *souls.* Soul-winning. Healing the sick is a *sign* that follows them that believe to draw unbelievers into the Kingdom of heaven. But in that same chapter of Mark's gospel, verse 15, Jesus opens His teaching with, ***'Go into all the world and preach the gospel to every man.'***

"Healing the sick merely for healing's sake is not God's intention. However, healing the human heart and drawing unbelievers to His love *is.*" He glanced down at his Bible. "Now, the fourth chapter of Ephesians tells us that God has endowed believers with gifts of the Spirit to equip us for the work of ministry and for the edifying of the body of Christ, till we all come to the unity of the faith and of the knowledge of the Son of God, to a perfect man, to the measure of the stature of the fullness of Christ.

"The work of *ministry*," he repeated for emphasis, "means that we must be mindful to spread the gospel whenever we're in public, praying for people. Throughout my experience in ministry, I've seen revivals come and go, with great signs and wonders drawing thousands to crusades. All too often in these revivals, too great an emphasis is placed on giftings and outward demonstrations of the Holy Spirit. However, when the signs and wonders start appearing less frequently, the attendance usually drops off and the enthusiasm wanes for the things of God. We're not going to let that happen with *this* revival.

"I'm excited to see front-page newspaper articles glorifying God for healing people through Chance Howard's hands, but I'd like us all to remain focused on spreading the *gospel*, not just performing healings. You see, with healings, there is no cut-and-dried method—it's a matter of faith between you, the person you're praying for, and God's will for that particular situation. But we will *always* know the will of God as it relates to the church, and that is to go throughout all the world, making disciples and baptizing them in the name of the Father, the Son, and the Holy Spirit. This is the Great Commission Jesus empowered us to do. I am thankful that we currently have twenty-one churches throughout Richland, Sumter, Lee, Clarendon, and Florence counties that have already enlisted in our outreach effort. While the highlight of our crusades is when we pray for the sick to receive God's healing, we should strive to see more people receive Christ as Lord. People will come to these crusades as a result of the media attention, and when they come, let's shower them with the true love of the Lord, alright? Whether they're coming to see a show or strictly out of curiosity, let's become living, breathing examples of the wonderful love of Jesus Christ. Amen?"

"Amen," the congregants shouted in chorus.

"In fact," Gentry continued, "let's all take a moment and pray for each other right now. I'm so thankful that we have strong intercessors at all these churches, praying for the success of this revival, because *nothing* is birthed in the Kingdom without prayer. However, I want to make sure this move of God gets down into the hearts of everyone involved, not just the intercessors. I'm praying for a move of God in your personal lives that will affect your family life at home, on the job with your coworkers, and everywhere else in between. I'd like everyone to take one person by the hands, and begin to pray for that person. Pray that God would touch your brother or your sister in His own special way and reveal to them how to not only minister healing to the sick but salvation to the lost. Amen?"

• • •

Travis had been half asleep throughout most of Pastor Gentry's teaching. The last thing on his personal wish list was sitting through some boring Bible lesson, and if he hadn't been brought here against his will, he would've ditched this service a long time ago. He could not understand why people felt compelled to sit for hours and let someone either preach hellfire and brimstone at them (which at least could be lively) or lecture from an antiquated book written thousands of years ago. After listening to Pastor Gentry's style, Travis had found the preacher to fall into the latter group.

Bo-oo-oring . . .

A small nudge to his ribs caused him to slowly open his eyes. He turned to his right and saw Eddie, trying to get his attention.

"What?" Travis whispered, leaning down to his nephew. Maybe Eddie needed someone to take him to the restroom or get a drink of water. Young kids always needed to make such pit stops.

"I'm s'posed to pray for you," Eddie whispered back.

"What?"

"I'm s'posed to pray for you," Eddie repeated, this time more insistently. Travis blinked a couple of times, trying to get rid of the sleep-induced fog blanketing his brain. Eddie was supposed to . . . *pray* for him? He looked to his left and saw Andrea and James facing each other in the pew, holding hands with their eyes closed. Their lips were moving softly; it was safe to assume they were praying for each other. Travis looked behind and all around him—everyone seemed to have paired off and was praying for one another.

Clever, Travis thought. *Audience participation . . .*

Eddie was now pulling on his sleeve. "Uncle Trav, I'm s'posed to—"

"I know, I know." Travis sighed. What harm was there in letting Eddie pray for him? Travis would be surprised if the little seven-year-old knew anything more than *"now I lay me down to sleep . . ."*

"Alright," Travis said, turning in the pew and taking Eddie's small hands in his. "You can pray for me."

Eddie beamed and scrunched up his face muscles, as if in deep thought. He stayed like that for about a half minute, then he began to pray.

"Daddy God, I know You're listenin' to me, 'cause You always do. I'm here with my Uncle Trav. He's my favorite uncle, y'know."

Travis grinned and closed his eyes, taking great pride in knowing Eddie favored him over his brother, Maynard.

"I like hangin' out with my Uncle Trav, but . . . but . . ." Eddie's little voice quivered. "But sometimes I get scared for him. He don't know You as Daddy God yet, and Mommy says everyone that don't know You will go to hell."

Travis's grin immediately vanished. He opened his eyes and stared at his nephew.

"I don't want Uncle Trav to go to hell, Daddy God. He jus' . . . he jus' needs to see You the way I see You. He jus' needs to love You the way Mommy taught me to love You. Okay? Can You show him how, Daddy God? That's all I want today. That's my prayer. Amen."

Travis released his now-sweaty hands from Eddie's small grip, speechless. Chills ran up and down his spine. The sensation frightened him; it was similar to when he was a kid and had stayed up to watch *The Exorcist* one Saturday night. He hadn't been able to sleep without nightmares for two weeks.

"You okay, Uncle Trav?"

What was all that talk about going to . . . *hell*? What on earth was Andrea teaching his nephew, filling his seven-year-old mind with such a horrible myth?

Eddie was tugging on his sleeve again. "Uncle Trav?"

Travis snapped out of his mini-trance and looked at Eddie. His mouth had suddenly gone dry. "Y-yeah?"

"You okay?"

The question was asked with the unbelievable naïveté of a seven-year-old, the same way the youngster asked why the sun never fell from the sky or why the ocean was always blue. *You okay?*

No, he was not *okay*. He'd just heard his nephew pray that his uncle wouldn't go to hell. What sort of twisted mind trip was that?

"Y-yeah, Eddie. Yeah, I'm okay." He cleared his throat. "I just need to go get some water . . . my mouth is real dry."

"You want me to come with you, Uncle Trav?"

"No," Travis replied, a little too quickly and a little

too harshly. He got up from the pew, having forgotten all about his article on church attendance. Having your seven-year-old nephew tell you, in so many words, that you were going to hell was not an easy thing to digest.

After pausing at the water fountain to relieve his parched throat, he stumbled out to the parking lot and made his way to Andrea and James's minivan. The vehicle was locked, but Travis sat on the back bumper and buried his face in his hands. He didn't know what was more terrifying—the first time he'd watched *The Exorcist* or hearing Eddie pray that his "Uncle Trav" wouldn't go to hell.

Chapter Fifty-four

When the sun rose the next morning and Pop still hadn't shown up at the house, Chance's initial concerns swelled to full-fledged worry. Whenever Pop got drunk, his surliness reached epic proportions and he became a magnet for violent activity. Making matters worse, the old man always kept a switchblade in his right sock, something he'd been doing ever since he returned from Vietnam.

At a quarter to ten, unable to wait any longer, Chance picked up the phone and dialed Telfair Williams.

"Telfair, this is Chance. You have any idea where Pop is?"

"Last I seen Bennett, he was over to Lucky's."

Chance groaned. Lucky's Liquor was one of Pop's well-known places to waste his money. "Telfair, you know Pop didn't have any business at Lucky's. You should've got him out of there—or called me."

"Got him outta there?" Telfair started laughing. The sound was like the furious beating of a raspy, hollow drum. "Chance, you know as well as I do, nobody can't make Bennett do nothin' he don't wanna do. I bin stopped tryin' to tell him what to do. As long as he pay me good money to take care of the yard, I ain't got no beef with him. 'Cause if he want to drink, he gon' drink."

"Well, do you have any idea where Pop is now?"

"Naw, can't say that I— Oh wait, now. He probably over to the Happy House."

"The Happy . . . *House*?"

"That's what we call it. It's a boardinghouse over in Bossier City. Lotsa tourists from the gamblin' boats go there to do . . . well . . . uh, y'know . . ."

"Why would Pop be in a boarding— Never mind. Telfair, listen—can you go get Pop? And bring him here . . . No, wait—can you get him and take him to our boat on Caddo Lake? Can you do that for me?"

"I respect what you tryin' to do, Chance. I really do. But I don't git paid for no shippin' and receivin'." The man made a brief noise that sounded like he was sucking his front teeth. The few front teeth he had left, that is. "A job like that's gonna cost you."

"Yeah, I get it," Chance said, sighing. "What's it going to cost me?"

Telfair made the sucking-teeth sound again. "A hunnerd bucks."

• • •

CHANCE WAS FEELING STRONGER, but not quite well enough to drive, so he called Mardy's Cab Service to take him to Caddo Lake. *Jacqueline* was moored in her regular spot, having been placed back there after being briefly impounded as evidence. If the case against Jucinda had proceeded to trial, the fishing boat would've still been kept under lock and key, but it appeared both sides would accept the plea bargain. As such, the boat was free to be used by its owners.

Aboard the boat now, Chance stretched out on a deck recliner, letting the sun's rays warm his body from head to toe. He had no doubt Pop would be here, because Telfair would definitely see to that. Telfair might not be the smartest handyman to have around, but he was a decent worker and his allegiance to the almighty dollar was stronger than a seeing-eye dog's loyalty to his blind master. Telfair would do just about anything if you padded his pockets right.

Closing his eyes, Chance dangled his legs over the side of the recliner and let his mind drift. When thoughts of Nina tried to find their way inside his head, he quickly replaced them with thoughts of Pop. He remembered the time Pop came home with the biggest fish he'd ever caught. Chance forgot how many pounds the fish had weighed, but it had been snared from the Gulf of Mexico a few miles out of the port of New Orleans. Pop had the fish gutted, stuffed, and mounted—for years that colorful trophy had been his pride and joy and the catalyst for many a story to narrate to admiring visitors. But when Jacqueline had died, Pop took the fish down from the wall and put it in storage. Jacqueline had never liked the big fish hanging on a wall in her house, and Pop, out of respect, guilt, or a mixture of both emotions, didn't have the heart to look at it anymore.

And then there was the time Chance had caught *his* first fish. He had been five years old, and he and Pop had been fishing on the banks of a small creek in

Nacogdoches. The two had been fishing peacefully for an hour when Chance had felt that now-familiar tug on the end of his fishing line. And then the lure had completely disappeared under the water's surface.

"That's it, Chance!" Pop had yelled. "The fish took the bait! The fish took the bait! Reel him in now, slowly . . . That's it . . . You got him now . . ."

Pop had allowed Chance to do all the work, excitedly calling out instructions from just a few feet away. When the fish's gills broke the water's surface, Chance had become as excited as Pop. Up until that point, all the fish that had been caught had been snared from the end of Pop's hook, never his own.

But at last—he was about to catch his own fish! He had scooted closer to the shoreline from his spot on an elevated ledge, eager to capture his long-awaited prize. But in his anxiousness, his bare foot had slipped on a wet tree branch. His forward momentum, coupled with the slippery footing, had propelled him headlong into the shallow water.

Chance's fall hadn't been dangerous, though, and once Pop saw that his son was alright, he'd started laughing hysterically. "You didn't catch that fish, Chance," he'd said, doubled over and wheezing for breath. "That fish caught *you*!"

A scraping sound on the side of the boat caused Chance to open his eyes. Sitting up on the recliner, he saw Telfair struggling to help Pop on board, albeit without much progress. Pop was unresponsive, like a deadweight on Telfair's arms.

"Here, let me help," Chance offered, before standing and realizing he hadn't yet regained full strength in his own limbs. But with the little help he *could* give, they were finally able to get Pop situated in one of the recliners after a few minutes.

"Pop, come on, wake up," Chance said, gently shaking his father's shoulders. Pop's eyes fluttered open and he began softly moaning. The puffy skin encircling his eyes magnified his bloodshot pupils, causing the upper part of his face to resemble a bad Halloween mask.

"Pop, come on, now. Can you hear me?"

"Wha's tha . . . Who's tha . . . ?"

"Pop, it's me. Chance."

"Chance . . ."

Chance looked at Telfair. "Listen, thanks for doing what you did. I know it must've been a lot of trouble to get him in your Jeep and all."

"Yeah—that old man weighs a ton when he passed out, drunk and all. But if you pay me to do a job, I's gon' do it."

"I know. Uh, I can take it from here, Telfair. Thanks again."

With a tip of his baseball cap, Telfair climbed off the boat and walked back to his Jeep. Chance glanced back at Pop, but the old man had closed his eyes, lost in another hangover-induced pipe dream. Sighing, Chance walked over to the boat's controls, started the engine, and steered *Jacqueline* out into open waters.

• • •

FORTY MINUTES LATER, Chance set down his two fishing poles and walked back to the other end of the boat. Either the fish weren't biting or he was a lousy fisherman, because he hadn't had so much as a nibble on his lines.

It's the fish . . . they're just not biting today, he lied to himself.

Pop was still dozing, but Chance knew how to rouse the old man. Taking the pail of water meant to hold the fish he should've been catching, he tossed it at Pop, splashing water all over him.

"What the—!" Pop's upper body jerked wildly as his eyes snapped open, and he began wiping at his face.

"Sorry, Pop, but that was the only way I could think of to get you up."

"What in the . . . Boy, is you crazy?" Pop shook his body back and forth, flinging droplets of water off him like a wet dog. "You ain't have to soak me up like this."

"Soak you up? Pop, you were already soaked. *Inebriated*, that is. Drunk as a skunk guzzling down a pint of Jack Daniel's."

"I don't drink no Jack Daniel's. I likes the—"

"*Whatever*, Pop. That's not what I'm getting at."

"Well, what you gettin' at, then?" Pop tried standing up, discovered his one good leg was still unsteady, and plopped back down in the recliner.

"We need to talk, Pop," Chance said, sitting down next to his father. "We didn't finish the conversation we'd started earlier."

Pop rubbed at his eyes. "I still don't know what you talkin' about. We didn't have no earlier . . . conver . . . earlier . . . conver . . ." He yawned.

"Yes, we did," Chance said, slightly lowering his voice. "You were telling me about Vietnam. About what you saw over there . . . and what happened to you over there."

Pop threw his head back and started laughing. "Now I *know* you's crazy, Chance. 'Cause I don't tell nobody about what went on over there."

"Yeah? And why do you do that? You think it's better to keep things bottled up inside? You think nobody can understand the horrors you saw? Huh? You think—"

"Watch that mouth now, Chance. You talkin' about things you don't know nothing about. You weren't there. You'd know why we keep silent about that if you was there."

Chance nodded, seeing that his plan was working like a charm. Pop had sobered up real quick once Chance kept pushing that Vietnam button. Now he had the old man's complete attention.

"I'm talking about things I know nothing about, is that right?"

"Tha's what I said."

"Alright. Then let me switch subjects and talk about something I do know about. Something that *you* haven't experienced."

"What you talkin' about, Chance?"

"I'm talking about what I've been doing for the last two years."

"What you mean? The last two years, you been running from Jucinda. Can't say I blame you, though. That woman crazier than a two-headed bat."

"Let me show you something, Pop." Chance leaned to his left and retrieved his duffel bag. He took out a black three-ring binder and handed it to Pop.

"Wha's this?"

"Just open it and read it, Pop. I would read it aloud to you, but you need to see it for yourself."

The binder contained Chance's collection of clippings from a half dozen newspapers in the South, describing various occurrences of unexplained, supernatural healings. The common thread woven throughout each article was the mention of a "man with no name and mysterious identity, who laid hands on the sick and produced miraculous results." The last paper in the collection was the *State*, showing Chance's picture on the front page as the identity of this mystery man.

Pop held up that copy and pointed at Chance, an expression of confusion and bewilderment clouding his face. "Tha's you . . . no, can't be . . . tha's you?"

Chance nodded. "That's me, Pop. The man they wrote about in every article."

"Can't be . . ."

Chance nodded again. "Nina was right to believe that God could heal her through the laying on of hands, because divine healing is real. It's as real as that paper you're holding."

"So all of this stuff," Pop began, thumbing back through the binder. "You tellin' me all of this stuff is true?"

"It's all true, Pop. I don't know why God is using me, but He is. I've seen crooked spines instantly straightened out, tumors disappear, blinded eyes opened, and crippled legs made whole again. And if you read that second-to-last article, you'll see that Lynn Harper was in a car accident and lost her eyesight for seven weeks. She was told she'd never see again. But as you now know, God completely restored her vision."

"How?"

"I laid hands over her eyes and spoke the Word of God over her. She was instantly healed. This is what I'm trying to tell you, Pop—this stuff is real."

"B-but Nina . . . it didn't work for Nina."

Chance took a deep breath. "I may never know the answers to some questions until I get to heaven. But what I do know is that she's now in a place where there's no more pain, and no more suffering. God didn't heal her while she was still here with us, but He did heal her."

"Hmmph. But why you? Why you, huh? If all this healin' stuff is true, why God usin' you?"

"I've asked myself that question a thousand times. I don't know why. It just is. Why does anyone question the cards we're dealt with in life? Didn't you used to tell me you have to play the hand you're dealt?"

"Reckon I did."

"Well, then, that's what I'm doing. It was a lousy hand at first—losing Nina—but now, I don't know. Now it's not so bad."

"How do it work?"

"What?"

"This healin' stuff. How do it work?"

"It works by faith, Pop."

Chapter Fifty-five

THREE DAYS LATER, Chance remembered something Lynn had said to him—Faith Community Church conducted healing services every Sunday night. And with that recollection, a vision appeared to his mind. He was standing at the altar of the church, speaking before thousands of people. He sensed there were more people, too numerous to be counted, because of the television cameras.

I'm reaching a worldwide audience with the words of healing . . .

One by one the people came down the aisle, forming a line that would pass before him.

Lay hands on them, Chance heard the voice of the Lord say. ***I have healed them through the blood of My Son.***

As the first person in line, an elderly woman walking with a cane, approached him, the vision blurred and his mind came back to the present. But he needed no more prompting to grasp the urgency of the vision—the Spirit of the Lord was still speaking to him.

I have healed them through the blood of My Son . . .

Taking a garment bag from his closet, he stuffed a

week's worth of clothes inside, then went to the bathroom and filled his shaving bag with all the essential items. Two years of living in motels, hotels, and the great outdoors had taught him how to get by with only the bare minimums.

Neither bus nor train would get him there by tomorrow evening, so he called the airport for flights leaving to South Carolina. The airport in Monroe didn't have a departing flight until ten the following morning, but Shreveport Regional had a midnight flight to IAH Houston, where he could then catch a connecting flight to Atlanta, and then on to Columbia.

"That's perfect," he told the airline agent. "Book it." Setting his bag aside, he walked down the hallway to the living room, where Pop sat in his easy chair, watching a fishing tournament on one of the secondary ESPN channels.

"You never tire of this fishing stuff, do you, Pop?"

"Fishin' is the perfect metaphor—"

"For life," Chance finished, taking a seat next to his father on the couch. "I know, I know. Listen, I'm going back to South Carolina for a few days."

The statement alone was enough to take Pop's attention from the TV. "You what? You going back . . . again? You gon' leave me . . . again?"

"Pop, I'm not leaving you. I just need to get some things in order."

"You can get things in order here."

Chance shook his head. "I've just been doing some thinking and some praying. This healing gift God gave me should be made available to more people, but I don't know the first thing about starting a healing ministry. But the churches I visited in South Carolina—they already have an outreach system in place. The seeds for believers to operate in divine healing have already been planted there, and from what I hear, are already producing."

Pop turned his attention back to the fishing tournament. "Sound like you already got your mind set, then. Ain't no need in you tellin' me."

"Well, my mind would be set, if I could leave without worrying about you starting drinking again."

"I told you. I ain't no—"

"Pop, listen. We're not going to argue about this. There's a problem and it won't do any good for us to act like there's not. We're just going to take it one day at a time, alright? I've left some brochures for some rehab centers on the kitchen table . . . and I want you to know that I'm behind you in this all the way. You and me—we're going to make it, you hear?"

Pop made no attempt to answer, but Chance knew his father had heard everything he'd just said.

"Because when I get back," Chance continued, "you and me got a lot of fishing to do. But as much as I love you, I can't be around you if you're still throwing your life away to that bottle."

A minute went by before Pop spoke. "When you coming back?" he asked softly.

"Real soon, Pop. And who knows? I might even take you to South Carolina with me. I'm told they got fish off the Atlantic coast that are twice the size of fish here in Louisiana."

At that, a wide smile spread across Pop's face. "You

don' lost your mind, boy. This here's Cajun country—ain't *nobody* got fish bigger than we do."

"Well, then, you'll just have to prove me wrong."

"I will, Chance." He glanced over at his son and Chance got the feeling Pop wasn't just talking about the fish. "I will."

Chapter Fifty-six

LYNN LOVED THE LARGE stained-glass windows adorning the east and west walls of Faith Community Church. She always looked to them as soon as she stepped inside the sanctuary on Sunday mornings, captivated by how the simple beveled glass planes reflected sunlight with such majestic beauty.

The window on the west wall depicted a small group of worshippers bowing down before a golden cross. The theme was simple, yet so profound: the center of Christianity revolved around Jesus's work on Calvary's cross. To that end, believers would forever recognize the cross as the place of ultimate worship.

The window on the east wall depicted Jesus's ascension into heaven, surrounded by the heavenly host of angels. It was a scene of ultimate triumph, one that always lifted Lynn's spirits whenever she saw it.

Because You got up, that means I can get up, too . . .

"Good morning, Sister Lynn," Arlene called out from her perch at the piano.

Lynn shook her head, smiled, and walked over to the piano. "Will there ever be a Sunday that I'll get here *before* you do?"

Arlene gave her a look that implied there would not. "I just love coming here early, spending time with Him," she said, as she started to play the beginning chords to "How Great Thou Art."

Lynn sat next to the music minister on the piano bench. "I think we must both be cut from the same cloth. I agree that there's *nothing* like quality, quiet time with the Father."

Arlene nodded, softly beginning to sing the words to the hymn in her rich alto voice.

You have such a beautiful voice, sis . . .

Lynn closed her eyes and reflected once more on God's goodness in her life—her miraculous healing from pneumonia at age two, having a wonderful human angel like Sister Imogene patiently teach her about God's love in Sunday school, hearing the strong call of God to the ministry during her teenage years (which subsequently kept her from succumbing to peer pressure), being placed as outreach director for one of the largest churches in the Carolinas, God protecting her during a horrific car accident that had killed the other driver involved, God using Chance Howard to heal her eyes from certain blindness . . .

The list went on and on, and by the time Arlene had finished the first verse, Lynn had slid off the piano bench and fallen to her knees, lost in worship.

"Then sings my soul, my Savior God to Thee . . . how great Thou art . . ."

• • •

"*I WAS GLAD WHEN THEY SAID to me, let us go into the house of the Lord,*" Pastor Gentry proclaimed, reciting from memory the first verse of Psalm 122. "God has blessed us to see another Sunday morning, not because we deserved to see it, but because His grace allowed it." He paused. "You know about grace and mercy, right? Many of you in here can testify that if it had not been for the Lord on your side . . ." He paused again, smiling as the congregation finished his exhortation in their own words.

Sister Arlene played a few chords on the Hammond B-3 organ, alert and ready in case her pastor needed any musical assistance. But Gentry looked at her with a slight shake of his head, indicating he wasn't yet ready for the assistance.

"I thank those of you who came out last Monday night to our special Bible study. May God bless all of you real good. I believe that when the body of Christ becomes unified and gets on one accord in our efforts to win souls for the Kingdom, great things happen. When we don't let denominational differences become bigger than our desire to fulfill the Great Commission, then *real* revival will break out all over the world.

"I was reading the praise reports from area churches' healing services on this week alone. Three cases of cancer, sugar diabetes, carpal tunnel syndrome, back pain, lupus, and a severe migraine headache case—all *healed* for the glory of God. Let's give Him a shout of praise for His wonderful works!"

Sister Arlene now played a looping chord in B-flat, soon joined by choir members beating tambourines and congregants clapping their hands and stomping their feet in spiritual praise.

"Church, what we're seeing happen here is not

some watered-down, out-of-date religion that has no relevance to everyday life," Gentry continued, tuning up the treble to his voice. He was now ready to preach.

"What we're seeing happen is the manifestation of God's Word. Where are my Bible scholars? The Bible says that if My people, who are called by My name, shall humble themselves and pray, seek My face and turn from their wicked ways, what will God do?"

"God will *heal* our land!" a member shouted.

"Say it again?"

"God will *heal* our land!"

"One more time, in Jesus's name . . ."

"God will *heal* our land!"

• • •

"MY GOD, YOU REALLY PREACHED today," Lynn remarked, passing by Pastor Gentry's office. The morning service had ended forty minutes earlier, but after either staying to pray for people at the altar, welcoming new members, or fulfilling other administrative duties, it was only now that most of the staff members at Faith Community could *pause* to catch their respective breaths.

"No, the *Holy Spirit* preached today," Pastor Gentry gently corrected her. "It had nothing to do with me—I knew God was going to show out today . . . I could feel it in my spirit early this morning when I woke up to pray."

Lynn leaned her shoulder against the doorjamb. "This revival . . . it's so awesome. I'm so excited about what God is doing. Every day, we're hearing more and more reports of healings, salvations, baptisms in the Holy Spirit."

Pastor Gentry nodded. "Acts 2:17—*'And it shall come to pass in the last days, says God, that I will pour out of My Spirit on all flesh; your sons and your daughters shall prophesy, your young men shall see visions, your old men shall dream dreams.'* These are the last days, Sister Lynn. We should feel so honored, and yet so *humbled* to be chosen by God to live in this dispensation of His Spirit. God could have chosen us to live during any time period—during the persecution of the early church, during the Crusades, during the Reformation after Martin Luther nailed his ninety-five theses on the door of the church, or during the Azusa Street revival in Los Angeles. But He chose us to live *now*, in the twenty-first century, right when I believe that Jesus is preparing His church as the bride, ready to meet the bridegroom."

"It's what we always prayed for," Lynn continued. "And we're seeing the fruit of those prayers coming to pass."

"And that's the key—prayer. I've been experiencing spiritual warfare on a completely different level over the past months, and I know others have, too. It's vital that we continue praying for the success of this revival. God is going to do exceedingly, abundantly above all we ask or think, but only according to the power working within us."

"Which is the Word of God in us, mixed with faith," Lynn said.

"Absolutely."

"Lynn?"

Lynn turned at the voice to see Arlene at the end of the hallway. Arlene, among other things, was the quintessential church worker—first to arrive, last to leave.

"Lynn, there's a telephone call for you. It just came in on the main line."

"Oh, okay. Forward it to my desk in ten seconds." She turned back to Pastor Gentry. "You know I could stay here all day and talk about the end-time revival, but it's been a long day."

"Sundays always are."

"And you need to take your wife, Shanice, out to dinner. Someplace real nice."

Pastor Gentry started chuckling. "Oh I do, do I?"

"Absolutely. Tell her I said hello and that I'll see her tonight." Lynn walked back to her office, wondering why someone was calling her on the church's main line. Most everyone who needed to contact her had her direct number.

"Faith Community Church, Lynn Harper speaking," she answered, once Arlene had forwarded the call.

"Hello, Lynn."

She instantly recognized the voice as Chance's, and for a few seconds she went speechless. Of course, she'd told him to call her anytime, but she really hadn't expected that he would.

"Chance. H-hello. How are you doing?"

"I'm doing real good, thanks. Listen, Faith Community is having a healing service tonight, right?"

"Yes. It starts at seven. Intercessory prayer begins at six. Why?"

"Well, it's just that I would like to come, if that would be alright."

"If that would be *alright*? Of course it would! As I've said, our altar workers and intercessors would be so inspired to have you minister alongside them. But you're still in Ruston, right? I mean, you can't possibly make it here in time for the service unless . . . unless . . ."

"Unless I'm *already* here," he finished. "Which I am. I just landed at Columbia Metropolitan."

"Y-you're here?" Lynn still could not fathom what Chance had just said. She was as surprised as he'd been a few weeks earlier, when she'd called him to tell him she was in *his* hometown.

He chuckled. "That's what I said, right? I figured that after all the times you spent following me around, the least I could do was return the favor. Listen, there's three more hours until intercessory prayer starts. Are you hungry?"

"Starving. I'm always hungry after Sunday morning services."

"Good. Would you care to join me for a late lunch?"

"Sure. I don't have a particular taste for anything, so . . ."

"Oh, I already have a place in mind," Chance said. "Know how to get to Five Points Diner?"

Chapter Fifty-seven

"YOU'RE LOOKING GOOD . . . I mean, um . . . *better* than the last time I saw you," Lynn observed, between bites of her hamburger.

Chance nodded. "I've spent some time out on the water, letting my body heal. I've had a lot of time to think, too. You know, the past two years have been crazy for me, and there were times when I just wanted to give up. But every time I would get to that point, every time I didn't think I could keep putting one foot in front of the other, God would let me pray for someone and I'd see that person get healed. An instant miracle, right before my eyes."

"Like when you prayed for me."

He nodded. "You never forget someone's face at that exact moment when they realize God has healed them. I can't even describe how many ways the human face can express wonder. Anyway, God would let me see someone get healed, and I couldn't shake the truth that someone's life had just been forever changed, and I played a small part in that holy experience. And then I'd remember how Nina would always tell me God was going to use me in the area of divine healing. She was right."

"Everything Nina told you has come to pass, hasn't it?"

He nodded again, taking a long pull from his root-beer bottle. "It's the most humbling feeling in the world, you know? Being used of God, being *chosen* of God to do a task that seems so great, so much bigger than you."

"I know how you feel, Chance. The call of God is supposed to make you feel a combination of things—somewhat fearful, excited, and alienated from everyone who can't see or understand your vision. The reason why the call is so great is because God's strength is made perfect in our weaknesses. The areas where we lack resources and abilities are the areas where His glory shines brightest."

"I can understand that. And I know I'll always miss Nina and the joy she brought to my life. But . . . but I realize that I can't waste the gift anymore. I can't waste the gift she played a huge part in developing within me, a gift that I know will help so many increase their faith in God. Not only would that be a tragedy, but it would mean Nina died in vain."

They were both quiet for a few minutes as they finished their meals, politely declining when their waiter asked if they wanted dessert.

"I take it Florence isn't here," Lynn said once the waiter had left, referring to the waitress who had identified Chance for the newspaper.

"No. I overheard her saying she didn't work on Sundays. Trust me, if she were here, you'd have heard her a mile away."

"She was that bad?"

"She wasn't that bad. If you could fit a muzzle around her mouth, she'd actually be quite charming."

Lynn smiled. "I didn't know you had a sense of humor."

Chance shrugged. "I haven't had much to laugh about lately."

"Maybe that could change." Lynn looked at her watch. "We should get going, especially since I need to stop by my place and change." She glanced at Chance, who was sporting a travel-comfortable athletic windbreaker warm-up. "Did you want to go back to your hotel and change, too?"

"I haven't booked a hotel yet. I called from the airport, right after I landed. I do have a suit in my garment bag, in my rental car."

"Oh. Oh . . . well, you could change at my place, if you want."

"Come back to your place? What would Pastor Gentry say about that?"

Lynn felt herself blush. "Oh . . . I didn't mean anything by that . . . I just . . . well, I thought that since you hadn't booked a—"

"Relax, Lynn," he cut in, smiling. "I was joking."

"Oh. Well, warn me the next time you're going to tell a joke, okay? I'm still getting used to the idea of you having a sense of humor."

• • •

THEY ARRIVED AT Faith Community Church at ten minutes to six. The parking lot was already filling with cars, as people from all over the area were coming to intercede for the healing crusade.

"This is amazing," Chance remarked, looking at the scores of people heading into the church. "And they're all here, believing to see the miracle-working power of God."

"What God is doing here is incredible," Lynn agreed. "Church attendance throughout eight counties is up twenty-two percent. People are stopping the handicapped out in public, praying the Word of God over them. We've bought over two pages of advertising space in the *State*, inviting the sick to come out and be prayed over. The response, as you can see, has been overwhelming."

"This is how it must have been in the days of the early church, in the book of Acts. At least on a small scale, anyway."

"It won't be on a small scale for much longer. We're hearing from churches all up and down the East Coast and as far away as California. The gospel is spreading and affecting even the staunchest of atheists. It's kind of hard to doubt when cancerous tumors are disappearing and blinded eyes are being opened."

They got out of the car and started to walk inside.

"Wait," Chance said, stopping. "I'd like to walk around outside for a while."

"You really do have a thing for the outdoors, huh?"

"I just like to pray surrounded by nature. There's something about looking up at the sky and . . . I don't know. I just prefer praying outdoors."

"That's fine. But at six-forty, come inside and ask to be taken to Pastor Gentry's office. I'll inform Brother

Roger—he'll be the Secret Service–looking brother in the front foyer—to take you there."

"Pastor Gentry's office?"

"With your healing gift, I think you'd be best utilized in the altar workers ministry tonight. But I won't be able to get you there without Pastor Gentry personally knowing about it beforehand." She patted him on the shoulder. "Highly gifted or not, we conduct our healing crusades decently and in order. We can't have just anyone at the altar, laying hands on people and praying for them. They have to be checked out, you know."

"Even me?"

She started to walk away, but turned back around and winked. "*Especially* you. But don't worry—I know an awesome man of God when I see one. And you are one awesome man of God, Brother Word."

Chance watched her walk inside before turning and walking the outer perimeter of the church.

Faith Community Church encompassed forty thousand square feet, with the main sanctuary housed at the center of the property. The surrounding area had been built on a tract of farmland on the outskirts of West Columbia, with trees and shrubbery lining the property to the south. It was an awesome structure, Chance thought, as he began meditating on the tenth chapter of Luke, the passage of scripture where Jesus sent His disciples out as laborers into the harvest.

Behold, I give you the authority to trample on serpents and scorpions, and over all the power of the enemy, and nothing shall by any means hurt you . . .

As Chance turned the northwest corner of the

building, he looked up and saw that the sun was setting in the eastern sky.

He paused, taking a deep breath before slowly exhaling. A calmness flowed within him then, a peace that let him know everything from now on would be alright. Looking at his watch, he saw that it was six-thirty-five, so he started back toward the front of the church.

Wait . . .

He paused as the voice of the Lord spoke clearly to his spirit, prompting him not only to wait but to look to his left and right. People were flocking to the church's front doors in droves, some praying loudly, others pushing others in wheelchairs, but all seeming to have a spirit of expectancy. Chance began walking back toward the parking lot, against the rush of the crowd, sensing the leading of the Holy Spirit.

What, Lord?

No stranger to the leading of the Spirit, Chance had been instructed by God many times before, during all those times he'd prayed for someone's healing. As a result, his sensitivity to the Spirit had heightened dramatically.

As he approached a light pole in the center of the parking lot, Chance stopped, sensing he had come to the place.

There was a lone car idling off to his right, which struck him as strange since it was the only car amidst the sea of vehicles with its engine still running. The person in the driver's seat seemed to be slumped forward, head resting against the steering wheel.

Is that guy just sleeping? Is he dead?

Chance began walking toward the car, quickening his gait since he didn't want to be late for his meeting with Pastor Gentry. Ten yards away, he noticed that whoever was behind the wheel was wearing a white baseball cap with an orange splotch in the middle of its front.

Five yards away, Chance saw that the orange splotch was a . . . *paw*. It was a Clemson Tigers baseball cap.

Chapter Fifty-eight

CHANCE CAUTIOUSLY APPROACHED the sedan from the rear. As he neared the passenger-side door, he could tell that the man inside was indeed . . . Travis Everett. But why would the reporter be *here*?

Chance looked at his watch. Six-thirty-eight.

He rapped on the window, hard, causing Travis to slowly raise his head and look to the right. A look of surprise came over him when he saw Chance standing there. A second later, the window rolled down.

"You getting the scoop on some story I should know about?" Chance asked, crouching down to see Travis better. He noticed Travis's eyes were red and puffy, with severe bags underneath. The reporter's clothes had two-day-old wrinkles in them.

Travis shook his head. "No story here. I'm just . . . well, I just . . ." He looked away from Chance. "I really don't know *why* I'm here . . ."

"How long have you been here?"

"I came here around three. Service was over by then, though."

"Another service is about to start in fifteen minutes, though."

Travis rubbed at his eyes. "Yeah, but that's strictly for the healing stuff. Lames and cripples—people like that. I was just tryin' to come to the regular worship service."

Chance knew there was *nothing* regular about Faith Community's services, but he kept that comment to himself.

"Why were you coming to the morning service?" he asked instead.

Travis shrugged. "Curious, I guess. Eddie, he told me . . ." He shook his head. "Doesn't matter, anyway. You wouldn't understand."

Chance looked at his watch again. Six-forty-five. Pastor Gentry would just have to wait. "I wouldn't understand what?"

"Nothing," Travis mumbled, though loud enough for Chance to hear. "You don't even know who Eddie is."

"I know who Eddie is," Chance spoke up. "He's your nephew. I prayed for him at Five Points Diner two months ago to receive hearing in his ears and strength in his ankles."

Travis gave Chance an incredulous look. "Y-you remember?"

"Of course I remember. I *never* forget the ones God heals using my hands, especially the children."

"Yeah, but how do you know it was *God*? What if Eddie's healing was just one of those unexplainable medical mysteries?"

"And what if it wasn't? What if God healed your nephew because of his parents' faith? What if that *faith* was the key that unlocked God's healing power?"

Travis began shaking his head. "I can't accept that . . . you can't prove it to me . . . nobody has ever proved that to me."

"Nobody needs to," Chance gently responded.

"What?"

Now faith is . . . the evidence of things not seen . . . "You proved it to yourself by showing up here this afternoon. Why would you be *here*, of all places, in a parking lot by yourself?"

Travis remained quiet.

"I believe God has been tugging at your heart. I believe the same way you pursued your mystery-man story is the same way God has been pursuing your heart. No man comes to Jesus unless the Father draws him, Travis. Are you telling me that you can't feel the Father drawing you to His love?"

There was no answer from Travis, and Chance sensed the moment of decision had arrived—the moment in every person's life when a decision about the gospel of Jesus Christ *must* be made. One either rejected the gospel or accepted it—neutral was not an option.

"Travis, there is one way I can show you how real all of these healings are, but you can only see it by faith."

"Faith . . ." Travis whispered, now breathing heavily.

"Faith," Chance repeated. "That's the key."

An eternity seemed to pass before Travis finally lifted his head. "Alright. I'm willing to try."

"Are you sure?"

"Yes."

"Alright then, come on," Chance said, standing back up to full height.

"Where are we going?"

"Inside. You can receive Jesus by faith anywhere, but since we're here we might as well do it among the company of believers."

Travis got out of the car and walked around to where Chance stood. "Inside? But like I said, that service is for people who need to be healed."

Chance put his arm around Travis. "That's exactly right. But it took me two years to learn a truth of God's love. You see, you *do* need to be healed. And so do I. And do you know where the greatest healings take place?"

Travis shook his head.

Chance touched a finger to Travis's chest, and then his own. "In the heart."

Chance took one last look at the sunset as they walked across the parking lot to the front doors of the church. The heavens had never looked more magnificent.

Reading Group **Guide**

1. "Strong faith in the area of healing or not, his present chest pains were real. *Painfully* real." How does your faith coexist with a painful reality? Does living or speaking in faith mean denying a physical experience? Why or why not?

2. "Ministry and emotional burnout mixed together like oil and water." How do you guard yourself against burnout in ministry—or in life in general? How have you made time and space in your life for Sabbaths such as vacation, recreation, and a day of rest?

3. What do you think—what *is* the "fine line between anger and stupidity in questioning the Almighty"?

4. Many people share Travis's awkwardness around people with disabilities. What experience do you have relating to children or adults who have special needs? How do you handle interactions with people who have some kind of handicap?

5. What is the worst possible handicap that you can imagine for yourself? What physical (or mental) capacity would be most difficult for you to lose (e.g., sight, hearing, voice, ability to walk or use hands, etc.)? How do you think your faith would respond to such a loss?

6. "It's one thing to believe for someone else's healing," Lynn realized. Why is it different—more difficult—to believe for your own healing?

7. What knowledge or experience do you have of divine healing? What do you think or believe about such miracles?

8. How would you minister to someone in Lynn's situation after the accident? Would you exhort her to greater faith, comfort her in her mental and physical anguish, encourage her to trust, bear her company in silence, or serve her needs in practical ways? Why?

9. Prayer, familiar scriptures, and recollections of her own faith history—how God had worked in and through her in the past—were an encouragement to Lynn in her darkest hours. What encourages you in such times—and how?

10. Would you allow a stranger to pray over you or someone you loved? Why or why not—or in what circumstances?

11. After the accident, Lynn asked, "Why me, God?" At the healing service, she wondered, "Why not me?"

When have you asked one of those questions? Did you feel like God answered you, and if so, how? How did *you* ultimately handle the question (and answer)?

12. Many of us acknowledge a *belief* in healing and other miracles—and then we are amazed when we see one take place. Why is that? What does it suggest about the nature of faith and belief?

13. What role do divine miracles have in God's work on earth today? What purpose did they serve in Jesus's ministry?

14. Rev. Gentry regards the newspaper article as "spiritual warfare 101." What does he mean by that?

15. Chance tells Lynn that his healing ministry is "more a principle of obedience than faith." What does he mean by that? What does that idea mean to you?

16. Salvation is free, Chance notes, but everything else God gives has a price. Our anointing is proportionate to our sacrifice. Do you agree? Why or why not? What has your own experience taught you about this aspect of God's empowerment?

17. Nina had thought it would show a lack of faith to go to a doctor to have her healing confirmed. Do you agree? Why or why not?

18. Nina was convinced she would be healed at the conference; Floyd Waters said Nina was healed; Nina herself experienced what she believed was healing. Then she died—and an autopsy revealed the cancer had killed her. How do you deal with such situations where you seem to hear God say one thing—and time seems to prove you (or God) wrong?

19. Chance experienced his calling and anointing as a burden. How have you experienced the call of God on your life or the gifts of God to be a burden? How have you responded to that experience?

20. Have you ever met someone like Chance—someone with great gifts who also had great needs? How can you—and the church at large—minister to such a person?

21. Most of us have a family member, friend, or co-worker who is a bit like Travis. How do you relate to that kind of "stubborn agnostic"? What strategies have you employed to share God's love and power with him or her?

22. What do you think about the follow-up strategies of Faith Community Church—the prayer calls, the emphasis on continuing in divine health, and on developing healthy living alternatives? Have you ever encountered a church that balanced belief in divine healing with such practical or "earthly" follow-up? What is the value—and biblical foundation—for such a holistic approach?

23. Chance had never felt led to lay hands on his own father to pray for divine healing. Why might a family member not be the best candidate for your ministry? What other reason(s) might Chance have for not sharing his gift with Pop?

24. What gift(s) has God given to you? How is it developing? What are you doing to cultivate it? In what ways has that gift ever made you feel like "some weird traveling sideshow"?

25. Lynn reflects that Shadrach, Meshach, and Abednego had a faith that would believe even if God *did not* deliver them. Many people would think this foolish. Do you? Why or why not? What is significant about that kind of faith?

26. What do you think: *Is* it God's will for all people to be healed and live in divine health? Why or why not?

27. As he sinks into the water, Chance figures he's probably dying—and he wonders, "This is my life?" If you were dying today, how would you sum up your life? How would you feel about its conclusion at this point in time?

28. By virtue of being alive, Lynn asserts, we can assume we have some unfinished Kingdom business. What is *your* part in God's unfinished business? What treasure is God unveiling in you?

29. Chance is startled when Lynn talks about his ministry. He doesn't really think of his itinerant healings as ministry. What gifts are you operating in that might be organized into a ministry?

30. Family, love, money . . . What would it take to make *you* happy?

31. Pastor Gentry's Bible study (see chapter 53) deals with a lot of issues related to healing. Which insights or arguments stood out for you? Why?

32. Compose your own litany of God's goodness, based on your own life. Allow that realization of God's grace to bring you to *your* knees in worship!

33. What do you think Chance meant when he told Travis the greatest healings are those in the heart?